THE PERFECT SONYA

Also by Beverly Lowry

COME BACK, LOLLY RAY

EMMA BLUE

DADDY'S GIRL

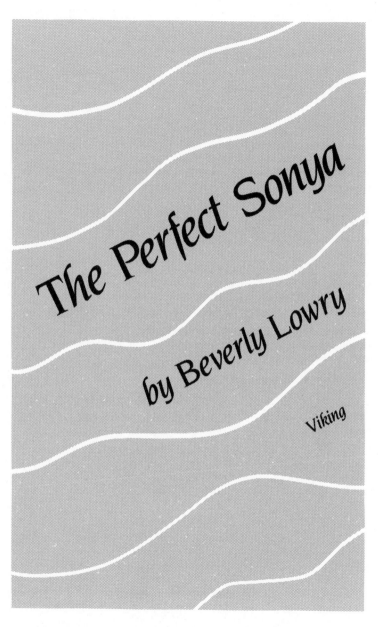

The Perfect Sonya

by Beverly Lowry

Viking

VIKING
Viking Penguin Inc., 40 West 23rd Street, New York, New York 10010, U.S.A.
Penguin Books Ltd, Harmondsworth, Middlesex, England
Penguin Books Australia Ltd, Ringwood, Victoria, Australia
Penguin Books Canada Limited, 2801 John Street, Markham, Ontario, Canada L3R 1B4
Penguin Books (N.Z.) Ltd, 182–190 Wairau Road, Auckland 10, New Zealand

First published in 1987 by Viking Penguin Inc.
Published simultaneously in Canada

Grateful acknowledgment is made for permission to reprint
excerpts from "Uncle Vanya" from *Chekov: The Major Plays*,
translated by Ann Dunnigan. Copyright © 1964 by Ann Dunnigan.
Reprinted by arrangement with NAL Penguin Inc., New York, N.Y.

The author wishes to extend her profound gratitude to the
National Endowment for the Arts and the John Simon Guggenheim Foundation
for their generous support.

LIBRARY OF CONGRESS CATALOGING IN PUBLICATION DATA
Lowry, Beverly.
The perfect Sonya.
I. Title.
PS3562.092P4 1987   813'.54   86-45842
ISBN 0-670-81413-X

Printed in the United States of America
by R. R. Donnelley & Sons Company, Harrisonburg, Virginia
Set in Janson Alternate   Design by Camilla Filancia

This book is dedicated to my brothers,
to Doris, and to my friends,
without whose steady and very loving attention
I probably never would have finished.

In memory, Peter Lowry.

THE PERFECT SONYA

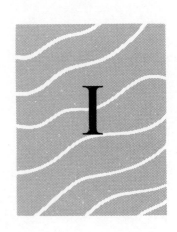

I

1

The bear was huge. Reared up on its hind legs, it loomed over her, beyond feet and inches, a dreamlike presence which did not yield to common measure: dark, still, more like the shadow of something larger than she might ever have imagined than a real bear.

Pauline held onto a wooden post a car's length away, refusing to come closer.

"It won't hurt you," her father said. He stood beside the bear, smiling, motioning her to come toward him, scooping his arm toward her and back. A black square camera hung on a strap around his neck. The camera was hers, a Christmas present. The Kodak, they called it. It was that long ago.

Pauline would have been eleven that year, twelve in August. Her chest was flat, her body smooth and hairless. She had that childlike swayback stance that punched her stomach forward and made her butt stick out, those zinnia-stem legs, knees knobby as chicken joints, her shinbones long with long feet tacked on at right angles like boxes, giving her a storky look. Already she was too tall.

The bear, stuffed of course, stood on a dusty Arkansas street in front of a souvenir shop, inviting the curious to come closer. On wooden sidewalks, barefoot Indians in feathered hats sat cross-legged, their wares spread out on blankets before their feet: turquoise rings and keychains, beaded belts, play tomahawks. The village was not real but manufactured for tourists, fake old, fake Indian, fake everything.

Her father crooked his finger and wiggled it. How could she stand it? Such a joke excuse for a father, like a miniature replica of a real man, a perfectly formed, walking, talking figurine. The top of his head came barely up to the bear's shoulder. Even then, when fathers loomed larger than bears, Pauline knew how ridiculously small he was.

Meantime she was growing, growing, all legs and arms and long pliant feet. That year her father was taller by maybe an inch or so. In two years she would pass him. When she was fifteen she bested him by inches. By then it was over. They were locked together in battle for good, size had been declared such an issue between them.

She shook her head and held on harder to the post.

Pauline looked like a Messican, Jack said, a tall Messican, with that dark skin, that nose and mouth. Everybody else in the family was white and short. Where did Pauline get her looks, he asked—asked *her*, as if she had anything to do with it—the woodpile?

He went over and smacked the bear on the shoulder. Dust flew. He had on his usual costume, jeans and skin-tight, pearl-snapped Western shirt, high-heeled cowboy boots and a 10X beaver cowboy hat with a high crown. People on the trip called him Tex instead of his real name, Jack Miller. They did live in Texas and so the name was geographically appropriate but about his size no one was fooled.

"See?" he said. "Stuffed."

He didn't have to tell her. She was eleven going on twelve: Didn't she know the bear was stuffed?

The bear's lips were drawn back, his teeth locked in a permanent snarl, his nose pinched so that it looked like a pig's snout with two deep wrinkles. All this was calculated to make the bear look ferocious, which it did. Then you were supposed to ignore that. You were supposed to go stand close, as if the face was somewhere else. Impossible. And all the rest was nothing compared to his eyes: glassy, vacant, yellowish gold with shiny flecks. Something was back there, an empty otherness Pauline couldn't stand, a promise of, who knew? Wherever she went, the bear watched her. He knew where she was and what she was thinking. She could not stand the thought of being close to him.

In her adult dreams things come after her. Things? A man, stalking her from out of the darkness. It is always nighttime in the dream, usually misting rain. She is in the city with friends. They have attended some meeting—convention, lecture, class, what the occasion is is not clear but the event is always benign, the spirit of the group quite friendly—and now they are all going home. Pauline, who lives in a different direction from the others, has decided to walk. Her friends try to dissuade her. The street is not safe, they say, dangers are everywhere, they are taking a cab and so should she. But she, having always been a daredevil kind of girl, a girl who believes herself up to whatever risks and dangers come her way, refuses. What could happen? Hasn't she always taken care of herself? Isn't she a lucky sort of person? And so in the dream she leaves her friends and begins to walk. And then on the way the horrible man (dark and dirty, sometimes driving a leaking, rusted-out car, old, with busted springs, a dripping transmission, a crumpled fender) comes after her, pursuing her from behind, close enough to feel. Too late, she turns. He is on her, smiling, slimy in triumph. She has nowhere to go. She feels not only terrified, but at fault and stupid as well. Doesn't she deserve what she gets? Didn't she ask for trouble, imagining herself endlessly self-sufficient and immune to harm? Why didn't she listen to her friends? The dream stops there, at the moment of greatest fear when she realizes the man has her and there is nothing to do. She wakes up whimpering, heart and gut turned to water. Then cannot shake the dream but goes through the next day still feeling the man's eyes on her, thinking *What terrible thing just happened?* Sometimes she can't tell if the feeling evoked by the dream is closer to fear or the erotic. Or if both are involved, one intensifying the other until her very core of self is shaken. The dream never leaves entirely but only lies in wait. After a while she dreams it again some other night. And does not reflect on what it means—she is an actress, after all—but only dreads its recurrence.

The bear's arms were extended in a wide embrace, talons clasped. People—tourists visiting the mock-Indian village, shopping for Indian souvenirs—took turns stepping inside the bear's arms to have their pictures taken, them and the bear, together forever. And so the bear is eternal, like Niagara Falls and Mount Rushmore, a concrete backdrop for the untrusting traveler's need for proof of what has been seen, done, experienced.

Pauline asked the owner of the nearby souvenir store if the bear stayed outside when it rained. The store owner laughed. "I don't guess he had a house to go to when he was living. And he sure as heck don't have one now." Jack laughed with the man. They both looked at her as if she were a funny toy. She did not hate him yet but it was building.

A small boy on the wooden sidewalk shifted his feet and loudly ahemmed. The boy was waiting for Pauline to get inside the bear's arms and have her picture taken so that he could take his turn.

Pauline shook her head no. She put her finger in her mouth, like a baby. Her father smiled. He was still in an agreeable mood, so far. Things could change fast.

"Hey," he said. "Watch me." He bent his head and went under.

Inside the bear's embrace, he rested his chin on the bear's paws and danced a jig. The camera bumped his chest. Pauline sucked her finger. He didn't have to show her. She knew the difference between a live bear and a stuffed one. He didn't have to make a fool of himself again. She hated this so much, everybody watching while she and her family did their dance, like performing monkeys in red suits turning flip-flops for change.

Mavis, who had been negotiating with an Indian for a string of beads, came up behind Pauline.

"Go ahead, honey," she whispered in Pauline's ear. Pauline pulled away. "It won't hurt you."

Her mother exuded her usual smells, sweet perfume and sticky lipstick, too many cigarettes and the other, her most persistent, the flowery aroma of bourbon. At the hotel, the three of them slept in two double beds in the same room. Before they left to come to the Indian village, Pauline had walked in on Mavis in the bathroom, sitting on the toilet, tossing down a water glass half-filled with bourbon. As she set the glass down on the sink, Mavis made a face and groaned, then flushed the commode so that Jack wouldn't know.

"Just go on and do it," her mother said. "It'll be over with before you know it."

She gave Pauline a shove. Pauline's finger flew from her mouth. She jerked her arm away. She thought she might be able to, but if she was going to, it had to be on her own. They would have to shut up or she would never. She took a step toward the bear.

Certain of her psychologically minded New York friends tell her the bear is a seminal, archetypal image, a metaphor for that which is most frightening to her and at the same time most seductive. No matter that intellectually she knows the animal is sawdust inside. No matter anything. Fear exists on the other side of knowing. Ghosts take their stand beyond words and facts. The erotic in particular is never accommodating, never comfortable, will not yield to predictability. The bear stands: an underground current, indecipherable, cosmic.

Other friends say the bear is a phallic image representing the erect penis. The powerful, primal push/pull. Meaning father of course, always and boringly forever.

Pauline knows all this and more; New York has taught her a great deal. But cleverness is not all. Nor does information necessarily invoke change. She is also efficient: smart enough to acknowledge the information she can make use of, canny enough to ignore the rest. In acting, emotions are useful. Memory serves. Sliding past her friends' slippery interpretations, she focuses on the pragmatic. Some possibilities are too dangerous to consider.

One step more. She looked up. The eyes. They never blinked. She could not make herself do it.

She took a step backward.

"I'll go," Mavis volunteered. Mavis started to push past Pauline.

"No, you won't," Jack said.

Mavis stopped in her tracks.

Jack came out from under the bear's arms.

"See?" he said, holding his own arms out wide. He was as small and as perfectly proportioned as a muscle-man doll. "Not a scratch."

Pauline tried to take another step. "I can't," she said.

"Why not?"

"I don't know." She was starting to whine. "Because."

Jack screwed up his face and mocked her. "Because why not, Pauline?" He swung his hips, imitating girlishness.

Pauline lifted her head, straightened her long braids, leveled her voice. "Because I don't know. I just can't."

In Baytown where she lived, she was known to be a daredevil, a girl who, afraid of nothing, gloried in danger and sought out adventure. A member of the town's junior swimming team, she swam distances, won ribbons, and for fun, after swimming practice did flips off the high dive, entering the water perfectly every time, practically no splash at all. Plunging carnival rides thrilled her; she liked the feeling when her stomach went to her feet. Enjoyed being suspended. Liked the air: leapt from rope swings tied so far up in oak trees even boys hesitated to go.

The trick to rope-swinging was to let go at the peak of the swing. Scared people waited, held on too long, waited for the descent to begin, then hit flatfooted and hurt themselves. Pauline trusted her luck, releasing the rope when she was highest, throwing herself into the air. For a moment, it felt like flying.

In water she was even more proficient. She swam in the bayou, which people said would give you hepatitis. Nothing happened. She could hold her breath underwater longer than anyone, swim to the other side of the bayou and back, water-ski when she was seven, ski on one leg at eight, on bare feet at nine.

All this was different from the bear. Except for the eyes, the bear was soft, untrustworthy, both fake and real. There was no way to measure its danger.

Her father came toward her. The camera swung.

Someone giggled. The boy on the sidewalk awaiting his turn.

Pauline, backing away, bumped into Mavis.

Mavis gave her a slight shove back in the direction of her father, sending Pauline's head and shoulders toward him. Pauline flexed her knees and bent her toes to grip the dusty street with her sandals. She was barely able to stop herself in time. Facing her father, her eyes met his.

They were all three within a few inches of the same height, something between five-three and five-five. Mavis was a squarish person of skewed proportions, large in the middle, tiny at the extremities, wrists thin as twigs, baby feet, tiny hands with fingers that tapered to points like the tips of candles. At school, when the health nurse came to give shots and measure everyone, Pauline turned out to be the tallest person in the fifth grade, a statistic the nurse found so amazing she told everyone. Mortified, Pauline was beginning to stand in a stoop. She felt like a freak.

Jack reached out to her.

Pauline buried her hand in the gathers of her skirt but her father found it. She hadn't wanted to wear a skirt but Mavis said no to shorts, they might want to eat someplace fancy. Jack grabbed her by the wrist and pulled. Pauline planted her heels in the dirt. Her braids flew behind her. She was strong. From spending all her time at the country club swimming pool, her skin was as dark as that of the Indians who sat on the wooden sidewalks selling things, her long dark hair tinged by chlorine a faint greenish gold.

She had not wanted to come to the Indian village in the first place. She had made friends with the hotel pool lifeguard, whom she'd promised to help that day, cleaning out the traps, seining leaves from the surface of the water. But Jack said she needed to see new things; she could swim at home. On trips, she had no power at all. She was expected to suspend her regular life totally and go look at things.

Strong but her father was stronger. He pulled. She couldn't help it. She was moving.

"You're hurting me," she said, still pulling back. His fingers were locked in a circle around her wrist. The pressure of his skin against hers burned.

"Only because you're so willful." He pulled harder. His face was turning red. She could see the spark of victory in his eyes. "It's stuffed. It's not real."

There was only one thing to do. Still pulling back, Pauline let her knees buckle. She crumpled to the ground, spineless as a dishrag.

Surprised, Jack stumbled. His left ankle was weak and it sometimes gave. He fell halfway with her, his bony shoulder crashing into Pauline's shinbone. Pauline quickly drew her legs and feet into her skirt. She rubbed her shin.

His face on fire, Jack jumped up. His cowboy hat was cockeyed. He fixed it. There was no telling what he would do now. He was springy and quick, like a whip. Pauline had a secret method of judging his moods. She watched the vein in his temple, to see whether it rose or just throbbed. The vein seemed on the verge of bursting. He took a step toward Pauline, then stopped.

The dusty fake street looked like a wax museum of tourists, everyone in their sightseeing clothes, no one moving. Beside Pauline, Mavis was a statue, hands up, mouth open in a perfect circle, like a comic strip version of fright. Only the Indians seemed unimpressed. They moved their jewelry around, maintaining a stolid demeanor, trying to look like the kind of Indians everyone imagined American Indians to be. Wise, unfazed, ancient. Like trees.

Pauline stood, brushed at her skirt and reminded herself not to take a step away from him. Retreat was a sign of weakness, and weakness only increased his powers to win.

The redness drained as quickly from her father's face as if someone had pulled a plug. The men in Jack's family died young, a family fact of which Jack reminded Pauline and her mother often enough. Most of them went in their forties; "Gone like that," he said, snapping his fingers. Pauline watched the pulsating vein in his temple, crawling down the side of his face like a worm. His temper was cooling, but the vein still throbbed.

Jack took the camera from around his neck and tossed it to the ground. *Her* camera. Dust puffed up around it.

"Fine," he said in a completely normal voice, as if they were discussing what to have for lunch, peanut butter or tuna fish. "Fine with me."

He lifted his hands to the bright blue Arkansas skies and made a face, twisting his mouth to one side.

"You made your bed," he said, smiling as if her fate were sealed. "Now you can lie in it."

The remark had no bearing on the circumstances; it was only a convenient exit line and a general statement of fact, denoting his truest feelings about her. All Pauline's life, Jack Miller waited for her to fail badly enough that his sentiment would make some dint in her defense against him. All her life she planned strategies to disappoint him.

He turned on his heel and, passing the bear, went to the end of the block. At the corner, beside a pretend saloon with wooden swinging doors, he wheeled around and faced her like a gunfighter. Thinking he might come back, Pauline drew herself up to her full height. But Jack only pointed his finger at her— pointed, let his hand drop, raised it and pointed again—and then turned and left.

Vacations never worked out, not ever. She wondered if other families really had fun the way they said.

They didn't go anywhere that often. With Mavis in and out of treatment all the time, they never knew when she'd be up to traveling. Mavis had this problem. Nerves, her family said. Pauline imagined nerves to be something like a rat in her mother's brain. Sometimes the rat slept, but when it wakened and began to gnaw, Mavis's brain turned to sawdust; her mother went away and left someone else behind, a stranger, made of stone.

And so mostly they stayed where they were, out from Baytown in the big white house on the banks of Cedar Bayou, with their dogs and cats and horses and one cow.

Only sometimes when they had a nice night together—it happened—playing Parcheesi or sitting in the porch swing watching stars and lightning bugs—the three of them grew first wistful, then sentimental, then dreamy. And when they got dreamy they did this family trick together—a balancing act, like three people on one bicycle on a circus high wire.

Exercising that familial skill, Jack, Mavis and Pauline forgot to remember how terrible other vacations had been and how they had vowed—sworn to God!—never to take another. They would have heard about other families' trips, to Colorado where you could ride a train straight up the side of a mountain, or to the Blue Ridge Mountains where the horizon was said actually to be blue. All the other families said they had such fun, swimming in clear cold streams, eating fried shrimp with drawn butter. Carried away, Jack would send Pauline to get out the atlas and, following major highways with their fingers, they would decide, like a regular American family, to take a trip.

Most vacations, they never reached their destination. The thread inside Mavis's mind started to frazzle or Jack got fed up with something—the heat, a mediocre motel, Pauline's need to go to the bathroom—anything would do. He might suddenly, in the middle of nowhere, stop the car, get out, look up at the sun and say, "If I wanted to be hot, I could have stayed at home," and they would turn around and go back.

The summer Pauline was eight, they actually made it to Carlsbad Caverns. Inside the cave, Mavis fell apart. Puffing like a steam engine, she had to be led back out by flashlight. Jack went with her. Pauline stayed to see the rest of the cave. When she came out, Jack was standing at the exit waiting, that vein in his temple thumping, his red face swollen with rage.

Pauline would just as soon they never went anywhere . . . although she did like certain features about hotels, room service and candy bar machines, the smell of the empty drawers, the swimming pool, some even with high dives. What she hated was the feeling that the success of a vacation depended on her, on what kind of time she had and how they watched her, how on the road they kept telling her to look, look, every time they passed a cactus or a tree. They never let her just sit there. She always had to say something or they either picked a fight or—worse—got swelled up and refused to speak.

Scenery was nothing. Nothing happened. Scenery was just out there.

Jack's Thunderbird was parked a block down from the Indian village. Pauline heard it start up. He gunned the motor hard. The other tourists went back to their looking. The boy waiting to have his picture taken stepped inside the bear's arms. He was only six or so. To get in, he did not have to duck.

"I ain't afraid," the boy said. And as he stood leaning against the bear's belly, hands in his pants pockets, the boy looked directly at Pauline. He smiled for the camera. His father snapped the picture and said, "One more, son, to be sure."

Pauline turned away. If she had a brother or a sister, she'd have been better off. There'd have been someone else around to keep her from feeling so watched and responsible all the time.

She had asked Mavis to have one, preferably a girl; she really wanted a sister. But a brother would do.

Mavis was old for a mother, forty. Jack was forty-five. Mavis hadn't said no to the baby. She hadn't said yes exactly—really, nobody had babies at forty—but she hadn't said no.

Pauline picked up her camera and, with her skirt, wiped the

dust from the lens. In the distance, the Thunderbird roared away. When he came to a paved street, Jack did something to make the tires squeal.

When her father went at her, Pauline never felt like crying. She could not fight and cry at the same time. But when the fight was over, the rest of her feelings came down and she wanted to go sit in a closet in the dark, press her eyeballs into her bony knees and—comforted by the smell of sour shoes and mothballs —cry all night.

She pretended to be rubbing dirt from her eyes with the back of her hand. Mavis sashayed over like a girl, fluffing her hair. Mavis was getting fat again, the first sign of trouble. After the fat stage came the stone-dead nothing time, when Mavis sat in a chair by the window with her bourbon and refused to move or speak. Sometimes Pauline slid her face down in front of her mother's to see what Mavis was looking at, but it was only the yard, the trees, nothing new. When the zombie stage had gone on a few weeks, there would finally come a night of whispers and telephone calls, of car tires crunching in the white shell drive and then silence. In the morning Mavis would be gone. Pauline would be alone in the house with her aunt, the great Wanda, her steady presence.

"It's okay, Mama," Pauline said. "Here," she said. "You take the camera." She handed her mother the Kodak and took her hand. "We'll get a cab home."

"Home?"

"The hotel."

Pauline led her mother toward a telephone booth beside the swinging doors of the fake saloon. The fat stage was not so bad. At least she was still normal.

Nobody used cabs much in Arkansas and so it took a long time for theirs to arrive. While they waited, Pauline let Mavis take one picture of her beside the bear, standing a safe distance away, her hands at her waist, clasped tightly.

Mavis pressed the red button and—too soon; she moved too soon, the picture would be blurred—lowered the camera. "He should like that," she said. And she smiled. Mavis had two looks, happy and sad. The greatest smile, up at the edges, like an angel on a Valentine. When she was sad, her face collapsed.

In the cab, Pauline pressed herself close to her mother. Now she would get to swim. Maybe the lifeguard hadn't cleaned the pool. Maybe Jack would stay gone. She and Mavis could order from room service. It was Sunday. They could lie in their beds and watch Ed Sullivan.

Mavis felt warm. Round and enveloping. Next to her mother, alone with her, taking care of her, Pauline felt safe and protected.

A nothing kind of incident, no lasting repercussions, nothing that hadn't happened before. Yet every second is as fresh to Pauline this minute as if she were standing on the street of the Indian village, eleven years old instead of thirty-two, in Arkansas instead of Texas, Mavis giving her that shove, Jack being his ridiculous self, pretending to be what he is not, with no picture of how he might appear to anyone else, locked into his own stubborn sense of himself, the big man, Tex, the Iron Duke. The motheaten brown bear is always close. Surely he invades her dreams. And she is still afraid. The bear's eyes pin her to the wall, even in memory, some twenty years later when she is grown, has moved, established a career, her own life. Even though she tells herself, *Stuffed, the bear was stuffed,* the memory sticks. Crawls lightly but surely up her spine like a feather-footed insect.

2

He was if not gone then going. Tubes were attached to every opening, wires exited the fold of his sheets. There was a plastic catheter bag, oxygen, a machine on his bedside table to monitor heart and blood pressure. Covered to his chin, he was breathing and that was all.

Pauline stood at the foot of the bed, hands knotted in fists at her hipbones, trying to find a way to dredge up some kind of feeling for the man, but what? She couldn't say. Surely something. He was her father after all.

The nurse had given her fifteen minutes. She'd used up ten standing there daydreaming.

Where was love, sorrow, or sadness? Or barring bigger emotions, perhaps a minor one, say regret? Nothing came. She felt like a store mannequin, frozen. Even regret had its standards, a minimal amount of retrospective hopefulness that with luck and more effort on both sides things might have turned out differently.

Things had gone exactly as they had to. When Pauline finally saved enough money to move to New York, she'd sworn no longer to think about what might have been. Her parents would never change. Gone was gone. Yet look at her, four feet from the foot of his bed, hands on her hips, ready for battle. He was blotto and she was still afraid.

His breath came fast, in shallow, measured pants; his skin pale and dusty, like a dried bone. Occasionally the left side of his face twitched, then nothing. The right side drooped heavily, stricken and still, as if pulled toward the pillow by fishhooks.

A nurse came in, checked some machine, drew the sheet aside to readjust a wire. As the nurse worked, her elbow nudged the stiff white sheet across his stomach and down, revealing his pumping ribcage, his moon-white belly, his inverted navel and, beneath it, a vertical line of hair which fanned out in a triangular shape. His catheter tube ran a dark yellowish brown.

Pauline looked away. The nurse paid no attention. His hair there was gray and wiry, like his mustache.

Memory was odd. Odd enough that the picture of Jack inside the bear's arms should stick with her at all, much less come to her now, when he was in this unthinkable condition, all but gone. The incident hadn't meant much in a general way, only that Pauline had behaved heroically by going limp, refusing to obey. And yet the day had ended badly. In the end, he had found a way to get back at her.

Briskly, the nurse covered her patient and smoothed the sheet under his chin. She floated to Pauline's side and patted her on the arm.

"Two minutes, dear."

She had left one arm out, his good one. That hand lay curled on top of the sheet. Moving two cautious steps closer, Pauline lifted the hand. It felt warm and very alive. She set it back down. Possibly she did feel something. Nervousness that he could no longer harm her, horror that whatever a person was could be sucked out so quickly and yet the body struggled on, mindlessly twitching and pumping. Fear for no reason she could think of. She had depended on him to be there for so long.

She adjusted her purse strap on her shoulder. There was no need to panic. She was a grown woman, thirty-two. Tenth Avenue was her home; Michael, friends, all the family she needed. She had a career, ambition, some small success, possibly more to come. Her agent, Arlene Amundsen—who laid claim to being the only Swedish Jewish theatrical agent in New York —assured her that if not success then steady work was ahead, no question about it. Her life was there.

His breath fluttered the hairs of his mustache. His jaw was smooth. Someone had shaved him. The nurse came in and said it was time to go. Pauline nodded and went out.

She did not want to be an uncaring daughter. She would like, when it came, to be able to mourn her father's passing. But the balance was fragile. She did not know how to care for her father—much less love him—even in his present condition, without yielding up to him all that kept her safe from him. And every time her mother asked her the simplest kind of question, Pauline heard, beneath the stated one, another request: come home, come back, be ours again. Her only choice seemed to be all or nothing.

In the hall, she leaned against the gray metallic door of the intensive care unit. She dreaded seeing Mavis, that wildly optimistic look, more fervent in bad times than good. In a crisis, Mavis accepted the only information she could bear to hear, good news at all costs, nobody dead or dying, nothing lost forever.

"Excuse me dear." Another nurse, with a tray.

Pauline moved from the door. She turned down the wrong hall, came to the lobby—full of people, a boy with a cart of flowers, volunteer ladies in candy-striped aprons, a woman standing alone, leaning against the wall holding a red bandanna with black cowboys and Indians on it over her face so that no one could see her crying—then retraced her steps.

Brackenridge Hospital, the best trauma treatment center in central Texas, Mavis said, quoting doctors. It probably was. It didn't matter. Dying was the same anywhere.

Returning to the gray door, Pauline started over, turning down what she believed was the correct hall. Her legs reached decisively ahead of her as she walked, her agile feet testing the ground like blind men's canes. Long legs, long feet, legs attached as loosely to her hipbones as if threaded by rubber bands, hips wide and shelflike, assurance in each step; a woman who trusted her body, whose body rarely disappointed her, one of those women whose posture and demeanor might be an illustration of how best to walk in order not to be considered a candidate for mugging. Assertive; strong and daring. Purse slung over her shoulder like a weapon, daring whoever would come at her to do so at his own risk.

In her mind she heard her father's flinty voice, taunting her.

"You walk like a man, Pauline," he used to say. "Why do you want to walk like a man?"

What had he expected, mincing steps? Shorter thighs, cuter knees? He asked her loaded questions all the time, then walked away, leaving her to wonder what in the world he wanted her to say or do. Stop growing? Shrink? How was she supposed to love a man like that?

Settling her shoulders, smoothing her impeccably cut, straight dark hair, she turned another corner and suddenly was alone. She listened to the heels of her leather boots echo against the pink native marble that was everywhere in Austin, atop the dome of the state capitol, in walls at the university, rising up against the changing horizon in the form of state and federal office buildings one after the other. The pink marble looked like tombstones.

Texas, home, slowed her down, turned her blood to gravy. She would not stay long. She would do her duty and go home. In the meantime she felt like an alien, on the moon. As if she were in uncharted territory instead of her home state.

She walked on down the hall, concentrating on listening to the sound of her boot heels clicking and not the ghost of her father's voice.

3

When she thought of it, Pauline still felt a mild sense of surprise that she had stumbled around and somehow found her career. Nothing had pointed toward it. In Baytown of course, she was considered to be not arty but an athlete. As a girl she dreamed of becoming a circus acrobat, flying from a trapeze. When she got older and gave up that idea, she couldn't think of a substitute. She could teach of course, PE or history. She was good at history. But teaching never appealed to her the way the circus had.

After high school she went to college in San Marcos, her major undecided, her roommate, assigned by the college, a sniffling, allergic girl who feared coolness, pollen and fresh air. Their room was like a closet, heat blasting away. Pauline spent as much time as possible away from the dormitory, walking the campus, studying in the library, swimming in the river. She had a hard time making friends.

By October she was ready to quit and go home. In six weeks' time, the only person she'd had a decent conversation with was her handsome uncle, Will Hand, who taught in the Science Department. They'd had coffee together, once. When Pauline invited him to go again, her uncle said it wasn't a good idea. She was a student now, not his niece. Her uncle was a principled man. Still, she'd been disappointed.

One cool, late autumn night when she had nothing else to do, she slid into a seat on the back row of the school theater, where auditions were being held for the semester's first play.

Having never acted in her life, she didn't think she'd actually read for a part. She didn't think anything. She just went. But the director—a huge-bellied man with a woolly mustache and a voice like a cannon—tended to pace the aisles during auditions, and so he found her. The play was *Tiger at the Gates*. He asked her to read for Andromache.

From the first, even sitting in the dark back there waiting, Pauline had loved the theater, its isolation, the immediacy of its risks and terrors and satisfactions, its quick daring intimacies and, when the play was over, its tearful farewells. She did not always love acting. Acting was a humiliating profession at bottom, especially during rehearsals when the director poked and probed and you had to try to come up with the same emotion evoked by the same lines, over and over again. But the theater itself was a new home.

Onstage the first time, she was nervous, as she had expected to be. She thought she might be sick. Her mouth quivered, her tongue turned dry. Then she began to read. A kind of quietness surrounded her speech. The director stopped snorting. She knew she'd done well.

A more seasoned actress—a junior—got the part of Andromache. Pauline played the laundress. One scene, no lines. Her only job was, in the first act, to walk across the stage from full stage left to stage right carrying laundry, listening to an emotionally fraught conversation between Andromache and Hector. She could tell the director liked her. "You are the Greek chorus," he declared, his deep voice filling the theater. "You listen. You know. You . . ." and his voice dropped, becoming more intimate ". . . have the only full cross in the production." Besides playing the laundress, she also worked backstage, doing props, helping beautiful Helen of Troy with her wig.

She'd worked hard, onstage and off, cuing actors, handling props, building sets, taking whatever part she could get. She wanted to be great, the kind of actress who created an entire life onstage, so that when she spoke lines they became her own and when she walked offstage it was to go someplace, not just make an exit. Moments were easy enough to come by. The rankest Little Theater amateur could, on a given night, come up with a great moment. But to develop a concept of a character and sustain that concept throughout the performance of an entire play, took art and study and concentration and focus.

She'd done it once, or come close, playing Sonya in an off-Broadway production of Chekhov's *Uncle Vanya*. There were moments she'd missed—Sonya's declaration of love for the fulsome Astrov, some lines in the scene between Sonya and Elena—but she had come close. Her reviews were good. One critic had called her "the perfect Sonya."

At last, the right hall. She turned a corner and there it was, the ICU waiting room, as crowded now as when Pauline arrived.

For a large county hospital, the waiting room was inexplicably small. There weren't enough chairs. Somebody was always stretched out on the floor. High on the the wall near the ceiling a machine meant to absorb cigarette smoke crackled constantly, like a severed electrical wire. The machine accomplished little. A pall of smoke hung in the air. In one corner, the family of a boy who'd been in a coma for a week ate sandwiches and brownies and drank canned diet soft drinks. The family—mother, father, a son and daughter in their twenties—was camping out in the waiting room, waiting for the boy to wake up. Everybody else in the room knew them.

Facing away from Pauline, Mavis, as blond as an advertisement for hair dye, was deep in conversation with another woman. Mavis's arms gesticulated wildly. Her blond curls bobbed. Mavis was large in the shoulders, with that rise across her back called a widow's hump. The other woman nodded her head, her face hidden by Mavis's bulk.

It was too soon. Pauline ducked into a doorway then turned around and walked in the other direction, stepping lightly to dull the click of her boot heels. There was no need to rush trouble.

She had left Houston ten years before in a twenty-year-old Chevrolet coupe with her two best friends, Robert and Dennis, both actors. In those ten years, nothing had changed. Mavis still looked like a child, that same light of feverish expectation in her eyes.

She came to the end of the hall. Another hall abutted, going left and right. After peering around in the corner in both directions, recognizing nothing either way, Pauline arbitrarily chose left, wondering as she went who designed hospitals and with what end in mind.

Robert was a thin balding character actor; Dennis, a handsome leading man type, beauteous as Bathsheba. The three had taken turns driving straight through, Houston to New Jersey, two days and two nights. At four in the morning in Newark, they ate crullers at an all-night diner, waited for daylight and sold the car. They took the train into Manhattan. It was all so exciting. They planned to be famous together, to live with intensity, to be accomplished actors. Pauline would play Cleopatra to Dennis's Antony, Robert would be everybody's comic relief.

For three years, they lived together in a one-bedroom cold-water flat, bathtub in the kitchen, toilet down the hall. Pauline slept on the living room couch, Robert and Dennis in the bedroom. Her friends were also lovers. More than lovers, it turned out; a couple. After ten years they were still together, as inseparable as Maggie and Jiggs.

Pauline's New York friends were family by now. Robert, Dennis, Michael. Her special friend Coco. Vicky and Patricia were a couple; Vicky an electrician who wanted to be a lighting designer, Patricia a costumer's assistant whose ambition was to own a shop and sell her own clothes. Bucky worked for diseases, heart, cancer, whoever was hiring. Miguel walked dogs. Eileen danced topless. Lazlo tended plants. They cooked together, celebrated holidays in traditional fashion, made huge events of one another's birthdays. This past Christmas they had all gotten together and done turkey *mole*. No food processor. Everything ground by hand in a seasoned *molcajete*. It took all day. None of them had children. Most pined to be in the theater but only a few had steady work. Felicia was an exception. Felicia had danced in chorus lines all over the city. Never out of a job, she made a good living. But Felicia knew she couldn't dance forever. "Besides," she said with a sigh, "I get tired of smiling all the time." Pauline met Felicia in an improvisation class at HB Studio. They did a scene together, Felicia as Blanche, Pauline as Stella. Felicia was great at improvs, terrible at line readings and picking men. She fell in love every other week, one bad choice after the other.

Pauline had met Coco through Felicia. Felicia didn't know what good friends Pauline and Coco had become.

The gray door again. A sign on the door announced the visiting hours, twenty minutes per visit, every four hours, strictly enforced.

She went back in the other direction.

Having reached the age when he could play the age he looked, Robert now worked all the time, but the beauteous Dennis had left the profession. Accustomed to being admired, Dennis couldn't accommodate himself to the condition all actors have to, in which appearance becomes not a personal attribute but a professional commodity. He kept getting his feelings hurt. An excellent cook, Dennis now owned and operated a home-based catering service with an emphasis on Mexican and Tex-Mex dishes, all the current rage in Manhattan. Like most New York actors, Robert and Dennis were talking about moving to California. In Hollywood, they reasoned, Robert could make a fortune.

A sign on the marble wall said SURGERY. An arrow pointed to the left. Feeling chilled, Pauline unrolled her shirt sleeves and buttoned them at the cuff.

She was still in her traveling clothes, off-white silk shirt, straight-legged bluejeans, round studs of lapis in her earlobes. Her caramel-colored knee-high leather boots, soft as a glove, had cost a full week's salary. It was June, too warm in Austin for silk shirts and high boots, but the hospital, like most of Texas, was air-conditioned to the teeth. She rubbed her arms.

She was not a pretty woman especially, not beautiful. But handsome, dramatic. Noticeable in a crowd. Her large, lush features assured her of a second glance, especially in high heels, when her face floated by above others like Peter Pan in midair. To emphasize her exaggerated facial features, she dressed with stylish plainness. No jewelry, no belt, little makeup, only mascara and a bit of powder. An actress had to know what she looked like, not only in mirrors. To calculate the effect she had on other people, she had to know what kind of person she *seemed* to look like and be. Some of this seeming was a result of artifice. Most was not.

Behind her, bottles clanked. She moved aside. Surgical attendants wheeled a patient by. The wheels of the gurney squeaked. The patient, in surgical green, was out cold, both legs in casts. Pauline flattened herself against a wall and let the stretcher and its entourage pass by. At the patient's side, a black man in a green paper cap nodded. Pauline nodded back. The man steadied the I.V. bottle.

The attendants all wore paper booties over their shoes. The booties made a soft crinkling sound on the marble floor. When the gurney and its entourage was safely past, Pauline went on.

I am, she said to herself, *Pauline Terry. I live in New York, walk as I walk. My feet. My legs.*

She had changed her name when she joined the union, taking her grandmother's name—Terry Pauline Steck—and turning it around. Equity approved. Pauline liked the sense a new name gave of being someone new. People thought she might be related to the great Ellen Terry.

Her hair was cut asymmetrically, parted low on one side, shorter in back than in front. Dark and heavy and straight, her hair took well to the blunt hairstyle. When her head was down, the longer hair in front fell over her eyes. The cut was great, but required frequent trims; it was too long now. But Mavis's frantic call had come in the middle of the night. No time for a quick appointment. If she stayed long, she'd have to have it shaped. She would never find anyone here to do it right.

When she was young, Pauline's exaggerated features and bushy eyebrows had driven her crazy. She had always had a messy and undefined look, too much of everything. In her twenties she had still looked unfinished, uncertain, soft around the edges. But at thirty, Pauline had begun to grow into her looks. Forgoing wishful thinking, she began to emphasize her assets: large and widely spaced eyes, long flaring nose and full mouth, those eyebrows, straight across her forehead, nearly growing together at her nose, like a slash drawn by a broad-tipped pen. In theater such a face is called a mask: large features, small bones, recognizable from the back row. Lucky you, directors said. Lucky girl. She finally gave up wishing to be pretty enough—small and delicate enough—to play ingenues. She began to wear high heels, liking especially to be tall at parties, meeting men's eyes straight on. New York helped. So many different kinds of looks, such varying definitions of beauty.

Still, she was amazed when she received compliments. Like most attractive but not especially pretty women, she had little confidence in her appearance. People said she should model but she had no marketable look. Excess made for dramatic shifts. Sometimes she looked fine, the next minute hollow-eyed and sad. Mirrors were a constant surprise.

With the fingers of one hand she lifted the long front piece of hair from over her eye and hooked it behind an ear.

She'd had help figuring all this out, from Michael in particular. It was Michael who had suggested she dress more simply, Michael who took her to have her hair cut, Michael who convinced her to leave off lipstick and stop plucking her eyebrows. Michael had a great visual imagination. In his mind's eye he could see in advance how things were going to turn out.

Spying a chair next to a water fountain, she sat and, crossing her ankles, let her legs stretch out. Lifting the clammy silk of her blouse from her back, she wrapped her arms around her chest and stared at a crack in the pink wall across the hall from where she sat. The crack looped around and joined itself in a shape not unlike that of a running dog. Pauline fixed her gaze on the bottom point of the crack, at the dog's front paws.

o   o   o

A former Marine from Brooklyn, Michael Caproselli was an actor when Pauline met him. He hadn't been an actor long, but by then he'd already grown tired of the grind: making rounds, cattle-call auditions, bad plays, stupid lines, endless rejections. For something else to do, he'd turned to teaching. Later, he became a playwright.

"I'll tell you something about that class," he said, some months after they met. "I wasn't interested so much in teaching *per se* as I was in seeing if I could *move* people." And he made a gesture in the air, like a child resituating doll furniture. Michael was an excellent actor—Pauline had seen him once in a night of Clifford Odets scenes; like a beauty queen he was so absorbed in himself, she couldn't take her eyes off him—but he had too many opinions to impose upon the world to do it for long. Actors had to take in more than they imposed.

Pauline had heard about the class from a friend. It met late, Monday and Wednesday nights from ten to midnight in a rehearsal studio he rented by the hour, midtown in the theater district. Skeptical at first—she didn't like taking class from amateurs—she knew from asking around that, like most fledgling actors in New York, Michael had never done a play in his life, his experience having been limited to scenework in class. To Pauline studying with somebody like that seemed crazy, like sending your watch to be fixed by a man who'd read a book on clocks, but Michael had studied with all the currently in-vogue teachers—Strasberg, Stella Adler, Uta Hagen, an obscure Russian woman named Mira Rostova whom only deeply serious actors knew about—and so students came to him. (Not that that was rare: acting students would go anywhere to have someone watch their work.) Friends urged her to go. Michael, they implied, was not an ordinary man. Pauline had nothing else to do that late on Monday and Wednesday nights and so she did. Besides, she was curious.

They had known each other six years, been married four. By now Michael felt to Pauline like the very ground her life was rooted in. Without him, where would she be? He had waked her up, changed her life and looks, taught her so much. Books, acting, life. No one had ever taken her so seriously. A student of the everyday, Michael watched her all the time, going to the bathroom, shaving her legs, changing her Tampax. Wanting, he said, to be a part of every minute of her life, he found nothing she did too trivial to be taken for granted. He told her she was beautiful, helped her learn to love the way she looked. If she would be an artist, he insisted, she must be an unwavering one. "If not a masterpiece," he said, quoting Cyril Connolly, "then nothing at all." Quoting writers, actors, philosophers Pauline had never heard of, he challenged the level of her expectations and, by challenging, raised them. By now his standards had become a substitute for her own. Anytime she made a gratuitous gesture onstage—what actors called indicating—she privately blushed, suffering the heat of Michael's scorn. He made her feel important, that was all, like a closely watched child.

She was living with Robert and Dennis when she met him, at night still listening through thin walls to her friends' arguments and subsequent lovemaking . . . getting nowhere with her career, working at a Howard Johnson's on Broadway, scooping out endless dips of ice cream, rehearsing scenes, memorizing, reading Boleslavsky and Stanislavski, going to improvisation or sense-memory class, studying body movement for the stage. She loved class and studying, and was beginning to feel herself slowly relaxing into a workable technique. But her life was stalled and she was in a slump. Nothing was happening, and it had been three years. Scenework was maddening, one chopped-up scene after the other, each done at fever pitch as if it were the whole point. She yearned to do a whole play again, to have that feeling of an arc of movement within an overall design. She had thought of going back to Texas, but for what?

Her hair was still long, plaited in a single braid. To Michael's class she wore a girlish outfit: gingham-checked blouse and matching full skirt, dangling earrings and, because of her height, flat ballerina slippers. Michael later told her she looked as cornfed as a Rodgers and Hammerstein musical.

And he. In his Spanish black boots and thick black wool sweater, tape-striped shirt, creased jeans, and perfect haircut—down his neck, across his face—black hair, dark eyes, that hoarse, whispery voice: Pauline had never seen anything like Michael Caproselli in her life. When she walked in, he was arranging chairs while students burbled among themselves, finding last-minute motivation for the business they planned to use in their scenes. Michael smoked a black cigarette, squinting as the smoke curled into his eyes. He waited for her to come over and introduce herself. When she did, he welcomed her warmly, shook her hand, then took his hand away and with its heel moved some hair out of his eyes, back in place. *Like a girl,* Pauline thought. *He's vain.*

In class, as he worked with other students, she studied him. The way he used his hands, drawing pictures in the air. And how he gave direction, holding an actor by the shoulders, whispering, standing so close the two of them seemed about to kiss, touching, always touching. As a teacher, Michael's cause was honesty unstinting: every moment explored, every emotion plumbed and discovered anew, no gaps; what the books called "moment-to-moment truth."

When her time came, Pauline did a monologue from *The Chalk Garden.* Michael didn't like monologues—acting was *inter*acting, he said; actors developed bad habits doing monologues—but since she was new, he let her do it. The scene went all right, not great. She was too anxious. When she was finished, Michael came up to her from the dark part of the room. When he walked, his boot heels clicked against the hard wooden floor. Above their heads, dancers rehearsed for an off-Broadway revival of an old vaudeville burlesque show. As Pauline waited, the choreographer yelled ". . . five, six, seven, *eight* . . ." and the high-heeled shoes began to pound against the ceiling, like riveting sledgehammers, the pianist's heel going *wham* as he pedaled out the rinky-dink tune.

Michael sandwiched Pauline's hand between both of his and sweetly asked her—whispering so that no one else in the class could hear—next week to do a scene, please, and not a monologue. Pauline could only nod, the breath having been drained straight out of her as quickly as water from an unstoppered sink. ("I'll swear," Michael said later, "when I reached for your hand there was electricity. A spark. Wasn't there? I don't mean some kind of symbolic bullshit, I mean the real thing. Between us, wasn't there electricity?" Pauline said well yes, maybe there was. Michael looked surprised. "You didn't *feel* it? How could you not *feel* it when I did? How could that happen?" Eventually Pauline said yes, in fact she had felt it. "Electricity," he repeated. "Real electricity?" Yes, she insisted. She had learned by then not even to try picking her way out of the exitless maze of his arguments.)

After class they went for a slice of pizza. Walking down Eighth Avenue, Michael spoke of acting teachers and technique, of individual performances. Geraldine Page was terrific, he said, but not as good as Kim Stanley, Kim Stanley was the best, did she agree? She did. Pauline listened, listened. Michael was zealous; committed; he had so much to say. And she to learn.

As they walked he leaned in so near to her his hair brushed her face. For emphasis—making points as he talked—he touched her gently, laying a finger over her arm, her hand, her arm again; and took her by the elbow to guide her out of the way of a drunken couple; and thrust his arm across her waist when she threatened to cross a street before the light changed and traffic cleared. Eventually he invited her to his room. ("You want to come up?" As if just thinking of it. "I may have some brandy.")

At his door, he pulled out a wad of keys, inserted one. The key fit but would not turn. He jiggled it, rattled the knob. "Sometimes," he said, cigarette hanging from his lips, black smoke drifting into his eyes, "I feel so incompetent as a man." Finally the lock gave. Pauline had never heard a man make jokes at his own expense. With every step Michael took, new territory appeared beneath her feet.

He lived west of Eighth Avenue in a hotel. No kitchen ("You grow up in a restaurant, you never want to smell food again"), nothing there but clothes and books. Not many clothes, but books everywhere, stacked on the floor and on every inch of available table and chest-of-drawer space. Curious, Pauline went to a stack and lifted one. She heard Michael's quick intake of breath. "Are your hands clean?" he asked. She set the book down. He poured a large amount of brandy in a hotel water glass.

She had her period. When she told Michael, he got a towel. The towel—white—she warned him, would not be enough; she bled heavily. Michael said not to worry and she did not. They made love a long time. When afterward Michael looked down and saw the long, Florida-shaped stain, he was annoyed. The stain had soaked through the towel and sheets to the mattress.

"My luck," he said. "Every woman I meet has her period."

Pauline soaked the blood from the sheets and towel but nothing would take up the stain in the mattress, not ice or club soda. Florida was permanent.

Worse luck, Pauline had used her last tampon during a break in the acting class. In Michael's bathroom, she folded the cheap stiff toilet paper into a temporary pad, laid it in the crotch of her underpants, and pulled her pants up as high up over her hips as they would go, hoping the paper might take care of the flow until she got home. She had done this many times before; it had never worked. She had not taken three steps from the bathroom when the makeshift pad slid too far back to do any good. She could feel blood seeping into her underwear and down her thighs.

There was nothing to do. Her menstrual periods were merciless. The first two days, the blood gushed, draining her of energy, making her a prisoner chained to pads, tampons, dark skirts, the quick dash into a bathroom to make a change.

Michael sat on the bare mattress, naked, smoking a black cigarette. "Will you tell me something?" he said, pointing the cigarette at the window.

She looked out. Beyond the grimy windows, there was nothing. Only grayish, darkened buildings. On top of one, the time and then the temperature flashed in red lights. "What?" she asked, feeling stupid.

"Why is it every time I want to know what time it is, the temperature is flashing and every time I want to know the temperature I get the time?"

"I don't know," she said. It had taken years of living with Michael to learn how not automatically to answer a question like that.

Michael's mood suddenly lifted. Indicating the stain on the mattress, he shrugged. "So I'll say I cut myself shaving," he said. "Forget it." And he motioned for her to come sit beside him. Pauline could never tell when Michael was kidding and when he was not. But at least he was true to his word. He never mentioned the mattress or Florida again.

By the time she got home, Pauline's underwear was soaked, her thighs raw from rubbing against the drying blood. A dark, curling streak had inched down past her knees. She rinsed her skirt and underwear and washed herself at the sink. The icy water froze her legs but it took the stains right out of her clothes. Using an extra-thick sanitary pad, she lay down on the couch and—legs apart to ease the chafing—fell instantly asleep.

That was the beginning. That quickly he had found out a great deal about her; that swiftly she had fallen under his spell. From the first, Pauline felt not so much in love with Michael Caproselli as drawn implausibly to him, and in six years nothing had changed very much. She still had not figured him out, still searched for the last, tiny puzzle-piece of self that might finally define him and help her get to what she thought of as the *end* of him. Once she'd done that, she thought it might be possible she'd even leave Michael. But for now he was still an exotic, an adventure, a rope swing; someone she would not have met in Baytown if she'd hung around the bus station for a month.

He was also exhausting. For the most part, Pauline's salary from various jobs paid their rent and bought their food. Michael stayed home and wrote. Sometimes she thought the reason she never minded this arrangement was that it tired her more to stay home than to be out working.

Michael's father was dead. His mother lived in Brooklyn, a subway ride away. But Michael and Pauline lived their own life, isolated, devoted to art and intensity, their marriage passionate, unconventional, and without family ties. It was what they needed. The more they were alone, the better off they were.

A man in a shiny black suit came down the hall. His pants were too short. He was wearing thin black socks which sagged at his ankles. He consulted a card, checked a room number, went on. Passing Pauline, the man gave her a brief professional smile. He had shaved himself so close his pale skin was raw. He smelled of cheap drugstore aftershave. Pauline nodded. Doubtless a preacher, making calls. Baptist, she would guess, possibly Church of Christ. Something hard-line. When he walked, he kept his head cocked to one side. Listening for angels?

She had vowed on the way down here to be shameless. To keep the past tightly gripped between her teeth. To forget nothing. She had promised Michael.

For a moment she lost the shape of the running dog. She squinted her eyes and, looking through her lashes, found it again, its nose pressed forward, hell-bent for leather. Unhooking her purse from the back of her chair, she pulled out a tube of colorless moisturizer and coated her lips.

4

A nurse slid by on silent white feet. Stirring, Pauline stood and went back to the waiting room. Mavis and the other woman were looking in her direction, heads screwed to the side like birds on a telephone wire, looking for weather clues.

Pauline waved as if she'd just seen them. The family of the boy in the coma were curled up together on the couch, settling in to take a nap. All except the mother, who looked as though she might never sleep again.

When she got closer and saw who the woman with Mavis was, Pauline quickened her step.

"Wanda," she said aloud. Wanda, standing, held out her arms.

Mavis was the baby of her family, Wanda a year and a half older. Besides Mavis and Wanda, there had been four other Steck children to survive beyond infancy: two more girls and a set of twins, boys in the middle named Rudolph and Randolph. Randolph—at birth small enough to cradle in one hand—died of complications from scarlet fever when he was three. Mavis and Wanda's two sisters also died young, one in her twenties in childbirth—at home, before the Stecks got their money and began going to hospitals at the least opportunity—the other at forty of ovarian cancer. Rudolph, the remaining twin, now in his seventies, was permanently ensconced in a Pasadena nursing home of dubious repute, his emphysema slowly sucking the breath and life from his lungs.

In the cemetery in Luling, stones marked the graves of

Steck ancestors who'd lived from ninety to a hundred years. The luck of the Stecks had changed. They had more money now and fewer years in which to spend it.

The prettiest and smartest of the sisters, Wanda had naturally curly hair and bright blue eyes which betrayed an intelligence she chose, for the most part, not to share. Like Pauline, Wanda knew more than she was willing to say. In her sixties, she was still slim, still attractive. She kept her prematurely white hair cut short. It curled around her face like a picture frame.

"Pauline, you old thing," Wanda said. "Come here to me." As Pauline moved into Wanda's arms, a flush of affection washed over her. She tried to speak but couldn't. She bent her head down to let it rest on Wanda's shoulder. With the flat of her hands, Wanda slapped Pauline's back in a steady, loving tattoo.

She should have known Wanda would come. Because she had had three husbands—a family scandal—and was always between marriages, not to mention being childless, Wanda always came.

Nurse Wanda, she called herself. When Mavis went for treatment, Wanda had always brought, for comfort, books and family stories, mostly about herself: how as a girl she wanted to be a movie star, how, because everyone treated her ambition as a joke, at sixteen she ran away from home to marry a railroad engineer who took her for a ride in his train and let her blow his whistle. Not exactly the silver screen but dramatic, the next best thing.

Wanda's hair smelled metallic. The bones in her back felt fragile as crystal, apt to break with unsure handling. Over the top of Wanda's head, Pauline could see Mavis peering up at her as if Pauline were the last friend she had in the world.

Pauline closed her eyes. When she opened them, Mavis was still staring.

"What do you think, Pauline?"

Mavis's blond curls shook as she spoke. Her lower lip trembled. She wiped her mouth with a tissue. Wanda stepped back, releasing Pauline. The smoke machine popped.

Pauline had two choices, to feed her mother a sugared lie or to throw truth in her face like a pan of dirty dishwater. There was no reason to give Mavis what she asked for, every reason to tell her the truth. She would have to know sooner or later.

"I think . . ." Mavis's eyelashes fluttered. She ducked her head and swallowed hard. Pauline hesitated. She couldn't. It was too hard. "I think we'll have to wait and see. It doesn't look good but you never know."

"Oh, thank goodness," Mavis said, and, fanning her face with both hands, she sat back, looking around to see if there was anyone else to tell. She wore a pale blue pantsuit with a long jacket. Nervously, she wrapped the jacket once again around her midsection, imagining the jacket disguised her heft. Her stomach was a melon, her hips like plates, her breasts a garden row. She had a huge colorless mole beneath her left eye, perched lightly on her cheekbone, as if about to take off and fly. Mole, wart; something. She'd had it for years. It seemed to have darkened and grown. Pauline had suggested she have it removed but Mavis hated doctors.

"Let's go get a bite to eat," Mavis said and, hugging her expensive white monogrammed pocketbook to her stomach, she stood up and took Wanda's arm.

Pauline walked behind the sisters. Wanda wore a sheer, belted dress which hugged her body and swung at the hem when she walked. Her hips still had a girlish curve. Her spine was straight. The heels of her shoes were high enough to emphasize the line of her calf. Mavis's pants strained at the seams. When she walked, her hips moved as one, like the body of a large animal, surging from one side to the other.

As an assignment for physical-image class, Pauline had studied animals at the zoo. Bears walked like Mavis. They took a step with the hind and front feet on their left side and then their right. This gave them their characteristic heaving motion—body going one way, pelt a beat behind going the other—and slowed their pace. Pauline made a mental note. If she ever wanted to use Mavis for a part, she would think not of her mother but the bear. Concrete reality first. Inner life followed. Good actors went by the rules.

Mavis turned back to see if Pauline was following. She motioned her down another long pink hall.

"Lord, Mavis," Wanda said. "I don't see how you find your way around in this place. It's bigger than the Astrodome. Do you, Pauline?"

"No," Pauline said. "I don't."

Mavis shrugged. "Smart, I guess," she said.

Moving to New York had not been hard for Pauline. She loved the city the same way she loved the theater, the way she was drawn to Michael, on the instant, gathering its risks and terrors to her like old friends. When she first got there, afraid of getting on the wrong bus or subway—terrified of ending up in unknown territory, maybe Queens or the Bronx—she stuck to sidewalks, depending on maps; her feet. Walking, always a careful observer, she learned the city's ways, how people behaved, what kind of language they used greeting one another or turning one another away, when a threat was meant to be taken seriously and when it was only an everyday exchange. She learned how the city itself changed, not just from one section of town to another but from block to block. There was a rhythm to each, a choreography. On the sidewalks, people swarmed, like migrating geese in formation, merging, separating, merging again. Subways never frightened her, she only had to learn the drill, when to step on, off, how to sway with the movement of the cars. She liked being underground, liked the fast pace and not knowing or being known by a soul, everyone pressed close, no one smiling or saying hello. All that was a relief, after Baytown.

There were things to be wary of: muggers, rapists, subway fires. Pauline took reasonable precautions. But she was not afraid.

o   o   o

Walking behind the two women, Pauline slowed her usual wide stride to a near standstill. Mavis and Wanda walked as if they had all the time in the world. And after all, they had a point. What was the rush?

There was no answer to the question. Pace was ingrained. When Mavis turned in to the cafeteria, Pauline moved ahead to get·their trays.

She waited for them and, when they got there, handed them their trays and let them go first.

"How do you like New York City, Pauline?"

They sat at a table with their food on brown plastic trays meant to look like woven bamboo. As it was the middle of the afternoon, except for two nurses the cafeteria was empty. Mavis had gotten a sticky sweet roll and coffee. Pauline and Wanda had iced tea. Mavis stirred artificial sweetener into her coffee. The sweet roll looked stale.

Wanda's question took Pauline by surprise. In her family, questions were rare. (By family, she meant Mavis's side only, the Stecks. There weren't many Millers left and those who remained had scattered. Jack refused to talk about them. His people, he said, were not for the most part worth killing. Bastards and cattle rustlers, he claimed with perverse pride.)

What Stecks called conversation did not include an exchange of information. They had no discussions and did not argue, but only made speeches. When in position to obtain it, a Steck grabbed the floor and did not yield until he had to. Other Stecks waited for the moment in which to step in—a break in the flow of talk, a breath taken, the unfortunate fit of coughing, the ill-timed drag on a cigarette, anything would do.

Their stories were all the same, trouble their topic: illness, personal deprivation, abuse, misuse, neglect, lack of appreciation. After a while, the subject matter became more specific.

They honed in on who among them had been *most* misused, neglected, unappreciated, hurt: whose arthritis hurt worst, who had the bloodiest childbirth experience. As competition grew more heated, tempers flared. Somebody was always leaving a family gathering swearing never to speak to a single one of them again.

But against the world, Stecks closed ranks. If one Steck had mistreated another, no Steck had ever treated another as badly as the world treated them all. On this one issue they were in common agreement.

"I like it a lot," Pauline replied. "In fact, I love it."

She sipped her iced tea. It was excellent. Good, freshly brewed iced tea was hard to come by in New York.

"How long have you been there now?"

Wanda's question was routine, a statement really, designed to extend the conversation.

"Ten years, about. I left in September. Remember, I worked at the Shamrock pool that summer, then went?"

"The year Mama died and my second divorce was final. I remember."

Wanda's second and shortest marriage was to a sharpy insurance salesman from Philadelphia. Always on the run, the salesman had gone from state to state in a westerly direction until he finally made his way as far west as he could go, to California. Once creditors got wind of his disappearance they flocked, as did the government, expecting back taxes. Even with her allotment from the gas wells, Wanda had to borrow money from all over the place to pay her half of the bills. Fortunately for Wanda, Texas was a community property state. For all she cared, Wanda said, the creditors and the IRS could sue the moon for the sharpy's half of what was owed. As for her, she was not forking over one more penny.

Her second husband had been a rascal, Wanda told Pauline, but oh my. And she rolled her eyes. Her face lit up and her voice implied all kinds of things. But when Pauline egged her on, Wanda clammed up.

Tubes were Wanda's explanation for the fact that she'd had no children. The women of the Steck family had become unlucky that way. Infected ovaries, cysts as big as baseballs, a dropped uterus threatening to come out like a baby. As a girl, Pauline had heard all the stories—told calmly, in loving and bloody detail as if it were some other people they were talking about and not themselves—and listened hard. Pauline was a big baby, nine pounds some-odd. Mavis had to have oh, well, just so many stitches. When Mavis talked about going into labor, she called it getting sick.

There had been other babies, stillborn and miscarried. Mavis had her hysterectomy the year after the family trip to Arkansas, when she was forty-one. Wanda had hers when she was thirty-nine. Gloria was said to have begun having hot flashes while still in her thirties, to have been beyond menopause at forty. Trouble in that area was a family curse. Pauline had no real way to know how much of all of this was true. But as a child of course she believed it all.

She lifted a piece of ice from her tea and idly put it in her mouth.

"By the way, whatever happened to Uncle Will?"

Wanda's third husband was the one Pauline knew best, her old college professor, Will Hand, well known in San Marcos for his absorbing lectures, his rolling voice, his old-fashioned handsomeness. Niece or not, like every other of his female students, Pauline had fallen under her uncle's mesmerizing spell.

Wanda set her iced tea glass down on the table with decided sharpness.

"Still in San Marcos, last I heard. Living on that creek . . . by his lonesome precious self, of course, he is his own best friend. You heard about his books?"

In the early 1970s, Will Hand had written a slim book, a combination myth and personal essay called *The Legend of Snake Creek*. The book had gained a good deal of attention among environmentalists and young people: hippies, flower children, back-to-the-land romantics. He had become a minor cult figure.

His book was listed in *The Whole Earth Catalogue*, its virtues praised, its importance rated up there with bean sprouts and brown rice. He had written one other book since *Snake Creek*, a collection of essays, but it had not attracted the attention of the first. Since then, there hadn't been much; an occasional article, nothing more. Pauline had read a few of the articles but neither of the books. Michael had read both.

"Yes," Pauline said. "We all know about his books. My husband"—the minute she said the word, she regretted it—"is an admirer."

Mavis cleared her throat and stirred her coffee. "How is your husband Michael, Pauline?" She asked. "Why didn't he come?" She fluffed her hair. "I'd like to meet him."

To avoid conversation on this subject, Pauline dropped her voice, made her eyes go blank. "Michael is fine. But you know how New Yorkers are. They don't like to leave the city." She focused on her tray.

The sisters grew quiet. Mavis shuffled her feet. Without the give-and-take of a story, they had no idea how to respond.

"So." She lifted her eyes and directed her attention back on Wanda. "Is Uncle Will still teaching?"

"I'm not sure. He was talking about not. After that first book, which made him not a lot of money but some, he built himself a house on a creek. We were still together, but not so you'd notice. I couldn't take it out there. Little? Girl, that house was tee-tiny, like a doll's house. I got the message fast. Your uncle likes being alone, that's for sure. Mr. Solitary. Read his books, you'll see." Her blue eyes danced.

"And what are you up to these days?"

Wanda pointed at her chest. "Me?"

"Yes."

Wanda brushed her hand through the air.

"Oh, honey, you know I can't stand to sit still more than a minute. When we broke up I went back doing needlepoint. I work at this store in the mall. I teach a class there and sometimes at Sears. You know"—she placed her hand beside her mouth as if telling a secret, but did not speak in a whisper—"I don't need the money. We none of us do. I just like to be out in the world. Busy."

Before they had any, Stecks had believed in money. If they had enough, they thought, everything else would fall into place. When fourteen gas wells were discovered on Mavis's parents' land in Luling, they all thought they'd found the end of the rainbow at last.

But money had been a big disappointment. No Steck was made happier by money. They bought more things, drank more, got deeper in debt, fought more. No one traveled. Their world was not broadened, nor was it made more complex. They drove bigger cars, air-conditioned their houses, bought fur coats they almost never got to wear, had aluminum siding put on and Butler outbuildings built. Their children went wild, bought diamonds and furs they almost never got to wear, squabbled over property and wills, had their ears pierced, their hair back-combed, their faces lifted. And that was all. For Stecks, money had been a major disappointment.

Mavis ate her sweet roll then mashed the leftover crumbs together with her fork.

"Well, I'll say this about Uncle Will," Pauline said. "He was an excellent teacher."

Wanda nodded. "No doubt about that," she said, and she looked away. "No question about it."

Mavis sighed. "That was good," she said. "I could eat about a dozen of those. They couldn't be too fattening, could they? They're mostly air."

She looked up at Pauline for affirmation.

5

She had just gotten in from work when Mavis called. It was two. Except for the small lamp Michael had left on for her to see by, the apartment was dark. Next to the lamp, a note. "Your mother called. She'll call again at two." A carefully drawn heart and then the initial M. Pauline grabbed the receiver after only one ring. Mavis was crying so hard Pauline could not tell what she was trying to say.

"Do you have pills, Mama?" she finally asked when Mavis had calmed down.

Mavis made a sound of assent.

Pauline gently instructed her mother to take her pills and try to get a good night's rest. "I'll be there, Mama," she said. "If not tomorrow, then the next day. Have you called Wanda?"

"Not yet."

"Then do that."

Mavis promised.

When Pauline was able to end the conversation, she turned off the lamp and sat in the dark by the telephone for some time. Home, she thought. Texas. She tiptoed to the bedroom door, hoping Michael might be awake, but he had slept through the call. In the dark, she took off her clothes and climbed in next to him, still smelling of chlorine. Automatically, Michael pulled her into the hollow of his long, slim belly. Pauline lifted her top leg to let one of his find its familiar place between her knees and, settling her pillow, lay on her side, staring at the wall.

Sometimes their bed felt like a cliff they both were perched on the edge of, thinking as long as they held on to each other, they were safe. Sometimes she thought the drop might be farther down than either of them could stand to imagine. It was bizarre, this arrangement they had made. Trying to be bohemian, they had managed simply to cut themselves off from their past. As if they'd been born that night in the rehearsal studio, he in his black sweater, she in her Baytown ginghams, no parents, no childhood, just the two of them, ready for anything. As if nothing else mattered: no three-act play to worry about, no general theme, only scenes, one after the other. Like snapshots in an album.

She drew her arms in to her chest. People had to have a picture of themselves to go by, something immovable to check against, a small inner mirror to consult. Pauline's mirror sometimes told her that the way she and Michael lived was dangerous, maybe even wrong. But why? And what were the risks? Mostly, she let those questions go by, content to use Michael as a guide, the way she palmed walls in the dark to find her way through the apartment. Michael was her fixed point and as long as he seemed so sure, Pauline could manage to do what she and Jack and Mavis had been so skilled at, back on their front porch those warm summer nights, planning vacations: she could brush doubt out of her mind and forget.

Only, sometimes—like now, alone and awake in the dark —she couldn't help it, she looked out over the edge of the bed and saw—beyond the window, into the air shaft—only darkness, the fall, no net. It was crazy. Crazy that she had never crossed the river and gone to Brooklyn to see her husband's mother. Crazy that Michael had never taken her, crazier still that she had not asked.

But in the beginning, Pauline had agreed with Michael, it was the only way. They had studied the terms of their marriage carefully, spending long nights trying to think through every eventuality. Their decision was, no family. The only way not to be sons and daughters forever was to break the tie cleanly. Their marriage was to be one of adult connectedness. No children,

Pauline said ever, Michael, temporizing, said at least for now. Michael went to Brooklyn but Pauline did not go with him. In six years, she had been back to Texas only twice. Rose Caproselli had never been to their apartment. It was always clean, clean enough, Pauline thought, for inspection by a mother-in-law. But Rose was not invited and did not come. On Christmas Eve, Michael went to Brooklyn, then came home to spend Christmas Day with her.

Michael turned over, mumbling something as he pulled up the sheet. Pauline went with him, fitting herself into the shape of him, pressing her breasts and stomach against his spine, her hipbones against his buttocks, her knees into the back of his legs until he lifted one and let hers through. Curling an arm over his chest, she cupped his breast in her hand. His mumble had sounded like a question. In case he was waiting, she answered him. "Yes," she said. "Yes." And with Michael as protection between herself and whatever was out there, she slept.

The next morning he was up early, as usual. Pauline tried to sleep but could not. Michael had taken the back room of the apartment—really only a storeroom, barely bigger than a closet —for his office. He was hunched over a stack of papers when she interrupted him.

"I have to go," she said. She was wearing her favorite robe, a lavishly embroidered silk kimono she had bought for pennies in a secondhand store.

Michael looked up and frowned. Michael rewrote his plays endlessly. None had ever been produced or read and would not be until Michael pronounced it perfect.

"If you have to, you have to," he said. He tossed his pencil onto his desk.

"He was playing golf—" When she started to tell him what had happened, Michael stopped her.

"Where is he?" He stacked some pages and turned them face down.

"Who? My father?"

"Yes."

"Austin. Why?" This was possibly his most irritating habit, stringing her along to create suspense.

"When's your plane?"

"There's one late this afternoon and another tomorrow morning. Why?"

"Do me a favor, go tomorrow?"

"I'm sure that's fine but, Michael, please. Why?"

He stood, took her by the shoulders, rubbed the place he knew was always tense. "I'm sorry about your father, you know that. Whatever touches you touches me. But I want to take you somewhere today. I want you to meet someone. All right?" He ran his thumbs across her eyebrows and brushed her hair from her eyes.

Michael's silky persuasiveness snagged her the way a hook gets a dumb, hungry fish. Pauline said yes, she would wait. But who?

"Trust me," he said. "Wear your good jeans."

On the BMT, he told her. The only other time Pauline had been to Brooklyn was to swim in a three-woman water ballet at a private club. The pool was too small, even for only three people. The swimmers kept bumping into one another. The audience was so busy talking they didn't clap for the flutter-kick flower, ordinarily a sure bet.

As soon as he stepped out into the Brooklyn air, Michael became another version of himself, a boy again, in a hurry. Forgetting Pauline, he walked ahead of her, skipping over cracks in the sidewalk, making jags around parking meters and door stoops, yelling to merchants in stores. Everybody knew him. All the merchants yelled back. He was wearing his black raincoat, fashionably big. The hem of the coat flapped around his legs like a cape. Pauline widened her stride but could not keep up. Occasionally he turned around to wait for her. Every time he did, Pauline was amazed. He looked flushed and irrepressibly happy.

Finally he turned in at a dark old brownstone in the middle of a block. At the top of the stoop, he waited.

Pauline took her time climbing the steps.

He met her halfway. "I'm sorry, Pauline. I get carried away. You know how I am. God, I hate it here."

He unlocked the door. They went into the hall and up one flight of stairs. Somewhere in the building someone was cooking cabbage. At the door marked 2B, Michael inserted one key and then another and another, turning a series of locks until the last one gave and the door opened.

"Nervous," he said.

He stepped through the door and began calling, "Mom?" until he heard an answer. Pauline came in after Michael, closing the door behind her.

The apartment was dark and cluttered. Heavy velvet draperies on the windows were closed. There was so much furniture in the room and so many pictures on the wall, the room looked like a store. Two couches, three wing chairs, two television sets, on top of one a digital clock with oversized numbers. Dark, elaborately carved mahogany end tables were everywhere, cluttered with family photographs and glass knickknacks. Paperweights with flowers trapped inside, figurines of perfect birds. Music boxes, ebony and carved. Albums, one on top of another. An ivory chess set, a coffee table made from a large, round brass tray. On the tray, arranged around the outer lip, small brass animals. Elephants, tigers, bears.

"You should have called," Pauline said in a whisper.

Michael pressed his hands down like an orchestra conductor asking for quiet. "Don't worry," he said.

Finally Michael's mother came out of a back room, smoothing her hair with her hand. As she walked down the hall she kept one hand on the wall beside her.

Like Michael, Rose Caproselli was tall. She'd kept her figure. Her large breasts were high, her short hips flat and firm. It was early afternoon but Rose was dressed elegantly, in a dark crepe dress and low-heeled shoes, stockings, gold earrings with a tear-shaped amethyst drop. Her makeup was carefully if dramatically applied, her complexion tinted olive, her lips almost purple, eyelids a deep blue, cheeks cunningly, not excessively, rouged. Coming from a part of the house even darker than the living room, she squinted. "Michael?" she said. She bent her free arm and set it on the rim of her brow. "Michael?"

Michael went to her. "You've been sleeping." He took her hands in his. Pauline felt afraid and out of place. She shouldn't have come. She should have dressed differently, worn a skirt.

"You know I never sleep in the daytime. Now who's here?"

Michael led his mother across the room to Pauline.

"This is Pauline, Mama," he said, holding hands with each of the women. "Pauline Terry. I've told you about her. Pauline, meet my mother, Rose."

Pauline held out her hand, but Rose, instead of taking it—could she see it?—turned away. She went over to an end table and from an ornate glass candy dish took out a pair of glasses. Pauline lowered her hand, jammed it into a pocket. The glasses fit into the sockets of Rose's eyes so tightly they seemed to be stuck. The lenses, thick as bottle bottoms, doubled the size of her eyes. She looked Pauline up and down.

"Your wife, Michael," she said sternly. "She's your wife."

Michael looked flustered. "Yes," he admitted. "My wife."

"So why didn't you say?"

"I told you her name." He looked to Pauline as if for help. "It's still her name."

Pauline felt like furniture, brought home on approval, being appraised.

"Michael tells me you do Chekhov," Rose finally said to her. "Sonya."

"Did." Pauline corrected her. "It's been a while."

"You're thin," she said. "But a good type for Sonya."

"You know the play?" Pauline could never get used to parents who had read anything beyond the funny papers.

Rose lifted her head. "Do I know the play, she asks. Of course I know the play. I've done Elena myself. *Vanya's* other woman. Sere-what's-his-name's wife."

Pauline turned sharply, first to Michael. "She's an actress?" And then, before he could answer, to Rose. "You're an actress?"

Rose took off her glasses and folded them shut with a snap. "You didn't tell her." Her glistening left eye blinked. A drop of water clung in the outside corner. Her pupils were lost in a cloudy glaze.

Blushing a little, Michael focused on Pauline. "I didn't want you to think that I'd . . . that I liked you because of . . ." He nodded in Rose's direction and, making a funny and endearing, self-mocking face—eyes to the ceiling, mouth turned down— gave it up.

Pauline did not let him know she thought he'd been charming. "But the restaurant?" she asked Rose.

From deep in her throat, Rose grunted. "The restaurant," she answered, "was his father's idea. The restaurant was a necessity. It kept us going."

Rose then turned her face in three-quarters profile to Pauline and, as if it were a speech she'd been asked to recite, launched into a monologue she'd obviously performed many times before. She knew, she said, why Michael didn't tell Pauline: because he was ashamed of her. He didn't think she'd been any good as an actress. Well, she'd seen Kim Stanley's Masha, and Kim Stanley's Masha didn't hold a candle to hers. Hers had stature, Stanley went for laughs and bitterness. When she paused for breath, Michael segued in, retaliating with remarks as cutting as Rose's, defending not only Kim Stanley but himself and his own judgments as well. Sparks flew. Neither let up. Michael looked happy, challenged, his eyes jumping with humor and admiration. Pauline watched, amazed. They sounded like her own family. Like the Stecks. They weren't angry and did not mean to hurt one another. This was simply the only way they knew to *talk*.

Rose turned on her heel and went to the other end of the living room, where she flopped into a worn wine-colored chair and looked off away from Michael and Pauline toward the front door, as if an audience were there. Michael motioned for Pauline to follow him. They tiptoed out. But Rose's diatribe neither cooled nor dwindled. Michael should have let her know he was coming, she snapped, so that she could have bought a little something at the bakery, a nice piece of cake or an almond torte. Michael didn't like her to talk about her career, he was afraid she'd get out her scrapbook and talk about the old days. . . .

Michael continued to defend himself, not in anger, only to keep Rose going. But Rose had the edge. Rose still had the practiced breath of an actress. She could recite a page-long speech without pause.

An archway led into the dining room, small and formal. The dining-room suite was made of deep red mahogany polished to a soft, satiny glow. Six chairs were pulled up to the table as if guests might at any moment come and sit down to eat. Against the far wall, a glass-fronted china cabinet held a set of ruby-red wineglasses and many place settings of gold-encrusted bone china. On a lower shelf were tiny liqueur glasses in various colors, red, cobalt-blue, deep jade-green. Beside the glasses two empty cut-glass decanters. All the glass pieces were immaculately dusted.

Against the long wall of the dining room, opposite the windows, a stack of cardboard boxes covered the wall. The boxes went up six high, nearly to the ceiling, two deep and eight across. Each box was marked NORTH AMERICAN VAN LINES: BOOKS.

Michael bowed and presented the boxes. "My library," he said. "There are this many more in my old bedroom. I didn't want Rose to have to fool with shelves, and so I left them in boxes." He had lowered his voice to a whisper so as not to interrupt Rose.

"I heard that," Rose said from the other room.

"Heard what?"

"My name. What were you saying?"

"How beautiful you are, Mama. How mellifluous your voice."

Rose harrumphed.

Pauline stood close to Michael. "But why didn't you tell me? What is this for?"

Michael cupped her face, took a breath, shook his head, then said, "I don't know."

Behind the darkness of his eyes and within the black smell of his tobacco breath, Pauline saw him, the real Michael, and knew he was telling the truth. A bubble of panic drifted up inside, from her stomach to her chest.

She moved away. "There must be hundreds," she said. "I can't believe it. It's a wonder they don't fall."

He turned to the boxes of books. "Thousands, actually." He began to count rows across and then down. "Including the ones in the bedroom."

He went to a stack two over from the door to the living room and handed a box to Pauline. His black hair swung down over his eyes as he worked. "Just set them on the floor," he said. He combed his hair back with his fingers and reached for another.

From the living room, Rose mentioned coffee. Michael handed Pauline another box.

"In a minute, Mama," Michael said. And to Pauline, whispering as if they were in a conspiracy, "This won't take long."

It was stuffy in the dining room. Pauline was beginning to feel closed in.

"What are you doing?" she whispered. "What is this about?" She heard Rose get up from her chair, go into another room and come back. Her step was crisp.

Michael handed her another box. "Please, Pauline, just a few more minutes. I have to show you something." When he came to the box one up from the bottom, he set it on the dining-room table.

"Don't scratch my table," Rose said. If her eyes were going, her ears certainly were not.

Michael's passion for books, of course, was no surprise. Pauline had known about it from their first night together. When there were books Michael wanted to buy, he got a job until he had made enough money to buy them, then quit and went back to writing once again. But Pauline had no idea there were so many.

"Are they catalogued?"

"You know me. I know where everything is."

He took a handkerchief from his pocket, wiped his hands, and opened the box.

"Nora?" Rose said. "My Nora was without peer." She set a cup on a saucer with a gentle clink.

Michael took a layer of folded newspaper from the box, then lifted out the top book. It was *The Burning Brand*, the journals of Cesar Pavese. The jacket looked out of style, but brand new. Michael set the book on the table, wiped his hands on his jeans once again, then lifted the next book from the box as carefully as if it were a rich child's spun-sugar Easter egg. He arranged the book across the palms of both hands and held it out to Pauline. The book was her uncle's, *The Legend of Snake Creek*. The one beneath it was *Straddling the Fault Line*, his second. When Pauline started to take the book, Michael pulled it back.

"It's a first edition. Mint condition. One of the few still unsigned."

"I'll be careful."

"That's not what I meant."

"Then what?"

"You're going down there. You might see him."

Rose had grown quiet. Pauline raised her voice. "Michael. I can't believe you asked me to put off going to Texas for this."

There was no extra air in the dining room. They were both beginning to sweat. Michael cautioned her to continue to whisper.

He cocked his head. "You know I wouldn't have asked if I thought it made a difference."

She whispered once again, following his lead. "Why would I see Will Hand? I haven't in years."

"He's your uncle, isn't he?"

"Was. By marriage. They're not even together anymore."

"But he lives near Austin."

"He used to. He may not now. It's a big state."

"But it's possible he's still where he used to be."

She tried to think of a way out and couldn't. "It's possible."

"And it's possible he may come to the hospital to pay a call. A family visit." He placed his hand on her arm and held her . . . not hard, but firmly. "I'm not saying he will, Pauline. I'm not telling you anything is going to happen. I'm just asking, that's all. Is it possible?' In Michael's vocabulary, firmness was a disguise for love.

Pauline lowered her eyes. And she was a fool for brashness, outrageous certitude, the unequivocating position. She yielded.

"It's possible."

Michael lifted her hands and gave her *The Legend of Snake Creek*.

The book was small and slim. On the cover an expressionistic painting of a creek with wavy grass on its banks and a smoky half-snake, half-woman figure, perhaps a ghost, walking beside it. The creek looked like a twisted blue hair ribbon. In the background two huge intertwined trees leaned in toward each other. The paper the jacket was printed on was pebbly, not shiny.

Inspired by the quietness in the dining room, Rose once again perked up. "Arkadina?" she asked the world, and she made a kissing sound with her lips. "Anyone who saw my Arkadina never forgot it."

Pauline handed back the book without opening it. "I'll do something to it," she said.

Unlike Michael, Pauline marked books with signs of life as she went. She liked to read in the bathtub, to turn down pages to hold her place, to underline passages that moved her. She read while she ate. Michael bought her used paperbacks to read, books she'd never have dared to attempt if he hadn't insisted. Henry James, Jane Austen, Hortense Calisher. Reading Edith Wharton, she retraced Lily Bart's footsteps all over the city.

Cradling the spine of Will Hand's book, Michael turned pages by delicately running his hand down the length of each one.

"Listen to this," he said. " 'I had not lived long on the creek when signs of ghosts appeared.' Isn't that just a fabulous opening sentence. *I had not lived long on the creek when signs of ghosts appeared.* Was there ever a better opening sentence than that?"

Rose was winding down. She'd soon sulk if they didn't go back in. Pauline shifted her weight and hooked a damp curl of hair behind her ear. The back part lay against her neck like a cap.

"Yes," Pauline agreed. "It is a fabulous opening sentence. Now can we go?" Her voice shook. Michael wrapped both books carefully in brown paper and tied them up with string, then set about restacking the boxes of books. Pauline went into the living room and asked Rose if she might have a cup of coffee. Rose seemed delighted. When Pauline volunteered to pour her own, she did not object.

They talked. Pauline asked Rose specific questions about her acting days—where, which theater, when, and with what other actors. Made calm by attention, Rose began again to tell her stories this time without anger. When she came to a stopping place, Pauline asked to see her albums. Rose directed Pauline to a nearby table. Michael came in and sat on the arm of Pauline's chair and Pauline flipped the pages of the album and they all three stayed that way for several hours. Finally, Michael began tapping his nervous feet. He said they had to go. Rose sighed. Pauline closed the book.

Michael went to his mother's chair, took both her hands, and pulled her to her feet. Rose came up out of her chair and into his arms as easily as a lover. Michael patted her.

"Mama, Mama," he said. "You are so bad."

Rose lifted her carefully manicured hands and softly slapped Michael's cheek. Her eyes were awash. "Idiot," she said. She clasped her hands together at the base of his skull and drew his head toward her and back. "Idiot."

When they let each other go, Rose looked in Pauline's direction. "I'm sorry I had no small something to offer you. Some other time, maybe."

"Maybe some other time, yes."

Rose held out her arms. Pauline went to Rose and hugged her. She smelled of lavender and coffee.

On the subway home, Pauline asked Michael no more questions, about the books, his mother, or Brooklyn. They rode home in silence. If he didn't know the answers, she didn't want to ask.

That night she had a dream about the two of them, sitting up in bed, side by side, each with a gun. The rule was, when one moved, the other could shoot. Pauline had already been shot once. Her chest hurt like anything but she could not give in to the pain. She had to watch for her chance to get him back.

The next day she left for Texas.

She had brought the books. They were still in her suitcase, tightly wrapped and securely tied.

Michael never accepted any explanation at face value but always looked behind words, searching for reasons. In his acting class, he insisted that students be ready to give specific motivation for the slightest change in facial expression. *Why smile?* he would ask. *Why at this particular moment do you smile?*

What did he have in mind, taking her to Brooklyn? Not just the books; he could have gone and gotten the books on his own. By breaking their contract, was he giving her his unspoken permission to do the same? Was he asking her to? And why had he hidden Rose away all this time if he was eventually going to let Pauline meet her, especially if she was going to turn out to be so great? Sometimes Pauline couldn't tell whether she loved Michael or hated him or what.

6

In the waiting room, Pauline sat close to the family of the boy in the coma and listened as the boy's mother told the story again. Like a wind-up toy, once begun, the mother could not stop. The boy had been in a motorcycle accident. He hit a curb in some funny way and went over the handlebars, landing square on his head. He wore a helmet, but the helmet was not protection enough. "He looks like Sleeping Beauty in there," the mother said. "I wish you could see him. Like Sleeping Beauty." Pauline thought she had seen the boy. He was the one on his side curling in on himself. He did not look like Sleeping Beauty.

They couldn't see Jack again for another three hours but when Pauline suggested going back to the motel, the sisters would not hear of it. Wanda and Mavis would not budge until after the last visitation at eight that night, the Steck method of doing hospital duty being one of constant vigilance, sitting at the hospital day and night until hospital personnel chucked them out, as if presence itself might have a therapeutic effect.

Feeling no compulsion to be a part of this family tradition, citing the long airplane ride, the need to unpack, the difference in time zones, Pauline excused herself to go to the motel to check in and take a nap. They were staying at the Villa Capri, a motel on Interstate 35, not far from the hospital. She had taken a cab from the airport. In the hospital garage she located Jack's pickup, paid the garage parking bill and drove down Red River, letting the air conditioner blow on her face. The radio was on, low, still tuned to the FM station Jack had chosen, which played country music with few commercials. On the seat beside Pauline a pair of Jack's leather driving gloves lay palm up, fingers curled. Pauline put the gloves in the glove compartment.

On the sidewalk in front of a huge, drum-shaped building, students from the university were lined up outside a ticket window. A poster announced a coming ZZ Top concert.

A year or so after Pauline left home, Mavis and Jack had sold the house on Cedar Bayou to U.S. Steel for a huge amount and moved into a condominium in Houston. More money. Jack went into cable television, rice, motorized water skis and real estate.

Every summer, Mavis and Jack took a two-week trip to a resort hotel in the hill country just outside Austin. The hotel had a lake, tennis courts, and two golf courses, plus organized indoor games for the less athletically inclined: something for everyone, like on a cruise.

It was at the resort that Jack had had his stroke, crouched over his putter on the seventeenth green of the golf course. Jack aligned the ball with the cup, missed the putt, and collapsed, instantly paralyzed on one side of his body, his blood pressure so high it went up over the range of the machine the Emergency Medical Service people brought to test him with. They drove him into Austin in an orange and white ambulance. The EMS driver said he thought something was wrong with his machine, he'd never seen blood pressure so high.

They had come to the resort in separate cars. Someone had driven Jack's truck into Austin. Mavis hated to travel in the truck. It jiggled. And if it rained, you had to jam all your suitcases into the cab. Besides, at the resort she and Jack liked to go their separate ways, Mavis staying in the air conditioning smoking cigarettes and drinking bourbon while she played bridge and mah-jongg, Jack golfing and, at night, making the rounds of Austin bars and beer joints. And so they had driven to Austin in tandem, he in his red and white longbed Ford Ranger XLT pickup, Mavis in her baby blue Seville.

Pauline liked sitting in the pickup, high above cars. Driving was one of the things she missed in New York. She turned into the motel parking lot and went into the office.

Mavis had forgotten to make a reservation, but there was no problem getting a room. Pauline charged the room to Mavis, took her key and drove to the back section of the Villa Capri. She pulled the truck into a parking spot. The motel had a Spanish look, like a lot of things in Texas.

The room was cool and dark. Pauline threw her duffel on a chair, took off her boots and jeans and, in her silk shirt and underwear, lay down on top of the covers. The curtains of the motel room were double lined so that no light came into the room. Pauline pulled a pillow out from under the bedspread and propped it so that her head was tilted. She closed her eyes.

In the picture Mavis took of Pauline and the stuffed bear on the fake dusty street in Arkansas, the bear—fuzzy and out of focus—could have been anything, a bear or its shadow, even a large bear-shaped sign. When they got their vacation snapshots back from the drugstore, Pauline examined the picture with her stampbook magnifying glass. As she had thought, the bear's eyes were on her.

As for herself, in the picture Pauline's legs drop down from the gathers of her skirt like sticks. Her long feet look like boxes nailed to her ankles. Later, swimming coaches would tell her how lucky she was to have hyperextended knees and long pliant feet, which together acted to propel her through the water like flippers. It was true, Pauline could shoot through water like a rocket. But she didn't like being told her feet were like flippers. In pictures of her as a child, she has the startled look of a girl whose bones have grown too fast for her understanding to keep up with.

When she and Mavis got back to the hotel, Pauline put on her bathing suit and went down to the pool. The lifeguard had already skimmed the leaves from the water and cleaned the traps, but he said it was all right that she hadn't showed up; she could help him the next day. The lifeguard, blond and muscular, his skin the color of pecan meat, had painted a stripe of white paste down the length of his nose to keep it from burning. When Pauline worked as a lifeguard—first at the Baytown municipal pool, then at the country club and finally at the magnificent fifty-meter pool at the Shamrock Hilton Hotel in Houston—her skin turned so dark she had to wear stockings meant for black women. The summer at the country club when she was in charge of everything—pool chemicals, traps, even sweeping the pool deck—her fingertips peeled from chemicals, her heels cracked from walking barefoot on pebbly concrete. It was the summer after she graduated from high school. She earned $1.50 an hour, enough to buy herself a clock radio and some clothes. She felt damp all the time. She always smelled of chlorine.

Water was great.

In addition to the lifeguard, Pauline made another friend on the Arkansas trip—a boy, nine, who looked exactly like Boy in the Tarzan movies. Same blond curly hair, those icy staring eyes and sweet curling mouth.

Having brought her Kodak, Pauline asked the lifeguard to take a picture of herself and her friend. In that picture, Pauline is a good head taller than the boy. Her wet braided hair is plastered down on her head, her eyes are puffy from chlorine, her bathing suit is hiked up higher on one side than on the other. The boy is hugging himself around the chest. They both have large, numbered safety pins attached to their bathing suits. Hers, crooked, is on one strap so as not to tear her suit. The boy's pin looks exactly right, squared with the hem of his bathing trunks.

A frozen moment, the boy and Pauline poised and restless, anxious to get back in the water, Pauline stiffly posing, standing face forward, awkward arms to her side, the boy looking up at her as though she were something scary he had to keep an eye on. Pauline's large eyes have a dazed look about them, her usual look, a willed innocence she later found difficult to give up. Her shoulders are tense. Her nose is too big. So is her mouth.

When she went up to the hotel room after swimming, Jack had not returned. Mavis was sitting on the bed talking on the telephone, her back to Pauline. In the ashtray a cigarette burned. Pauline waited, listening. This was how she learned things.

". . . not this time," Mavis said. "I fell off the roof last night. I think I'm too old."

Pauline shut the door. Mavis jumped. Turning, she motioned Pauline into the room.

"It's freezing in here," Pauline said. She ran to the bathroom.

She knew when Mavis said fell off the roof it meant the thing that happened every month and that that had something to do with having babies, but what exactly she had no idea. It was all a mystery. Nobody had told her anything. She could see well enough what was what, with horses and dogs all around. But it was hard to make the jump from horses and dogs to your parents. Mavis had given her a book. A fast reader, Pauline had gone through the book in minutes. When Mavis tried to explain, Pauline put her hands over her ears and ran out of the house.

She locked the bathroom door, then turned the shower on as hot as it would go, peeled her wet bathing suit down her body and kicked it away. Steam quickly coated the mirror over the sink and the glass shower door. She added a little cold water so as not to scald herself. Having a stand-up shower was great. Also, not being out in the country, she could get amazing water pressure and all the hot water she wanted without having to worry about running out. She could shower all day long if she wanted to.

She added a little more cold and got in, standing directly under the shower head until her skin warmed.

For a small test of her flexibility, she bent from the waist and reached to the shower floor for her shampoo. Limber as a rubber band, she could put her face against her shinbones without bending her knees.

The shampoo came in a tube. No one else in the family used this brand and so she got to have it all for herself. She squirted green liquid into her palm until her palm was full, then lathered the shampoo onto her head, pulling at her hair. The shampoo foamed up and made satisfying curlicues and peaks, like whipped cream.

Her stomach quickly turned red from the bullets of hot water pounding on her skin. Rubbing her scalp, she let the shower beat against her, then stood under it to rinse her hair. She ran a hand down her head to see if her hair squeaked. When it did not, she applied more shampoo, rolled her hair into a foamy doughnut on top of her head, and got out of the shower.

Eyes closed, dripping on the floormat, with a pink bar of hotel soap Pauline lathered herself all over, going in and out of her ears and around her face, between her legs and in and out of the crack of her buttocks, paying careful attention to every piece of skin: behind her knees, in the bend of the elbow, between every toe. When she was totally soapy except for her eyes and mouth, she felt for the shower door and got back in and rinsed herself.

This seemed to her the only way to make sure she was soaped up in every possible place before letting the hot water rinse the foam and dirt away, the only way to get truly clean.

The water ran down her face and over her flat chest. Suds whirlpooled and were sucked into the drain. With her palm she rubbed her head. This time, her hair squeaked. She raised her arms and pretended she was in the mountains in Colorado, standing under a giant waterfall.

Sometimes when Mavis was in her stone-dead stage or had a headache, Jack came into Pauline's bedroom to help her get to sleep. Sometimes he stroked her hair and talked to her, sitting on the side of her bed. When she was younger—three, four—he used to read her bedtime stories: fairytales about princes and princesses, "The Little Engine That Could," "The Camel with the Wrinkled Knees." They liked Raggedy Ann and Andy. Sometimes, later in the night, after he thought she was asleep, he came back. Pauline always closed her door but there was no lock and he did not bother to knock. When she heard the doorknob click it felt like some hot burning thing was turning her insides into flames. Silently she begged him to go away, not to come in, this one time to do something different. She pretended to be asleep but she could hear his breath. She could feel him watching, watching. Was her nightgown down over her thighs? She was afraid her eyes might twitch and give her away. She was afraid of what he might do or say. She concentrated on breathing deeply, evenly. She wished he would vanish into thin air . . . just disappear back into his lamp, like a genie.

In a stagey imitation of exhaustion, she would turn over, moaning as if in deepest sleep, then stay on the side of the bed away from him, facing the wall. (Making a place for him? Giving him the okay? Some room?) Sometimes he came closer, touched her arm, her shoulder, her face. She felt feverish and weightless, without bones, like a liquid. Sometimes he said things. Sometimes he got on the bed with her. One knee, then he sat. The mattress sank a little with his weight. He lay beside her. Surely no one else had a father like this. In stories they did not.

One time he did something else. As Pauline lay unmoving, he reached for her hand. She did not move. The only thing to to do was keep up the pretense, dead gone as if in the bliss of deepest sleep: no bones, her arm, hand, limp as dead flowers. He lifted her arm. She could not resist or he would know. He put her hand on himself. She wasn't sure at the time what was meant by "himself"; she only knew that what was happening shouldn't be and that the cool, ridged part of him she was touching—like nothing she'd ever felt before—was beyond what should be felt or looked at. But he was her father and she was supposed to be asleep and so she let it happen. She left her hand a while and then drew it away, feeling the cool ridges of him again as she sighed and dragged her fingers away, safely back into herself, letting hair flop over her face, pulling her two arms in close together under her chin.

Did he know? He leaned over and whispered to her, close to her ear; she could feel the moisture of his breath. "Feel that, honey?" he said. "Did you feel that?" Soon afterward, he slept;

snored. So far over on her side of the bed she almost fell off, Pauline forced her eyes open and, staring at the rose-print wall-paper, tracing the paths of the vines in and out of the white bordered diamonds back and forth and back and forth, vowed not to sleep all night.

She spit on her finger and wet her eyes, counted to one hundred without blinking. But she couldn't help it. Eventually, she could not of course remember exactly when, she fell asleep. Slept hard, no dreams.

In the morning, he was gone. Nothing was said. He might never have been there. Pauline stripped the bed and took her linens to the laundry room and jammed them down into the washing machine. A Mexican woman worked for them. Janie may have changed the sheets the day before but Janie never asked why Pauline wanted them washed again. No one said anything. Pauline told no one; not even, in a way, herself. She didn't want them to tell her anything; she knew enough. There were things it was better never to think about.

In the hotel bathroom, she rubbed herself dry with one white towel then wrapped another one around her head the way she'd seen movie stars do. Her robe was on a hook on the bathroom door. She put it on, wrapping the belt tight around her waist, tying it in a firm knot, and opened the bathroom door. Her mother was still there, sitting against the headboard of her bed. Pauline waited to be noticed.

When the telephone rang she had no idea where she was. Arkansas, she thought at first. New York?

She reached for the phone. It rang again. The Spanish furniture told her she was in Texas, at the Villa Capri. She expected Mavis.

But of all people, it was Will Hand, calling from San Marcos. She had forgotten how deep his voice was. He was polite as ever. He asked for Wanda. They spoke of Jack. He said Wanda could not call him back, he had no telephone, but that he would try her again the next day. He said he was happy to have talked to Pauline. They said good-bye and that was all.

When she hung up, Pauline lay in the dark with her hand on the telephone, wondering why Will Hand had wanted to get in touch with Wanda. Wanda had such a look in her eyes when she spoke of him.

At five, the telephone rang again. Mavis. She and Wanda had been in to see Jack. There was no change in his condition.

"He just lay there, Pauline," Mavis said.

Pauline said, "I know, Mama. I know. There's nothing you can do and that's hard."

"I just thought you ought to know," Mavis said.

Pauline thanked her for calling.

Mavis and Wanda were staying for the eight-o'clock visit. Pauline said not to wait for her to eat with them.

She ordered a cheeseburger and iced tea from room service. The room-service boy was fat with blond curls. He wore gray jazz oxfords. He left abruptly. The cheeseburger was not hot. The french fries were stale. Pauline ate everything.

When she finished, she turned out the lights so that when Mavis and Wanda came back to the motel they would think she was asleep. Later, when she was sure they were in their room for the night, she turned on the television set and watched late-night talk shows and—flipping from station to station—pieces of old movies.

The wind started to blow. Outside her window, she could see only the motel swimming pool and more rooms. The pool, lit up and sparkling, looked like a green neon comma. Low clouds covered the moon. The wind ruffled the surface of the swimming pool, making choppy waves. The parking lot was deserted.

There was one thing Pauline and Jack used to do together that was fun. They used to stage jalapeño-eating contests, sitting across from one another at the kitchen table with a clock and a bowl of peppers between them to see who cried first. Pauline loved hot food and so did Jack, but straight jalapeños took nerve. She'd look at her father and crunch into one, feel the heat rise up to her nose and eyeballs and steam through her brain, and bear down. It took all the strength she had to keep her eyes from watering right away.

Sometimes she won, sometimes he did. All in all, she thought they were about even.

She stared at the pool.

Mavis still hadn't noticed.

Pauline tied the knot of her robe a little tighter. The towel on her head slipped. That never happened to movie stars. She took the towel off and hung it on the bathroom doorknob. Mavis had put on her pink nylon nightgown, even though the sun was still out.

Pauline moved closer. "Who was that?"

Mavis took a long draw from her cigarette and frowned, as if trying to decide who Pauline was. "Who was what, honey?"

"On the telephone."

Mavis looked at the telephone as if someone were inside it. "Oh," she said. "Just Wanda. Gassing." She motioned Pauline over. "You have a good swim?"

Pauline went to her mother's bed and sat down, dangling her legs over the side. Mavis's skin felt warm and soft, like a sun-ripened tomato. Pauline waited for an invitation to move closer.

"Snuggle, honey," Mavis said. Pauline pulled her legs to her chest and curled up into her mother's armpit, trying to turn her bony arms and legs into cute soft ones, like the dolls and teddy bears Mavis bought her, which Pauline never played with.

"What you been doing? Swimming?" Mavis stuck her nose in Pauline's hair. "Pew-ee, honey. You washed your hair and it still smells like a bottle of Clorox." She jiggled Pauline by her shoulders and pulled her closer. This was another great thing about a vacation, getting to snuggle with her mother in a strange bed. If Mavis wouldn't get fat, Pauline thought, she would be as beautiful as a movie star.

Pauline told Mavis how she and the boy stood on the side

of the pool with their backs turned to the water, counting to ten. One of them threw a penny over one shoulder into the water then both dove in. They kept score, who found the penny the most times. Pauline won. Once, the penny had fallen to the rim of the pool drain. The drain was the deepest spot in the pool, ten feet. Pauline's eardrums felt like they might burst when she dove for the penny but she got it.

Mavis rubbed Pauline's legs to warm them. She wasn't really listening but she didn't interrupt.

"You hungry, honey?"

Pauline said she was.

"Look in the drawer," Mavis said, pointing at the desk. "There should be a menu."

They ordered from room service, all the things Pauline loved, fried shrimp and Coca-Cola, french fries and apple pie with ice cream. Pauline put her pajamas on under her robe. When the food came, Pauline ate the pie first, so that the ice cream wouldn't melt before she got to it. Mavis didn't eat much. She picked at her shrimp and toyed with her pie, drank her Coke and ate a few french fries dipped in ketchup. Pauline loved fried shrimp maybe better than anything.

After eating, they sat in one bed together, against the headboard. Pauline turned on the television set. Ed Sullivan was on. Pauline didn't much care for Sullivan or any shows featuring variety acts. Liking to be absorbed, she preferred stories, "Playhouse Ninety," "Alfred Hitchcock Presents."

But Mavis loved the Sullivan show. Jugglers, ventriloquists and dog acts made Mavis happy. Shari Lewis, clowns. *"Look at that!"* she would say. *"Can you beat that!"* And her eyes would light up like stars on a moonless night.

When Pauline and Mavis finished their drinks, Pauline went down the hall barefoot to the Coke machine to get them another. Mavis poured hers into a glass and added bourbon. Pauline drank from the bottle. It made her feel strong and useful to take care of her mother, like a real daughter.

She didn't drink much of her second Coke. She listened to

Mavis's ice clink against her glass as she lifted it and set it down, lifted it, set it down. When Pauline closed her eyes, they burned and teared from the chlorine.

She fell asleep after the Sullivan show, watching a scary story about a crippled woman alone in a big house, a threatening telephone call, noises from the bushes. When Mavis wakened Pauline, the television set was still on but the sound had been turned off. Pauline had been dreaming, something about Jack she couldn't remember.

"Honey." Mavis pinched her arm. Pauline sat up. In the dream Jack was smiling, but the smile had not been friendly.

Mavis had the telephone book on the bed, open to the yellow pages.

"I found him, honey," she said. "This is where he is. You have to call."

With the tip of her long red fingernail, Mavis pointed to an ad for a place called Bump's Billiards. "He won't talk to me but he's there."

While Pauline slept, Mavis had redone her makeup, combed her hair and dressed. She was wearing a blouse of Pauline's which a second cousin in Louisiana had sent. Somehow the cousin got everything wrong. In November, not August, the month of her real birthday, her cousin had sent the present and a birthday card addressed to Pauline. Made of burnished gold polished cotton, the blouse had a deep sweetheart neckline with bust darts. At eleven, Pauline had no bustline and the shoulders of the blouse were far too wide. The blouse was meant for a grown woman, not a girl. But Pauline loved the blouse. She had wrapped the gift in tissue and put it away in a drawer, to save for the time she could fit into it.

Without asking, Mavis had brought the blouse to Arkansas. She was wearing it. Too small for her, the blouse was ruined. There was a rip in each corner of the sweetheart neckline, not in the seams but the fabric.

Mavis looked down. Seeing the rips, she covered them with her hands. "I can fix it in a jiffy, Paulie," she said. "In a real quick jiffy." A lie. Mavis couldn't hem a skirt. She handed Pauline the telephone book. "Here," she said. "I'll dial for you."

"What do you want me to say?"

"Just ask him to come home, honey, that's all. Tell him you want him to come home. He'll do it for you."

"I don't want to."

"Here. I'll dial for you."

Mavis dialed the number and handed the receiver to Pauline. Pauline put the receiver to her ear. She hated talking to strangers. She looked up at Mavis, hoping if not for sympathy then reprieve. Mavis nodded encouragement. Someone answered, a man with a gruff, impatient voice. Pauline cleared her throat and shakily asked for Jack Miller. The man yelled out Jack's name and then he was there.

"Daddy?"

"You change your mind?" He sounded as if he had been sitting there all this time, waiting.

Her voice trembled. "We want you to come home," she said. "We had fried shrimp and we want you to come home." She sounded like a baby. She felt like a baby and, at the same time, the oldest old woman who had ever lived.

Mavis puffed fast on her cigarette.

"What'd he say, honey?" she said when Pauline hung up.

Pauline told her Jack was coming home. Mavis smiled her sweet smile, as happy as if the jugglers and clowns had come back on TV.

Pauline got into her own bed and pulled the covers up.

When Jack came home, she was still awake. He told Mavis how he had won the pool match. His voice was shrill and tense from victory and drink. He ate Mavis's leftover cold shrimp and french fries and then the two of them went down to the hotel nightclub to listen to the piano player. Before they left, Mavis tiptoed over to Pauline's bed. "Dead to the world," she whispered, and they left.

Pauline was not surprised about the piano player. The poster in the lobby said he was acclaimed and fabulous, direct from Paris, France. While Jack was checking them into the hotel, Mavis had mooned over the poster. Pauline knew then and there that Mavis would eventually find a way to leave her in the hotel room alone and go over to Jack's side to hear that piano player.

Once they were gone and the room was quiet, Pauline slept.

Telling this story to Coco some fifteen or twenty years later, Pauline ended with a shrug. "It wasn't so bad," she said. "I don't guess I can complain."

They were sitting on Coco's bed, smoking dope and drinking zinfandel, eating French bread with anchovies. Coco's mother was Jamaican and so his skin was dark, like strong tea; his hair frizzled but not kinky.

"Oh, go ahead," Coco said. "Complain."

Coco was great. Sometimes Pauline thought that, of all the men she'd been with, she loved Coco best. When they were together, nothing else mattered. No strings, free-fall forever: they held on to one another a while and then let go. If they ran into one another on the street, they spoke and went on. At parties, they chatted like casual friends or nodded and joined separate conversations. Sometimes Pauline thought perhaps she and Coco might even be that other elusive thing, in love. Other times she knew it was so. Then felt silly. How could it be love when they hardly talked?

Besides, there was Michael. Pauline could no more imagine leaving Michael for Coco than Coco could see himself turning away the druggy, cast-off women who came to him for love and money. Coco had an army of girlfriends, all in need, many having been mistreated by people he knew; colleagues, other musicians. Coco took care of the women, loved them in his way —expertly, patiently, precisely—gave them money. The women went on and then, inevitably, came back again. Once, leaving Coco's building, Pauline had seen one of them getting out of a cab. The woman looked like a bruised pansy. She wore a see-through blouse, skintight jeans and six-inch high-heel shoes with wooden soles. Her purse was huge, like a worn leather suitcase. Looking up at the building as if expecting Coco himself to come flying out of a window, the woman told the cabby to wait. In her stiletto heels, one arm clamped on her bulging bag, she brushed past Pauline, going for cab fare.

Pauline and Coco had their good times. Their dope and anchovies and all the pleasures flesh could yield. Maybe not real love, but something.

Ordinarily Pauline slept easily and well, but when one season gave way to the next or a new wind blew in, she walked the floor. Now she sat back down on the bed, wishing she'd taken Coco's advice and brought some grass to smoke.

Eleven, twelve. One in New York. Too late to call Michael. She lay down on top of the covers and finally, sometime after two, fell asleep with the television set still blaring. In the night, wakened by the air conditioner's snowy blast, she slipped her legs under the sheets, took off her silk blouse, and pulled the covers up. The bed felt huge. She was used to Michael cupped into her midsection or she into his. The space felt like weight.

In her sleep, she ground her teeth and dreamed of a tall glass building she could not get to the top of.

7

In the morning, she opened her door to put the smelly tray of food outside. The wind whistled quietly. Weather could turn violent fast in this part of the state. She washed her hair and blew it dry, artfully combing the front part to make it fall right.

She was at the hospital in time for the eight-o'clock visit. She'd been right about Sleeping Beauty. The mother sat at the boy's side, holding his hand and telling him stories.

The next day she continued this routine, watching after Mavis, talking to Wanda, visiting Jack, returning to the Villa Capri, walking the floor. Nothing changed. Mavis talked a blue streak and grasped at every straw. Pauline told stories about New York. Wanda asked questions to keep the conversation going and then did not listen to the answers. On the third day, Pauline began to pace the marble hospital floor. Mavis begged her to be still; she couldn't. New families arrived, all on the far edge of hysteria. Pauline called Michael. He was unusually sweet. When he asked about the books, she said it didn't seem likely she'd run into Will Hand, but of course there was still time. Michael said he thought he'd finally gotten a scene right. Pauline said she couldn't wait to hear him read it.

By the fourth day, she'd grown cranky. Bad weather still threatened but so far no rain had fallen. The wind and thunder were beginning to seem like a bluff.

They were in the motel coffee shop having breakfast— Wanda eggs, Mavis waffles and bacon, Pauline cereal with low-fat milk and a banana—when Wanda put her hand on top of Pauline's.

"Why don't you take the day off, Pauline? You haven't been in Austin for a while. We'll be all right here."

It was eight. The sky was gray. Clouds obscured the sun. Pauline didn't look at Mavis. "Are you sure?"

Wanda shooed her with the back of her hand. "Go. Go. Only watch for thunderheads." She nodded toward the window. "I believe it's going to storm. My hip is about to kill me." Wanda's arthritic hip was an infallible weather predictor.

"Well, I wouldn't mind moving around a little if you don't mind. I'm not used to being so still."

"We'll be fine. Just watch the skies."

Pauline picked up her banana.

"It's been threatening all week. I don't think it's coming."

"This little baby never lies." Beneath the table, Wanda patted her left hip.

"That's okay too," Pauline said. "I love weather. We don't get thunderstorms in New York." She stood. "I think I'll do that, drive around a bit, maybe go take a look at my alma mater, see how it's held up."

Mavis looked uncertain. "But . . ." she said.

Wanda waved her on. "You go on, honey. We'll be fine."

In her room, Pauline put mascara on her eyes, recombed her hair and changed her shirt.

It was eight-thirty when she drove from the motel parking lot out onto I-35, going south in the red pickup. The interstate was busier coming into Austin than going out. By the time she got to Buda, she had passed four highway patrolmen parked beneath blooming oleanders watching for speeders. The truck had a radar detector but Pauline didn't know how to use it.

At the Bunton Overpass, she ate her banana. At Kyle, she threw the peel out the window. The sky went through radical phases, darkening then turning unnaturally bright.

She hummed along with country tunes without knowing the songs. On the seat beside her lay Michael's books.

At the first San Marcos exit, she checked her hair in the mirror. She hooked some wandering strands behind one ear.

She hadn't lied to Wanda about her love for unruly weather. She especially liked the hours before a storm hit, when anything seemed possible.

At the second exit, she turned west on Highway 80, toward town.

II

8

The San Marcos streets were damp and slick. The college, no architectural delight to begin with, had become more hodgepodge than ever, the one fine old building on campus now all but blotted from view by a gray modern monstrosity with tombstone-shaped windows and a vaguely pre-Colombian, humpbacked roof. The theater building, round, painted red, with decorative wrought-iron railings for adornment, was uglier than she had remembered.

From a college policeman, Pauline learned that the school was on break between the end of the spring semester and the beginning of summer school. Downtown was deserted, damp and gray. No students eating Jack in the Box breakfasts, too early for shoppers.

She drove down the hill from the college to the town square. She was stopped at a traffic light on the square deciding where to go next she saw his truck. The same one: the rattletrap pink International. There was a dog on the seat beside him, head out the passenger window a foot. It couldn't be the same dog, not after ten years, or could it? The same breed at any rate, a sheepdog. Pauline could see the dog's tongue, pink and thick. His eyes were covered with a mop of hair. She could almost remember his name. A game of chance, not Domino but something.

At the stoplight, he shifted gears with one hand, then leaned out the window to scan the overcast sky. His hair was parted in the same place, just off center and smoothed to either side in old-timey movie star fashion, like Rudolph Valentino. But Will Hand's hair was wiry and would not paste down. It lifted at the tips like wings.

He drew his head back into the cab of his pickup and ran his finger down the length of his cigarette, sliding ashes into the street. When he turned in her direction, Pauline ducked into the shadows. She drew the books closer.

The day was cool for June in Texas, as cool as New York had been when she left. Wanda's hip doubtless had it right; something was bound to happen. The sky had turned a faint gray-green across the top. Along the horizon to the west, a line of low purple clouds hung along the crest of the hills.

A man in a yellow slicker approached the corner of the sidewalk beside Pauline's truck. There was a new pizza parlor on the corner and across the street an empty building, its broken display windows taped along the cracks. The man in the slicker looked at Pauline and then at the traffic light. He pointed.

Pauline's light was green. She shrugged at the man in the slicker, pressed her foot on the accelerator and started to go. The light changed again. She put on her brakes and Will and his dog went through. The man in the slicker crossed in front of her. In addition to his rain gear, he wore black rubber boots.

Bingo. He used to wait for Will in the pink International all day in the faculty parking lot, his shaggy head out the window to his shoulders, his tail whapping the seat when anyone passed and called his name or sang the song about the dog named B-I-N-G-O.

The pink pickup eased across the intersection, bucking a little when the gears changed.

A banner strung across Hopkins Street announced a rodeo the next week. Planted on the lawn of the courthouse, a huge thermometer indicated the success of a community fund drive. The red mark climbed halfway up the stem of the thermometer with a month of fundraising to go. Small-town events, wars on disease, kids in the street with collection cans: she'd been away a long time.

The courthouse looked the same, dull yellow brick with a dome of such fake bright silver it seemed to have been covered with aluminum foil, like the windows of trailer houses whose residents aim to preserve air conditioning at all costs. At the peak of the dome, a silver woman in a long dress held a pair of scales and pointed toward the east.

The light changed and Pauline followed Will, hanging back so that he would not notice. A scrim of moisture hung in the air, beading up on the windshield. Pauline turned on the wipers. The blades scraped at the glass. She turned them back off again.

At the bank, the time flashed in lights: 9:38. A number of bulbs were missing in the eight; it might have been a three. Will did not signal. In front of the post office doors, he parked. Pauline started to turn in beside him then lost her nerve. She drove on by, turning her head so that her hair covered her face on his side.

What was she after? Restlessness was tedious, like an itch. It set her teeth on edge. She could always ask him to sign Michael's books.

She drove down the street to a service station, turned left, went around the block, came back to the post office and parked next to the truck on the passenger side. The dog looked around at her once, then turned back to focus his attention on the glass doors of the post office.

Pauline rolled down her window and gave it a try. "B-I-N-G-O?" she sang quietly. Unimpressed, the dog looked straight ahead.

Pauline watched with him. The glass doors were tinted gold. Like mirrors, they reflected the two trucks back to themselves.

Once every semester, to show students how the land around them had been formed, Will took his Conservation class on a tour through a cave west of San Marcos. The cave had been turned into an amusement park called Wonder Cave. There were billboards saying "See an earth quake from the inside out!"

The billboards announced the distances to and from Wonder Cave north and south on the Interstate for miles, like Disneyland.

Wonder wasn't much of a cave—no dripping stalactites in tortured shapes, no gothic formations—mostly just dull red rock. This was because—she remembered so much of what he had told them, so little of other classes—the cave was dry-formed during an earthquake which had taken place, as Will explained to them, some 35 million years before.

He was an actor plain and simple, one of those professors who were never content merely to lecture but felt the need— had the knack—to spin and weave. Will performed his class, using voice, pause and gesture, for dramatic effect, teaching through narrative.

During the earthquake, huge boulders fell down into the crack in the earth and wedged the earth apart. A fault line and many caves smaller than Wonder were created. In the cave, the students looked up to see the wedge rocks jammed into place over their heads. Beneath the wedge rocks, concave stones on one wall of the cave matched convex partners on the other, like matching pieces of a jigsaw puzzle waiting for some gigantic hand to fit them back together again.

There was no need to worry, Will had said. The crack in the earth would never heal. The wedge rocks were permanent . . . as permanent, he said, as anything gets. The young students shivered to think of time behind them, without them.

They knew about the fault line already, but not in a scholarly way. The fault line separated this part of the country as definitively as if someone had drawn a line, coastal plains on one side of the fault line, hill country on the other. On the hill country side there were other, smaller caves, which daring students with flashlights sometimes went down into. One late fall night a boy being initiated into a club was instructed to descend into a cave alone with only a candle to light his way. The boy was to stay fifteen minutes. When half an hour passed and the initiate neither returned nor responded to shouts down into the cave, a seasoned member of the club went in after him. The boy was found slumped over on the floor of the cave, unable to move or speak. The rescuer directed the beam of his flashlight onto the wall. There, coiled on a limestone shelf, some two hundred hibernating rattlesnakes, piled on top of one another, sleepily hissed and rattled their tails. Both boys had to be helped out. The first boy was never able to describe his experience. The words rose up in his throat and would not come out.

The glass doors opened. He was dressed as always, in a long-sleeved Western shirt buttoned to the neck, and underneath, a white cotton T-shirt. The only time Pauline had seen him in anything else was one unusually cool fall day. Students had put on sweaters as protection against the chilly north wind, only to find the the perverse and unpredictable Dr. Hand dressed in a short-sleeved summery shirt.

His jeans were too short to be fashionable and he wore the same custom-made boots and, at his waist, that wide leather belt with a turquoise stone for a buckle. His waist was narrow, his hips slim and lithe. He had a surprisingly citified kind of walk, heel-toe, chest leading. Very proud, almost a strut. Who did he imagine was watching?

Sorting his mail, he put groups of letters between his fingers, tucked several magazines and a large envelope under his arm and came toward the truck. The wind ruffled his hair, lifting it into a fan. His forehead was smooth and high, his skin deeply tanned, his hair the color of iron.

Pauline sat forward on her seat, closer to the steering wheel. She felt scared and happily wicked, like the last child to be found playing hide-and-go-seek.

The dog's tail slapped the seat.

"Dr. Hand?" She cleared her throat. "Uncle Will?"

He looked up and turned the left side of his face in her direction. Pauline rested her chin on her arm.

She had been charmed by his asymmetry the first time she saw him at a family picnic, head tilted to one side as he heaped his plate with barbecued ribs. Will and Wanda weren't married then—Wanda had been unable to locate the sharpy salesman to get her divorce—but they were "going around together," as people called it.

He had lost the sight in his right eye in a childhood accident involving a BB gun and so he walked in a kind of list, left shoulder leading. At the picnic, Pauline had not known about the eye. She had only noticed how he leaned and watched with fascination as he turned his whole head when he talked, focusing on the other person. Something about this touched her strangely. He reminded her of a dolphin she once saw in an aquarium. The dazzling intensity of the one eye.

When Will walked past his truck, the dog reached out and licked the ear on his blind side.

"Oh, Lotto," Will said. He wiped his ear.

"It's me, Uncle Will," Pauline said, suddenly feeling like a child. "Pauline. We spoke yesterday, on the telephone."

"Yes, I know who you are," he said. "You cut your hair."

"Yes." With her fingers, she drew her hair out of her eye. "I did."

"Well," Will said, and he reached his out right hand. "How are you, Miss Miller? How is your father? What a surprise."

They shook hands like men. And steadily, as they held one another's hands, Pauline looked into Will Hand's good eye and, as she told him with great evenness where she was living and how Jack was doing, she began to understand what she had come for. Once she knew, she grew calm. And in no time she passed the information on to Will, not in so many words but with the steady gaze only a fool could fail to recognize.

Will was no fool. He also was not easy. He responded only to her words. "I'm sorry," he said, "to hear about your father."

"It's a terrible thing," she said. And the shadow of something dark and potentially dangerous quickly flew in and out of her consciousness, like carbonized paper shredding, splitting, drifting to the sky.

Occasionally Pauline had what she could only think of as psychic flashes: sudden visions, a snatch of what might be a certain person's future . . . might be because she thought of her visions not as absolute truth but as imaginative extensions of the present, a leap from one possibility to the next. One of the questions she always asked herself when working on a character was, "What will this person be like in twenty years?"

It might have happened now, but Pauline forcibly closed her mind. The dark thing left as quickly as it came.

"Yes," he said. "It is terrible." He leaned on his hand, propped on the door of her truck, and lowered his head, paying respects.

"And you? You're still teaching, I presume."

He shook his head. "As a matter of fact, no. We are happily on leave, Lotto and I." At the sound of his name, the dog slapped the seat with his tail.

"I wondered if that was Bingo."

He turned to the dog. "Lord, no. This is Bingo's son."

He returned his attention to Pauline. He looked confused. It was a temptation to focus on the wrong eye; the false one was so invitingly still. He frowned. "I've forgotten what I was telling you."

"You were saying where you live."

"Yes." He rubbed his chin on his sleeve. "When the first book came out, I bought a piece of property out east of town on Snake Creek." He nodded in the direction he had come from. "You know that creek."

"No. I only know about your book."

"It's beyond the Blanco," he said, giving the river its Spanish pronunciation. "I live on the creekbank, precariously pitched, as is my wont. Lotto keeps me company. I've bought a bit of time. He and I will stay until the money runs out. Or until Hollywood stops thinking it can make a movie out of a slim book of myths. Then I'll go back to telling young people like yourself about the politics and vagaries of moving water."

She loved the way he played, using show-offy language. There was a new crease in his forehead running from just above his left temple to the inside edge of that eyebrow, near his nose. When he frowned, the crease deepened.

Pauline shook back her hair.

"Could I come see it?" She swallowed a bubble that had formed in her throat. "The creek, I mean. And your house?"

Will slid his finger down his cigarette and looked back in the direction of the square, as if to check for witnesses. Though his hands were blunt, his fingers had the precise delicacy of a craftsman.

"It's not much of a creek. And not much of a house."

Pauline suddenly felt intrusive and silly. Someone else could be waiting for him at home; a woman, possibly a new wife. She was too bold. He might have something else to do.

"Hey," she said. "What an idiot. I didn't mean to be pushy. It comes from living in New York all this time, I expect. I'm too forward."

"I didn't think you were being forward. Or pushy."

"No?"

He looked at his feet then back at her. "Maybe a little forward. But I can stand it."

She made a wide gesture with her arm.

"Well, a girl's got to try. And I have the day."

"The ladies let you leave?"

"The ladies suggested it. One of them."

"The ladies are relentless."

"Yes."

He looked at the sky. "It's supposed to rain. Possibly storm."

Pauline studied Will's reflection in the gold windows of the post office. One boot heel was busily tapping. "If you have something else to do?"

"No." The boot heel stopped. "I came to town to get the mail. I was going to go back home to sit on the porch and read catalogues."

She waited.

He flipped his cigarette into the street. "It's out the Luling highway," he said. "Follow us."

"I'll be right behind you."

They started their trucks, backed out and after circling the square, turned back down Hopkins again, going east. Pauline followed her uncle closely so as not to lose him. He drove slowly and with caution, routinely checking his rearview mirror to make sure she was still behind him.

Pauline opened the glove compartment and laid Michael's books on top of her father's gloves.

They crossed the river, which ran through the middle of town and brought to San Marcos its yearly supply of summer tourist trade: families, church groups, clots of hormone-crazed young people looking for a cheap good time. Three pale boys in tractor-sized inner tubes floated from upstream toward the bridge, splashing one another and drinking beer. Along the riverbanks, elephant ears taller than basketball players stood on either side like loving guardians, their green buttery leaves flopping softly in the wind. Spring-fed, the river was glassy all the way to the bottom. Roots of water hyacinths and underwater grasses could clearly be seen from deep down, drifting with the current. The temperature of the river, whose originating springs were located just blocks north of downtown, was the same all year, cool but not forbiddingly cold. In winter, when the temperature of the damp air dipped lower than that of the water, the river looked like a long winding stewpot, clouds of steam boiling from its surface and rising into the trees, dissipating in wispy peaks among the bare branches of cypress, willow and sycamore trees.

Namesake to the town, the presence of the river yielded to the town its unabashed sense of physicality. In summers, in spring, and on any fall day warm enough, near-naked sun and water lovers in cut-offs and bikinis tossed Frisbees and oiled one another's sleek smooth legs and arms. San Marcos, the poor man's Cancun, where sensuality bloomed like crepe myrtles.

When she was in college, Pauline swam in the river all year

long, upstream first—to build her wind and warm her stiff shoulders—then down, pressing hard to outstrip the free ride of the current. She never knew how far she swam. It was hard to measure in the river.

The softball fields on the other side of the river were gone, the grandstands flattened, the ground resodded. Nothing had been built as a replacement. The field was bare. As Will took the curve and crossed the railroad tracks, the sky suddenly brightened, turning almost pink.

Pauline wondered if Will and Wanda were still married. Wanda never exactly said. How did Will know to call the Villa Capri? Only Wanda would have have told him. Not that Pauline had anything to say about it if they were. Being married herself. She only wondered.

Beside a bigger-than-life stone steer standing next to a restaurant called Sirloin Stockade, Will stopped for a traffic light. When the light turned green, he drove through, passing under the interstate highway Pauline had driven in on. The wide-eyed steer had a sign on his side in place of a saddle. The sign advertised today's special, lunchtime C.F.S. with salad bar, $3.99.

She didn't feel she was punishing Michael by going off with her uncle, but then again, maybe she was. Or maybe she was following his instructions.

Just beyond the interstate, a huge gravel truck passed her, flying. The truck tailed Will for half a second and then zoomed by him as well. Gravel dust spattered against Pauline's windshield.

Married but not faithful. She was tall. She liked ice cream. Marriage had not become the definition of her life but only a distinguishing possibility, one of many. It was possible to ignore even a birthmark from time to time.

If Michael hadn't made her swear, she might not have swung so far in the other direction. "Either we're together," he said. "Or we're not. One affair," he warned, "and it's over." She swore, then answered his challenge as if it had been a double-dog dare to ride a rope swing across a deep, dirty ditch.

Within a week, she had fallen into bed with a mediocre actor she met at a cattle-call audition. Two days later she and Coco shared a joint and began their long affair. There had been others. A scene partner at HB Studio; a physical-fitness expert she met over brownies at Chock Full O'Nuts; her boss at the Shipwreck, a fat man with bone spurs. Some she didn't want to think about. Mostly now, however, she saw only Coco.

Will passed a huge new shopping center and then a small grocery store Pauline remembered, a dilapidated frame building with handmade signs in the windows advertising sales. Strung across the width of the window, feathered roach clips hung like laundry on a wire. Except for the roach clips, the store looked the same. Beyond the grocery store, a U-Haul company. Storage units for rent. A car repair shop with a congregation of wrecked, rusting cars out front. A shuttered Seventh-Day Adventist church. Slam-a-Rama, a by-the-hour batting cage. A taco stand.

Before her marriage she had been fairly conservative sexually, one boyfriend at a time. Now she was not promiscuous exactly, but an adventurer. Several boyfriends at one time meant secrets. With escalating risks, more danger. The corresponding proliferation of excuses, lies, layer upon layer of deceit, once the first lie has been told.

A gray hearse approached. In the direction they were headed, there were several country graveyards just off the highway, one modern—flat ground, flat stones, no trees, designed for the convenience of mowing machines—the other a Mexican cemetery with wonderfully ornate stones featuring angels and on every grave bright plastic flowers blooming year-round. Like a death fiesta.

A patchy stream of cars followed the hearse. The rear of the hearse was empty.

Lies were her protection. Armored, she could live her own life, have her own feelings, be who she was, apart from Michael. In quiet times, when she examined her justifications, Pauline knew they lacked the heft of truth and sounded more like lame excuses than a defense. She would swear off, then meet someone. And life would start all over again.

Will bobbed his head, checking his rearview mirror as if to make sure she was still back there. They came to the Blanco River bridge. The Blanco, green and sparkling if less clear than the San Marcos, rolled between cypress and sycamore trees, going east and then south. In less than a mile, the two rivers joined to make their winding way south together, eventually emptying into the Gulf of Mexico. On the grassy banks of the Blanco, narrow intersecting motorbike trails had been etched. Closer to the river, a short, dumpy man in brown workclothes sat on the gnarled and twisted roots of a cypress tree, idly fishing.

Unbuttoning her blouse the first time, Coco had asked if Pauline loved Michael. Breasts bare, as she slipped out of a sleeve, she had said yes. "Of course, I love Michael," she had said. "Why else would I have married him?"

And she did. A kind of love. One that had in it the necessary undertow, pulling in the opposite direction, against ease and natural inclination. To last, love needed friction.

A boy on a bicycle pedaled toward her in a special walking lane on the side of the bridge. The boy, a Mexican, frowned at Pauline. His black hair drifted in and out of his eyes. The wind was against him. Pauline wondered if the boy had been to the funeral on his bicycle.

Beyond the bridge, the land flattened. Fields of maize stretched on both sides of the road. Some fields had been harvested and turned but not rowed up. There was a large pasture, a silo, grazing cows. The sky held on to its unnatural pinkness. Pauline turned on the radio. A beer commercial celebrated homegrown hops. She turned it off.

In her rearview mirror, west of downtown lay the purple line of the hills. In that direction, within a few miles of the town square, the land became pale and rocky, rich with limestone and minerals, deficient in mulch and loam. Topsoil thinned and became blowing dust. Rainfall was chancier, rivers turned to sometime streams. Trees grew gnarled and stunted. Goats roamed the countryside. After the hill country, the true west began.

Unlike the rest of the state, things changed fast in central

Texas. Soon, in the direction they were going, the land would grow flatter still. To the south and east, cotton grew in black gumbo. Only miles beyond that was a sandy area, once riverbottom, where in cool months farmers grew lettuce and peas. To the south, within a few hours, lay beaches, Corpus Christi, fabulous sunsets, the gulfstream-warmed Gulf of Mexico.

She passed a sign indicating the road to a trailer park.

Will stuck his hand out the truck window, indicating a right turn onto a gravel road which ran straight into a thick grove of hackberry and sycamore trees. To the left of the highway there was a long curving gully, a winding scar in the flat green ground. Pauline had heard about flash floods in this part of the state, as rockbottomed creeks and rivers overflowed and sent water straight out into the countryside to etch out a gully like that. She'd heard about people drowning in their cars while they sat at a stop sign making up their minds whether to save the car or get out and swim for it. But in the years she was in school in central Texas, rivers had remained calm.

She turned on her right-turn blinker.

To the left of the gravel road was a plowed field. More maize. The maize had dirt-brown heads, like corn but not as tall, with tassels on the top. At least she thought it was maize. Some kind of grain. Will would know.

Michael was in New York, a thousand miles away. There was no way he would ever find out. As for her lies, some voice in her head told her good people did not play dishonest games, but the voice was not loud enough to distress or sway her. She didn't know where the voice came from. Or what good was. She never thought of her adventures as betrayals. She wasn't sure if being good was even important. And she thought, deep down, Michael knew.

As she turned into the trees, she saw that in addition to the hackberries and sycamores, the grove included cypress and willows: water-loving trees. Snake Creek was in there somewhere.

Will pulled into a cleared space next to some low trees and drove through a stand of Johnson grass, then an outcropping of wild red poppies and the yellow and brown wildflower called Mexican hat. Lotto's big head flopped like a beach ball. Pauline swerved to miss a tree stump. It was a good thing she'd brought the truck. The Cadillac would have bottomed out on the first turn. Will wheeled to the right. Beyond his truck, from within the trees—up in them—a house suddenly appeared, silvery blue, like a dream treehouse.

He parked his truck between two support beams on the concrete-floored space beneath the house. Pauline pulled in behind him. When Will stepped out of his truck, Lotto stayed where he was until Will came around to the dog's side, opened the door and gave a command.

The big dog loped toward Pauline. Will called him back. Lotto obeyed. Pauline got out of her truck.

"What a spot," she said.

"Come." Will held out his arm. "See my castle."

He escorted her down a narrow path between Mexican hats, firewheels and poison ivy, fingertips at her waist, as if guiding her onto a dance floor.

He taught water-related subjects, Water Conservation, Ichthyology, Marine Biology and one class he had designed himself called simply Rivers, a two-hour course which, along with Biology, fulfilled students' science requirements, making it popular. He told them how rivers were formed and how they drifted, moving south, and what was left behind, and about their own underground water supply in central Texas, how delicate the balance was between use and overuse and how important it was to pay attention to that. He stressed not history so much as sources, resources, patterns of interdependency and usage.

Much of the ecological life of central Texas went on beneath the surface. The land from south of San Marcos to far north of it was fed from underground, a natural supply of groundwater which, captured within the porous limestone, leaked through the fortunately placed fault line into a deep reservoir. The aquifer provided precious clear water to people from north of Georgetown to west of Uvalde. The aquifer was large but, as Will warned them time and again, a resource could run out if attention was not paid, care taken. His warnings were suffused with hopelessness, as if he were certain no one was listening.

Having torn down a small cypress farmhouse which needed clearing, Will had made a deal with a farmer to keep the wood. He'd built the house himself. Showing her around, he apologized for the mess, clothes tossed on the unmade bed, several pairs of muddy boots lying sole-to-sole on their sides. "If I'd known I was going to have company . . ." he said and let the sentence drop. Breakfast dishes were piled in the sink: a black cast-iron skillet crusted with eggs, a plate, coffee cup.

Wanda was right. The house was meant for one—living room and bedroom, doll-size kitchen and bath. The furniture was old, unmatched, most of it with a Western look. The arms of the couch were shaped like wagon wheels. The coffee table had interlocking horseshoes engraved on the footrest. There were no pictures on the walls, only floor-to-ceiling shelves filled with books, most of them old with frayed spines and no jackets.

Near a window sat an overstuffed upholstered chair and matching ottoman. A protective wall of books and papers surrounded the chair. A brass floor lamp cast a cool circle of yellow on the back of the chair, highlighting a torn spot. Stuffing poked out.

Beyond the sliding glass doors leading into the living room, a deck extended across the width of the house. The deck, which overlooked the creek, was as big as the living room and kitchen combined.

"Two things," Pauline said.

"What?"

"I worked for an architect for a while. The man was vain but I learned a few things. One"—she made a circular gesture with her arm—"you mean to live alone. Two, you'd rather be outside than in. Witness the size of your deck."

Will nodded, surprised and a little embarrassed. "You're too young to know so much," he said. His eye twitched.

"Not so young," she said. "Thirty-three in August." She lifted her hair from her eye and hooked it behind her ear.

He turned away. "Let me show you the creek."

He held open the sliding door.

Her heart dipped but did not sink. He was only directing, making sure it was he who determined the rhythm and pacing of the action, and not she. That, she was used to. Eventually, she would find a way to switch roles with him. Meantime she did love to hear him talk, that eloquent and self-conscious floweriness only men of Will's generation could get away with, having learned their tricks early on, at the foot of some preacher's pulpit.

Pauline stood on the high place just past Will's house looking down at the creek, which ran some thirty feel below their feet, pretty much straight down. The banks were slippery and sodden. The creek ran clear and high.

With his thick forearm, Will motioned toward the sky.

"For once," he said, "the heavens have been generous. Usually, great sections of the creek are blocked with algae and muck. This year we've been lucky."

Pauline kicked a rock down into the creek. The water looked inviting. "Is there," she asked, "a swimming hole?"

Across the creek was a reddish high bluff. A steady trickle flowed from the side of the bluff into the creek. As it dripped, the water made a high, crystalline sound. Other than that, the world around them was quiet.

Will lit a cigarette, burying the match in some mud. He spoke softly, drawing deeply.

"A pool or two deep enough to lie in. Not swim. You're looking at one." He blew the smoke away from her. Beneath them in a small pond, something moved. The silver whip of a fish tail.

"What's that?"

"Nothing that will hurt you. Crawfish, perch. Minnows. Sometimes a cat wanders up from the river, gets trapped. Snakes give you plenty of room. Though I keep a close watch. A moccasin will come at you if he sets his mind to."

South of the house the bank was rockier. Seep streams

caused the water to froth and bubble along the edge of the creek. Ferns grew thickly where the springs emerged, one doubled up on the next. Beneath the ferns was a soft layer of dark green moss.

At the top of the bluff, a bush grew in cascading layers down the side of the bank, its branches arranged in staggered horizontal planes. Exotic red flowers with long centers drooped from its limbs.

Will pointed it out. "A Texas buckeye."

"I'm disappointed," Pauline said. "It looks rare. Lush and jungly."

"That's what it is, at any rate. I'm surprised you didn't know."

She shook her head. "I'm a bayou girl, you know. We grow swamps where I'm from."

Trees came together over their heads in a thatch of wildness so thickly bunched you could not see the sky. Mustang grape vines wound around bushes and trees in a dark tangle. New green grapes hung from the vines. The air was damp enough to swallow. Pauline shivered. It was perfect. Uncivilized and perfect. The creek ran steadily, patiently winding its way through rock and mud and slabs of the bluish rock Will called blue clay toward the river. The hospital and her father might be a thousand miles—another planet—away. She and Will could be the only two people on earth.

"Is it named Snake because of its residents or its curves?"

He turned his good eye on her and silently scolded her like a child.

"You didn't read my book."

She blanched, then turned coy. "What can I say?" She raised her arms toward the sky, and lied. "I bought it. That was as far as I got. At least I bought it."

Far away, thunder rolled quietly but persistently.

"I did some research on the creek. I knew about this place and that it was for sale. The old boy who owned it agreed to give me first refusal on the land. I'd done him some favors. But I had to raise the money, which took time, and some very fancy footwork with the bank. I got to wondering, while I was clearing the land—before I even bought it—if anybody else had lived on the creek and if so, who. I couldn't find out much, but I did turn up the barest bones of a myth about *a* Snake Creek, which I took the liberty of assuming was mine. A large assumption. There are some thirty-three creeks in Texas named Snake. I added some fancifulness of my own. And there you have it."

"I heard about the book, saw you in the *Times*. Heard you got famous."

Pretending embarrassment—she could see he was pleased—Will mashed out his cigarette and squatted, rolling his weight to the balls of his feet. He picked up a small stick and, cocking his head away from her, began to draw in the dirt, digging a trench between his feet, then sat back on his heels Indian style. Pauline lowered herself to his level, imitating his squat. But she could not put her heels to the ground.

"More famous than rich," he said. He winked his good eye and drew wavy lines intersecting the trench.

"Tell me the legend."

Pauline did not understand men but she knew how to please them. Her current job was as an underwater swimmer at the Shipwreck Inn, a bar in a tacky section of Fort Lee, New Jersey. The bar was decorated in pirate-ship garb, nets, masts, treasure chests, Jolly Rogers and, on the walls, lacquered pictures of sea captains.

In a sealed tank behind the bar, Pauline did her act, swimming underwater in a sequined mermaid suit, turning flips and doing surface dives, waving to men she could not see, doing hula moves with her hands, bending her back so that her body became a hoop snake slowly turning, lying on her side on the sandy bottom, head propped on one hand, casual as a water resident.

Every night she took the bus across the George Washington Bridge to get to work. Her hours were from eight to one, with an hour off for dinner between ten and eleven. It wasn't bad work. It paid the rent. To collect her paycheck she didn't have to talk to anyone. No pleasantries, no idiot conversations.

She liked night jobs, sleeping late, coming home when the world was sleeping, slipping into bed next to Michael's unresisting warmth. It left her daytimes free for auditions, making rounds, taking class.

From inside the tank, the world was a blur. The men could see her clearly enough, but to her they were watercolor movement, a head, burning cigarette, a raised glass. They merged, one into the next.

Sometimes on the street someone recognized her. "The girl at the Shipwreck," they said, pointing. Pauline acted dumb, went on.

"Indians," Will said, "were the first inhabitants we know about in these parts. I've always felt the creek was haunted. I can't say why. There have been no visitations, no poltergeists or clanking chains, but when I walk the creek, something down there begs my attention. A presence picks at the mind. I look around, thinking it's a possum or an armadillo, a rabbit or a lost dog, but nothing is ever there."

Above them, a tall thin cottonwood swayed in the very slight breeze, its leaves shimmering in the sunlight like bright paper fans. The day had turned clear and blue. Except for occasional thunder, the possibility of storms seemed remote.

Will looked beyond Pauline, downstream toward the creek.

"And so," he said, "I imagined or created or"—he shrugged —"who knows, recreated perhaps, a murder."

Pauline's cranky knee, twisted in a high school softball game, was beginning to ache. She found a root to sit on.

Will pointed his stick at her. "Of course the book is not all ancient myth. This is modern literature after all. The legend is a story within the story of a newly arrived inhabitant of the creek, a man who, upon discovering the myth, follows the thread of its mystery and in turn begins to question his own motivations in moving to such a lush, overgrown and only marginally secluded spot . . . the man, the writer, having himself grown up in harsher circumstances. It's an old idea. A man searching for an honorable life, one he can live with."

"What does he find?"

"More questions."

"Another book?"

He laughed. "Well, yes. Or . . ." He thought better of his flippant answer. "Knock wood. I hope another book." He rapped a tree trunk.

"What's wrong with comfort?"

"It feels to the man, the writer, like an expensive accommodation."

"The man, the writer." She pointed toward San Marcos at some imaginary, invisible man. "*Him,*" she said.

"Yes," he said. "*Him.*"

"I see," she said. She was pushing him. He didn't like it. She shifted directions. "And the Indian legend?"

He looked off into the distance.

"It's an old tale of betrayal, revenge and expiation. One spring, so the myth has it, an Indian woman took a stone axe and hacked her husband and her husband's mistress to death. I imagined the murder taking place down the creek from here, where the ghostly presences are strongest. The woman planned afterward to hang herself from the limb of a bald cypress tree, but the gods—jealous of their power—would not allow it. The murderess was turned instead into a snake; thus the name of the creek. Winters, the snake-woman sleeps underground, biding her time. In spring, she emerges to look for her victims once again. That's why, Miss Miller, you must allow the vengeful cottonmouth plenty of room." Again he pointed the stick at her. "Revenge accepts no conciliation." He lowered his voice playfully, imitating the voice of doom. "It only takes its toll."

Above their heads, sycamore leaves shivered, making a dry, rattling sound. Pauline smiled at his little joke.

"So if Madame Snake finds a substitute, she takes out her need for revenge on that person?"

"Innocent standbys happen along." He had a habit of occasionally biting his lower lip, holding it between his teeth a moment then letting go. With age, his mouth had thinned.

"A fairytale of horror."

"The deaths didn't end there. The husband's mistress—his wife's sister by the way—was pregnant at the time of the murders. The unborn baby died in his mother's womb and, in swift succession, so did the murderess's daughter, who happened on the scene and ran off toward the river. On her way, the girl tripped on a mustang grape vine, fell into the river and, carried downstream, quickly drowned. Two cypress trees now stand where she died, signifying the death of the innocent children. A bloody tale. All the ancient shibboleths. Betrayal, incest, infanticide." He shook his head.

"But," Pauline said, "she was his sister-in-law. That's not incest."

"You come from a more liberal-minded generation than I. Would you accept 'sibling rivalry'?"

When he joked, he did it teasingly. When he came on like God, he sounded like Charlton Heston as Moses. Which he knew.

"So the book didn't make you rich."

"It did better than I had expected. It somehow struck people's fancy, especially young people. The times helped. All those environmentalists, romantics. But no, not rich by any means. It bought me some time, as I said. And brought me a grant. And of course," he shook his head, "there's Hollywood. I'm grateful for those dreamers."

"And now?"

"There was one other book, not so successful commercially, although what reviews it got were positive. And now—well, I'm in a time of . . . I am, oh, *pausing,* I suppose. I've gone far enough writing about the land and man's place on it. What I'd like to do is fiction. To me, that's mankind's great accomplishment, that and poetry. But poetry I leave to the poets. I'm stuck with prose."

He paused and looked away, embarrassed and amazed to be talking so much about himself. Pauline waited, wondering why it was men were so seldom satisfied with their accomplishments, yet at the same time seemed to need to believe their achievements had never before been matched or possibly even dreamed of. Will's dissatisfactions were familiar.

He doodled with his stick to keep from looking at her.

"I'm working on a less fanciful piece of work now, commissioned by a university press to introduce a glamorous book of color photographs. It's nothing particularly new, another essay. The shifting rivers, our loss, stories I've heard. As you might have learned from my class, Miss Miller, I am not a man of ideas, so much as a lover of narrative." He pointed a finger. "If you ever listened to a word I said."

"I listened. I remember. Not everything but actually, if you'd like to know, a great deal." She paused. "It's not Miller any more."

"Oh?" He cocked his head at her. The good eye squinted then widened.

"I changed it when I joined the union. I'm Pauline Terry. My grandmother's name was Terry Pauline Steck. I was named for her. Terry Pauline Miller. Except her they called Polly. I switched it around and dropped the Miller."

"What union? What do you do?"

The rewards of patience. At last she had her opportunity to take him beyond kinship and the past.

"Two unions. I act, that's one. When, if, I get a job. Right now, under the protection of the other union, I swim. AGVA, the union that comics join, and nightclub clown acts. And swimmers in bars."

"You swim for a living?"

"Enough to get by on. I turn flips underwater in a glass box behind a bar, wearing a green sequined mermaid suit and plastic wig. I tell watery jokes with flicks of my tail . . . around my neck a string of plastic jade, very pretty. I breathe from plastic tubes hidden in the sea grass. I've learned to do it so that no one knows. People think I live underwater. Which is, of course, the whole idea."

He shook his head.

"A use of water you maybe didn't think of." She shrugged. "It's a dumb job, but it's a living."

He had a kind of Indian look, his eyes dark with no centers, his nose high and hawkish, his forehead broad and flat. He watched her intently, as if trying to remember something.

"I remember," he said, "you were a lifeguard, and swam on teams. You worked at that fancy hotel pool in Houston."

She nodded.

Every time either one of them brought up the past, even in the most offhand, unacknowledged reference, something happened between them. A stab of the forbidden. Like ice on a bad tooth.

"I went to New York wanting to be an actress. I still want to be an actress. I am an actress. I've done a few things. But when I couldn't get steady work, as almost no one can, I auditioned for a water ballet. The company toured, then had a short run in the city, in the Coliseum if you've ever been there, on Fifty-ninth Street?"

"I know what it is. I haven't been there."

"A very short run. People don't come to New York to see swim shows. Imagine, a three-foot deep, twenty-five-meter-long plastic pool in the Coliseum with two dozen swimmers—we were called leggy mermaids in the one review we got—doing a water routine to *Swan Lake*. Talk about mankind's great accomplishments. We wore white caps decorated with petals meant to look like feathers. Our suits had fluffy tails. We were cultural in the extreme."

Will chuckled. She had him now. He was charmed and amazed.

"Before we dove in—understand: we plunged into a three-foot plastic pool like Hawaiian rock divers doing swan dives into the ocean—we actually danced. Not funny dancing. The real thing. I mean, *ballet*. We were swans in costume, pointing our bare toes, fluttering our arms to the famous tune. You know . . ." She hummed a bit of the pas de deux then shook her head. "I can't believe it myself sometimes but, well, it was a job. When the show closed, someone told me about the job at the bar. I never would have thought I'd end up performing underwater in a bar. But that hasn't been my only surprise."

"Do your parents help?"

"You mean money?"

"Yes."

"They would."

"You have a need for independence."

She matched him. "And you for solitude."

He dodged it.

"You said you'd done some acting. Anything you're proud of?"

Pauline rolled her eyes. Proud of? She would have taken anything, any job, any play, any theater. His question was a test. He meant to find out how serious she was, which translated by his definition into how virtuous.

"This and that. I've been at it a while. I work pretty regularly, as a matter of fact. I don't like to be still. One thing in particular I am proud of. A small, old off-Broadway company did a production of *Uncle Vanya* I was in. We got some attention for a while. Do you know the play?"

"Chekhov. Of course."

"I played Sonya. It was my best part."

"The faithful niece."

She bowed her head. "Long suffering my specialty, listening my forte."

"Madame star."

"Hardly. We opened upstate in Saratoga Springs first, during the summer season there. Stayed three weeks. In the fall we had a limited run in the city. I had to audition four times. I thought Macon McAllister would never give me that part."

"Who?"

"Our director. A good man."

Macon hadn't been sure about Pauline. She'd had so little New York experience. But he was fearless.

"Now remind me, the other woman's name is . . . ?"

"In the play?"

"Yes."

"Elena. Sonya's mother is dead. Elena is married to Sonya's

father, Serebryakov. The happy couple come to the family house where Sonya lives and works with Vanya, her mother's brother. Things happen and, as always in Chekhov, don't. Elena was played by an established actress you might have heard of, Dorothy Carruth? Red hair, white skin, black eyes, gorgeous?"

Will said he had not.

"Dorothy left New York for Hollywood some years ago, like most actors, to get work. She did a comedy series out there, a couple of specials, a mini-series. She's one of those actresses people see on the street and think they know but can't quite place. To play Elena, she got the same salary as the rest of us, which came to one-fourth of her usual pay scale. Her agent said Chekhov was boring, and Dorothy was crazy. He said when she got back to Hollywood nobody would remember her. He ended up being right. But Dorothy had her heart set on doing theater again."

In Saratoga Springs, the company had been housed in dormitories at Skidmore College. Pauline and Dorothy had shared a small ugly room, institutional green with one window, one shallow closet, a sink and a mirror in one corner, toilets and showers down the hall. Isolated from their homes and families, rehearsing long days and nights, the cast grew quickly close, like a family. The only friction among them was between the actors playing Vanya and Serebryakov. Serebryakov was played by a Hollywood actor even more famous than Dorothy, a man who had starred for several years in a television courtroom drama in which he played a cranky but principled lawyer. The actor was moody, his accent all wrong, but he was easy to work with, and generous enough. Their Vanya, on the other hand, was a Method purist who had studied with Strasberg and could quote Stanislavski to the semicolon, who loved Russians and art and hated television and money. The two men were natural adversaries, but, considering their roles, their enmity if anything only strengthened the production.

"And the play was well received?"

"In Saratoga, we were a smash. Every night we felt blessed.

Not to get too moony, but it was special. We thought Chekhov himself might have approved. Saratoga's a resort town. People go there for the baths, the horse races and to take a holiday. Our production played before the racetrack opened or we might not have drawn so well. As it was, we filled the house every night."

They'd all had a wonderful time in Saratoga Springs, eating and drinking together, breakfast in the middle of the night, dinner at three in the afternoon, baths in the hot springs, an occasional massage, parties given by patrons of the ballet company also in residency. For six weeks, they'd led a shared life.

Using techniques learned in acting classes, Pauline had done her homework on Sonya, including a detailed biography, down to early childhood: what kind of baby Sonya was, when she walked and talked, what her mother was like. She knew exactly what kind of clothes Sonya would be wearing now if she were transported into the future: where she would shop, what she would eat, what kind of perfume she might wear.

Dorothy, on the other hand, confined her work to rehearsals. "I work when I'm not working," she explained. Yet Dorothy was the first to learn her lines. Once she had learned them, she never forgot.

At night after rehearsals Dorothy wrote letters, listened to the radio, polished and repolished her nails. Daytimes when she wasn't on call, she went for walks, paid for massages, shopped, went downtown to neighborhood Saratoga bars to cheer for the Dodgers when they were on. She'd brought an endless muffler she was knitting, also a china cup and saucer to paint. Dorothy was a woman of many talents.

"The thing I like about California," she said, "is, you can be an amateur and not be embarrassed about it. Everybody takes class."

Coming in one afternoon to find Pauline hunched over what she called her Sonya notebooks, Dorothy bent down and whispered in her ear.

"God's breath, Pauline," she said. "That's what genius amounts to. Watch Olivier, do you see technique? The man's a receptacle."

In their dormitory room late at night, the two women lay side by side in their lumpy single beds and in the dark talked one another to sleep, gossiping, giggling, confessing fears and dreams like high school best girlfriends. They swapped earrings and socks and consulted one another on makeup and diet tips. Dorothy knew everything about hot rollers. Pauline helped Dorothy do her eyes a new way, using purple, which Dorothy had shied away from thinking it clashed with her hair. Dorothy was in her mid-forties then, the veteran of two marriages and a number of long-term love affairs. She looked more durable than she was. Underneath, she was fragile. When she smoked—one cigarette after the other, fast puffs, each cigarette smashed to smithereens when she was finished—you could see it.

They had felt like sisters. Closer than sisters, insisted Dorothy, who had one.

It was Will's turn to ask leading questions. When Pauline did not continue, he egged her on.

"In the end, as I recall, everyone leaves. No one is left except Vanya and Sonya."

"She's no glamour girl, Sonya, but she's great. No fireworks, quietly great. One of Chekhov's brown-haired, low-burning women, like an all-night candle. And in the end, loyalty has its reward. She gets the last word."

"Which is?"

"I mean, she has the final speech in the play. Greatly coveted by actors."

"I know she does. I adore Chekhov. I'm asking you to do it for me."

"The speech?"

"Yes."

"You want to hear it? Here? Now?"

"Of course. You're an actress. Please."

"No." Momentum had shifted again. She felt oddly embarrassed. "No."

"Pauline." He touched her arm. "Please?"

She looked down at his finger pressing into her flesh, at the hairs of her arm closing over his fingernail, short and blunt and very clean, and then up at Will. In his seeing eye she finally found the response she had been looking for when they were parked in front of the post office. In his own way he was answering now, saying yes, yes of course, yes all along. She should have known. History made her shy. Will was no help. He had been able to blunt her usual perceptiveness with his impenetrable and well-crafted bluff.

She looked back off toward the creek. He took his hand away.

"Let's see," she said.

She wanted not to act the speech, but only to offer it quietly to him. It seemed a brazen gift. She set the scene.

"It's night. Everyone has left and Vanya has told Sonya how sad he is and she says, 'What's to be done, we must go on living!' " Pauline cleared her throat. An audience of one was much more difficult to play to than a full house. She took a breath. "And then she says, 'We shall go on living, Uncle Vanya. We shall live through a long, long chain of days and endless evenings; we shall patiently bear the trials fate sends us; we'll work for others, now and in our old age, without ever knowing rest, and when our time comes, we shall die submissively; and there, beyond the grave, we shall know' . . . no . . . 'we shall *say* that we have suffered, that we have wept, and have known bitterness, and God will have pity on us; and you and I, Uncle, dear Uncle . . .' "

Will sat perfectly still, listening. From below, she could hear Lotto panting, the creek trickling; around them, the wind faintly blowing. Speaking the word *uncle*, she'd felt that cold stab again. He nodded. She went on.

" '. . . shall behold a life that is bright, beautiful and fine. We shall rejoice and look back on our present troubles with tenderness, with a smile—and we shall rest. I have faith, Uncle, I have fervent, passionate faith. . . .' " Pauline stepped out of character once again to explain what was going on. "Sonya kneels in front of Vanya and puts her head on his hand and says, 'We shall rest.' Telyegin starts playing his guitar. Sonya goes on. 'We shall rest! We shall hear the angels and see the heavens all sparkling like jewels; we shall see all earthly evil, all our sufferings, drowned in a mercy that will fill the whole world, and our life will grow peaceful, gentle, sweet as a caress. I have faith.' " Pauline hesitated. Will had turned from her. "Are you still with me?"

He looked annoyed. She had broken the spell. But now she really had him. She could probe the moment beyond the ordinary, extend it and, if she chose to, snap it shut. She returned to the speech as if there had been no interruption.

"Vanya starts to cry. Sonya wipes his tears. These are Stanislavski's stage directions. 'Poor, poor Uncle Vanya, you're crying. . . . You have had no joy in your life, but wait, Uncle Vanya, wait . . . we shall rest. We shall rest!' Then"—Pauline rearranged herself so that she was in three-quarters profile to the creek—"there are background sounds. The watchman taps. The guitar keeps playing. Vanya's mother makes scratching noises with her pen. The old nurse Marina clicks her knitting needles. And Sonya says it one more time. 'We shall rest!' " Pauline looked around full face at Will. "Pretty terrific, don't you think? The writing I mean, of course."

She could hear his breath.

"I love," she said, "those background indications of everyday reality. Needles, pens, guitars. The small proofs of continuing life. Everyone has left. Only Sonya, Vanya, the servants and the everyday noises remain. Reality. It's enough." She felt stirred. "Life, life, life," she said, tossing her head. And she laughed out loud. "Enough is enough."

Will laughed with her. He tapped his small stick against his boot like a cigarette. And Pauline felt suddenly apprehensive, the slightest rumbling, like the far-off thunder. She had done more than charm Will. He looked too serious, as if he might cry.

He cleared his throat. "Ah, well, yes," he said. "But rest? At my age, I don't know."

She shook her head. "I loved doing Sonya. I'd jump at a chance to play her again. Others, too. Maybe Irina in *The Three Sisters*. I'm tall for Nina, though I did do her once in a showcase production of scenes. I felt gawky and odd, like a fish out of water. Someday, if I have the stuff, I'd like to take on Arkadina. Chekhov is addictive. You keep wanting to go back to him."

Michael had seen her Nina. He said it was her best performance. Her awkwardness, he claimed, gave her characterization a special poignancy. Easy for him to say. She felt ridiculous.

Flushed with success, Pauline plucked a blade of grass and rolled it between her thumb and forefinger.

"Well, Miss Pauline," he said. "I am impressed. And have there been other parts? How do you fare on the rich-and-famous scale?"

"No other great ones. Flops here and there that never opened. Showcase productions which actors stage for attention and experience. I used to want to do ingenues. I was once cast in a showcase production of *The Glass Menagerie*, a horrible mistake. I got the limp right and the accent. Otherwise, what a mess. I was taller than the gentleman caller, which we might have been able to use, but the actor couldn't handle it. I can't play suicides or victims. It's hard for audiences to think I can't handle misfortune's every arrow and sling. I have this appearance onstage of strength and survival."

"And in life."

"That I can't say."

"I'm telling you."

"Sometimes it's a mask."

"You wear it well."

Will tossed his stick down the creekbank. Lotto raised his head as if contemplating fetching the stick, then gave up on the idea and went back to sleep.

Pauline leaned against the tree.

Thunder again. She looked up at the sycamore. A huge glistening black bird sat on a limb that looked too slim to hold the bird's weight. The bird looked at the sky and let out a shriek. The shriek was wild and high, the sound of a jungle bird.

"Damn grackle," Will said. He threw a rock toward the bird.

"It feels like we might be the only people on earth."

"That's why I like it."

"Don't you get lonesome?"

"We're ten minutes from town. It's not exactly the out-back."

"I know but—"

"But in the winter, even so, sometimes yes . . . when the trees are bare and the creek gets backed up. There is a feeling of stasis those times, which I find difficult. That plowed ground you saw on the way out here is some I've leased. I farm that, plus another tract beyond it, toward Uhland. I have plenty to do. Except in winter. Lotto keeps me company."

At the mention of his name, the huge sheepdog slapped his tail against the ground without raising his head.

"Why do you farm, for food?"

"Not for food, no. I have a small patch I eat from. The rest? An inclination toward the difficult. Some need to keep at what I know best, without having—God forbid—to move back to where I learned how to do it, chopping cotton in the West Texas sun." When she made him uncomfortable, he relied on eloquence to help him escape. Then shifted to humor. He winked his good eye. "I can hoe, Miss—Terry was it?—as fast as I can walk."

Once again, he had deflected the intimacy they'd taken so long to establish and nudged the conversation back into the seductive and overfamiliar Texas rhythm of men making boasts to women, women listening, men tossing out kernels of wisdom and experience such as "I can hoe as fast as I can walk," to which the listener could provide no intelligent response. She could only be amazed and say something silly and schoolgirlish like, "Is that so?"

He took her hesitation as an invitation to continue.

"The memory of chopping cotton kept me in graduate school until I got a degree high enough to assure my never having to do that again. Since that time, everything has been better. But I'm in a constant state of ambivalence, trying to find a balance between a need to return to what I know and the even stronger need never to go back. But"—he brushed at the air as if to shoo away a fly—"I'm talking too much. You're a young woman." He turned his left eye on her. "You don't need to hear the story of an old man's life."

"Not so young. It just seems that way. Because of family."

"I was sixty last January."

"Not so old."

"Did Wanda tell you I was here?"

"Yes."

"How did it come up?"

Pauline brushed back her hair with her hand.

"I asked. Why did you call?"

He squinted, as if deciding whether to trust her. "We keep in touch."

"I didn't know you were younger than Wanda."

He put his finger to his lips. "She'd kill me," he said, "if she knew I let it slip." He thought a minute, frowned—deepening the crease that angled across his forehead—then decided to go on. "We were fine together, Wanda and me. It's just that women—" He stopped himself. "Most women like people. And comfort."

"Speaking of which . . ." Pauline looked at the creek.

"Yes?"

"Water may mean lectures and book prefaces for you, but I can't imagine what it's for if not to get into. You want to?"

"No, but I'm happy for you to. You're not wearing good shoes, are you? The bank's muddy. I have boots."

Pauline wore jeans, a terrific black silk T-shirt Michael had bought her, bright red jelly sandals. "These weren't good when they were new," she said. The T-shirt was from a small, expensive shop near Fifth Avenue, so fancy it kept its goods hidden in the back or shut up in drawers like illegally obtained goods.

A small yellow and white cat wandered up and rubbed itself against a leg of Will's bluejeans. The cat, Will said, had shown up one morning and hadn't left.

"I don't ordinarily care for cats," he said. "But Eggs has style."

Pauline started down the creek bank, catching hold of small trees and roots to keep her balance. Halfway down, when she saw she would slide in her shoes, she took them off and threw them up the bank to Will.

"Watch for poison ivy," he said.

"I'm not allergic." She looked back up to see if he was coming with her.

He was standing at the top of the bank, looking down. "You never know," he said.

"That's what my mother says. 'You never know, you just never never know.'" Pauline shook her head and clucked, imitating Mavis.

In the fall, after Saratoga, Macon McAllister had restaged *Uncle Vanya* in the city for a limited run. The cast reassembled. Dorothy gave up a small part in a mini-series to do Elena again. Her agent had a fit. But Dorothy followed her heart.

The company was small but established, and so in New York they attracted a fair number of reviews, even in magazines. The production was generally if mildly praised. Some thought Macon had strained the play's conventions to make it seem modern but most were kind. Response to performances of individual actors was spotty. Astrov did well, as did Pauline, who received excellent notices for her Sonya.

"The perfect Sonya," the best one said, *"she listens admirably. Other actors go blank when not speaking. Miss Terry, like Sonya herself, turns listening into an energetic act almost palpable in its intensity."*

Some of the other actors fared less well. Serebryakov was taken down for his accent and citified gestures, "like a Bronx policeman lost in the steppes." Some critics found Vanya's performance too inner-directed and mumbly, reminiscent of Brando at his worst. But about Dorothy reviewers were in unanimous agreement. No one liked Dorothy. One review said simply that she was a duck out of water. Another used the word *ludicrous.* Pauline thought Dorothy was brilliant. Maybe she was too close to the situation, maybe they all were. But she could not enjoy her own good reviews for feeling bad for Dorothy.

The night after the first reviews, Dorothy swirled in the

backstage door like Duse, carrying two dozen blood-red roses, her wildly frizzed red hair resplendent against the jade green of a floppy silk jumpsuit. As cast and crew stood silently waiting, she plucked roses from her bouquet and distributed them, one by one.

Later, in the dressing room, Dorothy reached for Pauline's hand. Dorothy's skin was ashen and without light. She looked old. The two women sat before the dressing-room mirrors, saying nothing.

Her Hollywood agent had known his business. Having interrupted the momentum of her career, when she went back to Hollywood, Dorothy did not work for a year. Pauline and Dorothy exchanged postcards for a while. Dorothy's messages were too cheerful to take at face value. She was busy, busy, she said, throwing pots, raising orchids, tending a vegetable garden and painting china. "Tell you what," one card said. "I don't miss it. Sometimes I think I hate acting. If I didn't need the money . . ."

Beyond those few exchanges, Pauline and Dorothy had not kept in touch. Their friendship was like those passing moments of connection people have in the city, on the street, in stores, across the aisles on public transportation. A glance, the recognition, then nothing. The revolving door whirled around and out they went.

Arlene Amundsen had come to a performance of *Vanya*. "You're an interesting type," she'd said backstage, sizing Pauline up like a leg of lamb. "The older you get the more interesting you'll be." Arlene reprinted the review saying "the perfect Sonya" and sent it out all over town. Within the business, Pauline's work was remembered.

One good part in ten years' time wasn't bad. Besides *Vanya*, she'd done a six-episode part in a daytime soap, some work dubbing films, an off-off Broadway flop, several TV nothings, other plays that never opened. She wondered what had happened to Dorothy. She hadn't seen her name in trade papers since.

She dipped her feet. The creek was icy. Will said it would be up to her knees in the deepest part. She wanted to taste the seep springs on the other side and so, to cross the stream, she stepped on a slab of blue clay. The clay was softer and slicker than Pauline had expected; she felt her foot catch, then give. She slipped fast and came down hard. A hunk of clay broke off with her. She slid toward the water and then into it.

Sitting on the trunk of a fallen hackberry, Will laughed.

"You all right, Missy?" he said. It was only an instant, a slip of the tongue perhaps, a name he perhaps gave to any girl foolish enough to step down on slick blue clay in Snake Creek. Whatever his reasons, the nickname was hers.

Pauline laughed with him. "I'm fine. Just wet. Which I'm used to."

She stood, careful to avoid the clay. The T-shirt clung to her chest. She pulled the silk away from her skin. Beside the clay was a section of gravel riverbottom. Pauline moved to the gravel and began taking off her clothes. Soaked, the jeans were difficult. She had to crank her hips back and forth to slide them down.

She was neither modest nor kittenish about nudity. Swimming in the water ballet had yielded its benefits, for one this casualness about skin. She had been shocked at first, seeing how, like wet chorus girls, the swimmers walked around in makeup and no clothes, fixing their caps, squirting eyedrops in their chlorine-damaged eyes, warming small bottles of eardrops under hot running water to make the thick liquid loose enough to flow. Doctoring one another for an ear infection that went around, one girl held another's head to the side to squeeze the medicine in, the other shrieking when the drops hit. All of them naked, like monkeys in a zoo picking fleas. The shock wore off quickly enough. Before she knew it, Pauline was one of them, standing sipping a soft drink wearing only the feathered bathing caps for the *Swan Lake* number, leaning toward a mirror to correct her "Ritual Fire Dance" makeup not wearing a stitch.

Modesty had been a relief to be rid of, that silly girlish skittering for clothes, that futile desperation trying to cover everything, breasts and pubic hair, with only two hands.

Out of the corner of her eye she watched Will. He took another cigarette from his shirt pocket and tamped it. Like her, he feigned nonchalance, as if this happened every day, his niece and former student shedding her clothes in the middle of Snake Creek.

Pauline slid into the water and lay on her back. When the cold water hit, her nipples hardened. She shivered and ducked them under. Beneath her, more mounds and slabs of clay. Arms afloat, she arched her neck and let her head drop back until her face was under, hair drifting behind like seaweed. She blew air out of her mouth then pressed her face to the surface, enjoying that delicious moment when the water peeled down the sides of her face.

Knowing he was watching, she avoided looking at Will. She felt calm. She had led him to this point and now that she had him, she could go on with the adventure or let it go. It was the first time that day she had set herself apart from time, him, need and inclination, keeping something of herself safe from all forms of harm.

The flow of the creek burbled in her ears. Somewhere in the distance there was a rumbling sound, maybe more thunder, possibly something going by on the river below. From living in New York so long her skin was pale. She lowered her hand into the creek. It looked like a white rock.

Something moved in the trees above. She felt more than saw it, a sudden disturbance, wildly flapping. Pauline looked up in time to see a huge bird flying low. The bird was a blue-purplish color, its wing span wider than a hawk's. One flap of its wings took the bird up into a hackberry tree, its long neck in an S-shaped curve, feet and legs dangling behind. As it went, the bird let out four shrill warnings, crowlike but more emphatic. Another flap, the bird soared and was gone.

She sat up. "What was that?"

"My great blue," Will told her. "A heron. It has a nest nearby. The great blue feeds on fish." He turned his good eye on her. "You stay in that creek too long, Missy, it may feed on you."

"I look like a fish, I'm so white. I've never been so white."

"You're a city girl now."

She stood. Will picked up her clothes and came to her. Lotto hung back, watching.

Pauline did not know much about love, only passion. She had had love affairs that pulled her heart from her chest and made her feel she was flying. Coco, for one. Michael. From that first night at the hotel, she and Michael had gone at one another like athletes in a match. They still did, after six years, sometimes setting aside entire afternoons for marathons of lovemaking. That was how she thought sexual love was supposed to be: difficult, oppositional.

And this was what she knew to do with the energy she felt rise up in her in the presence of men: lift her hair from her eyes, fall into their beds, feel them fit themselves inside her. But in love?

She imagined love to be a safe and perfect world. An enclosure of warmth and shared goodwill. Sometimes she felt it onstage with an actor she trusted, who she knew would return a line even if she muffed it; that cool, dark circle of certainty, enclosed by footlights. In real life she waited for that perfect world—her version of Oz—magically to appear. She wondered if she would love—even fall in love with, the way people talked about it—Will Hand.

He handed her her shirt. "You know my rule about students," he said and he raised his hand and laid it on the side of her face, cradling her jawbone.

Beneath his hand she clenched her teeth.

"Much less," he went on, unaware of her annoyance, "my niece. Vanya would never."

"I'm not your student," she said firmly. "And Sonya was a part I played. Besides, you aren't my real uncle, only by marriage."

"Which doesn't count."

"Which doesn't count. Right."

He took his hand from her face, dropped it to her breast. She shivered. Will helped her up the bank, showing her places to put her foot where the roots of the trees were knotted in such a way that she could use them for stairs.

Pauline lifted her long naked legs and, with her arms as levers, pulled her way easily up the bank.

It was up to him to decide what counted and what did not. It was his house. And he was older.

In Will's bed, though she had dried herself quickly with a towel, Pauline made a wet spot in the shape of herself. Will kissed and touched her before he undressed entirely, keeping his jeans on, and the belt with the turquoise stone, until the last minute. A patient lover, he spoke into her ear, using old-fashioned declarations of love and adoration, telling her how sweet she was and calling her darling.

Except in plays—mostly English—or in jest, she had never heard anyone speak the word *darling* before. She wanted to hear him say it again and again.

He held her face and kept his Indian eyes on her and after a while she knew what he wanted and gave it to him. She did not close her eyes or look away but, knowing she would not be with him long, freely shared with him the secret part of herself, laughing, looking straight into his dark centerless eyes as she came, delighted to discover it could still happen that way, in the old-fashioned way, without the dope, him on top, inside her. When he came, she hardly knew.

Afterward he got her a glass of ice water and asked her to do scenes for him. She knew a great many. To show off her ability to do a dialect, she began with Juno's "murthering hate" speech from *Juno and the Paycock*, then switched to Southern and did Maggie's bitter diatribe in *Cat on a Hot Tin Roof*. "More," Will said, "more." She gave him Lady Macbeth washing her hands, Charlotte Corday's description of the murder of

Marat, and speeches spoken by heroines she would never play —Ophelia, Miranda, Blanche. Then Tom's opening monologue from *The Glass Menagerie*. He asked her to do Laura from the same play, but that had been too humiliating an experience to repeat, even in fun. She did *Alice in Wonderland* instead, first the Queen of Hearts—bellowing *"Off with his head"* into the silence of the afternoon with such gusto that Lotto wakened and whimpered—and then the Mad Hatter inviting Alice to have more tea, Alice saying how can I have more when I haven't had any yet. She had played the Mad Hatter in Houston, the Queen of Hearts in a New Jersey children's theater workshop. Will asked for more Sonya. Pauline did her scene with Dorothy, in which Sonya confesses to Elena her love for Astrov. Taking both parts, she went back and forth from steadfast Sonya to the loving, glamorous Elena. Imitating Dorothy, she felt her friend's presence slip into the room. She wondered whether, given the choice, Will would prefer Dorothy to herself, Elena to Sonya. Most men would.

She sipped her water and chewed a piece of half-melted ice, put the glass on a bedside table and, sitting cross-legged, did Desdemona.

In Houston, she had worked as assistant stage manager on a production of *Othello* the summer before she went to New York. It had been a good summer, working at the swimming pool during the day, staying up until all hours at night, rehearsing, performing, working backstage. As assistant stage manager she had cued actors as they learned their lines and so she knew *Othello* practically by heart. As she spoke the words of the speech for Will, she remembered the speech patterns of the actress who played the part outdoors in Hermann Park years before. *If it were now to die,* she said, the words spoken in a high, questioning vibrato. And then the actress's voice began to slide, down through *'twere now to be* until, when she came to *most happy,* her voice toyed with its bottom-most register, implying an attitude of seductive sensuality regarding death. Pauline wondered then and now what it might be like to have that feeling.

Thunder lightly rolled. Will put his hands behind his head, leaned back on his pillow and watched her.

She wasn't sure what would happen next. Will was vigorous, but surely age had taken some toll. Pauline waited. And after a while he let her know. When she threw up her arms and said, "Enough, enough," he pulled her to him and they made love again.

As a lover he was skilled. His erection was not as firm as a younger man's but that never mattered as much as men thought. He knew other things to do, lifted her buttocks just so, doing this and that with his hands and mouth. Unlike Michael, who collected her orgasms like trophies—even rating them, congratulating himself if she became particularly passionate—Will's attention seemed fixed on a more distant and somehow less exacting point. When he came, he ducked his head, moaned, as if in regret, and closed his eyes.

Lotto lay bored and panting on the front porch. Sitting up in bed, Pauline could see through the living room to the deck where the big dog was. Clearly, Lotto had seen it all before.

In the city, the night of the red roses, Pauline and Dorothy had played one more scene together, which no one knew about, not even Coco, with whom Pauline shared most of her secrets. The two women had tested their friendship that night to see how much intimacy it could stand . . . had in fact tested that friendship to death, possibly, Pauline thought, out of pure cowardice and the need to return intact and without regret to their separate lives; in order not to deepen the friendship more.

In Dorothy's hotel room that night the two women made love. It happened only that one time, but once was enough. Not that anything was said. The two women agreed without speaking of it to let the friendship, if not the memory, go. If they'd been neighbors, even if they had lived on the same coast, they doubtless would have eventually been able to laugh all of this away and would have come back together again as friends, but they were so far away from one another and the friendship was so new that humor, time, never had a chance to work their negotiations. They were not lesbians; it was Pauline's only sexual experience with a woman, and, according to Dorothy, hers as well. They both had simply felt the need, on that hard night, to push the intimacy they had discovered as far as it would go. Wanting to see what would happen, that was all. They just wanted to see.

Remembering the feeling of Dorothy's lush, soft white breasts against her smaller, pointed ones, and the way Dorothy's full belly fit between her angular hipbones, and how it was to yield to feeling without wondering about differences or risks, Pauline still felt uncommonly moved, as if cold water had been sent down her spine, robbing her of breath.

With men, there was a moment before sex began when the two lovers stared one another down. Who was up to the challenge, how far would they go, who had the most stamina, the greatest desire? Making love with Dorothy, there had been none of that.

Then Dorothy had disappeared from her life. People came, went.

Will moved his hand slowly, in just the right place.

12

In a borrowed T-shirt and her underwear, Pauline sat on a tree root, watching crawfish make darting zigzags in the creek. Mavis called crawfish ditch-dwelling cockroaches. This image had endured in Pauline's mind. She could eat crawfish in *étouffée* and gumbo but never boiled whole.

Suddenly the crawfish scattered. As one, they dove, digging their way into the mud, sending a cloud of silt up after them.

Pauline looked upstream. The danger the crawfish had sensed swam into the silt. A snake, princely calm. Its head rode the surface of the water like the leading arc of a well-paddled canoe. Its long curved body made a gentle whipping motion. The whipping sent the snake smoothly forward, hardly disturbing the surface of the creek—a ripple now and then—and making no noise at all.

Will came up behind her. His mood had changed after he left her in the bed. Either embarrassed or annoyed with himself, he had gone off with Lotto. Pauline had never understood men's inclination to grow morose and churlish after sex. Was it that they expected something they never received?

She pointed at the snake which, headed for the river, had swum past the buckeye.

"A moccasin," he said. "See the triangular shape of its head and how it swims with its head out of water."

"It's beautiful."

"Perhaps, but don't be deceived. Rattlers are tame in comparison."

"Somehow hard to believe."

"Just because you swam there."

"I guess."

The snake dove into the water, resurfaced several feet downstream then disappeared.

"As long as you keep your distance."

The secluded beauty of Snake Creek was dangerous. Off her city-trained guard, Pauline had begun to think a poisonous snake would not harm her, that if she went to it the snake might open its mouth white as cotton and not strike but greet her like a companion, she and it having swum naked in the same spot. She felt like Mavis, all eyes.

"What you're sitting in," Will said, "may bite worse than the cottonmouth. See the five-pointed leaves? That's poison ivy. It's all over down here."

Pauline stood, brushing at the back of her legs. "I told you," she said, "I'm not allergic."

"I always give the vine plenty of room myself. Poison ivy's a curse. As soon as you think you're safe, I swear to God, it gets you. It happened to your Aunt Wanda. She'd played in the stuff as a child. One day, she must have been forty, she was picking berries and reached into a patch. She had blisters full of water up and down her arms and into her eyes. She couldn't see for days. It left scars."

Pauline didn't want to hear about Wanda.

"Well," she said, "there's nothing to do now. If it's going to get me, I'm in the soup."

"Speaking of which, I'm fixing lunch. Come on up." He passed her by and climbed the creekbank without her, leaving her to make her own way.

In his cast-iron skillet—which in her absence he had washed—Will pan-fried a steak he had thawed for himself. They shared the steak and some green beans and tomatoes from his garden. Ordinarily, Pauline ate little more than yogurt and fruit for lunch, but today she felt furiously hungry and ate more than he.

On the table he had set an open sack of oatmeal cookies for dessert. The cookies weren't good, but Pauline ate six, breaking them apart, eating small pieces.

While they ate, the day suddenly turned dark. Holding their forks in midair, they looked up at one another. It was barely past two o'clock. More thunder. Will switched on an overhead light and went to the window.

"It figured," he said.

"It's been coming."

"Yes."

"Wanda warned me."

"Her hip?"

"Yes."

"It never lies."

He stood looking out, still as a statue.

"I should call."

He turned. "I don't have a phone."

"I could drive to the store just past the bridge, but first I have to know. Can I stay?"

"Overnight?"

"Assuming nothing has changed, I can make it all right with them for a night, if you want me to."

"Of course I want you to. I just wonder if you should, beyond the situation in Austin. The ground is sodden. There's no place for this water to go, except up and out."

"Not *of course*. Do you want me?"

Will gave her his dolphin stare. "I shouldn't think you need a new flirtation."

"Then I'll go and make sure there's been no new complication, then make it all right with my mother. I'll tell her I'll be back tomorrow."

Will gave her some clothes. She hitched up his jeans with a belt and put on a cowboy shirt and a rain slicker.

"Maybe I should go with you."

"No. I'll be fine." Lies were easier to tell without an accomplice.

"Be careful."

"I will."

Pauline drove to the store, leaving Will standing in the kitchen looking out. She called the hospital. A nurse at the ICU nurses' station told her there had been no change in Jack's condition. And then she left a message for Mavis and Wanda at the Villa Capri, saying she'd located her college roommate and was staying over.

Lies weren't so bad while you were telling them. When she got back to Will's house, Pauline took a shower.

She had not heard her parents come in after going down to listen to the piano player from Paris. Next morning, she was the first one up. She tiptoed past them. They slept without touching, Jack spread out in a wide X, Mavis curled on her side so close to the edge of the bed it seemed she might fall off. Jack wore only his boxer shorts. Mavis had pulled the sheet to her shoulders. Pauline could see one pink nylon ruffle, down on her arm.

After they'd had a night out together, their breathing was loud, his nasal and rattly, hers a chesty growl. The room always smelled of bourbon, and Jack and Mavis breathed together, as if orchestrated. The draperies were drawn. The room was dark. It could be any time. The pool might not even be open yet.

In the bathroom, she put on her bathing suit, which was still wet and cold from the day before. Shivering, she stuck her legs in, trying not to let the suit touch her skin, then quickly pulled the bathing suit up over her chest and tied the straps around her neck. The suit froze her chest, making her nipples turn to nailheads. She needed to go to the bathroom but was afraid the noise would wake them.

Over her suit, she put on her terry-cloth cover-up. If the pool wasn't open, she could go to the hotel coffee shop and eat breakfast.

Carrying her rubber sandals, her hairbrush, two pennies and two rubber bands tucked into her palm, Pauline tiptoed to the door. Her hair hung loose down her back, nearly to her waist.

She had grabbed hold of the doorknob and turned it when she remembered her key. She started to let the knob slide back in the other direction when, as the latch clicked, Mavis spoke.

"I see you," she said, as clear as anything. "Get back in bed." Her voice was gruff and low, the way it was late at night after a party when she had smoked too much.

Pauline's heart plunged. She turned to answer. But Mavis's eyes were shut. A drop of saliva fell from the corner of her mouth. She was dead asleep, still clinging to the edge of the mattress.

Pauline turned the knob again and, leaving her key, slipped quickly out the door and into the hall.

The pool was not open, but the lifeguard let her come inside the fence and use the bathroom. She helped him skim leaves from the surface of the pool with a special rake, then plaited her hair. Long braids, behind her ears, down to the bottom of her ribcage. The sun was already warm. Her hair smelled like shampoo, her skin like sleep.

It was still too early for the pool to open and the lifeguard had something to do inside the hotel, so Pauline went to the coffee shop to have a doughnut and a cup of hot chocolate. The hot chocolate had a large dollop of whipped cream on top. As she sipped the warm liquid through the cream, Pauline felt a mustache forming on her upper lip. The doughnut was large and sugary. The waitress called her honey, like Mavis. She wondered if Mavis could actually see and hear her in her sleep. Feeling completely grown, Pauline signed her room number to the check. When she went back outside, the gate to the pool was open. No one was in the pool. The lifeguard was sitting in his high chair, listening to a portable radio and staring into space.

Never happier, Pauline opened the gate to the swimming pool and went in.

People said not to swim after eating, but she never got cramps. In the water, nothing bothered her. The lifeguard waved. Pauline went to the basket room, got a basket, put her hairbrush and shorts and cover-up and shoes in it and pinned the numbered safety pin from the basket to her bathing suit, trying to thread it through the same holes she had made the day before so as not to ruin her suit. She had hidden the pennies in a small well in the concrete beside the aluminum legs of the lifeguard chair. When her friend arrived, they would play the diving game again.

Some things she got tired of, swimming, never. Texas winters were not long but she wished for summer all year long, so that she could swim her life away, until she was grown up enough to leave. She loved the swimming-pool world, its smells and rules, the regulating sound of the lifeguard's whistle and how she felt swimming underwater, protected and strong, unreachable, as she pulled water behind her with her strong arms, staying under until it seemed her lungs would explode. She could dive for pennies for hours and never get hungry or tired.

She began doing laps, her best stroke, the crawl. She thought she must look terrific, braids streaming behind her like exhaust from jet propulsion. On the Baytown junior swimming team, her specialties were distance swims, two hundred and four hundred meters. She sometimes did the one hundred as well when another swimmer didn't show, but she was better at distance than sprints. On the relay team, she did breaststroke in the mixed medley. She never missed workouts. The coach said she had a great attitude. But nobody in Baytown cared that much about swim meets. Everybody liked football.

Happy, she swam back and forth, pulling her arms straight down as her coach had instructed, her long feet fluttering in time with her arms, against the water, every third stroke turning her head for air.

At the end of the pool, she touched the concrete with her fingertips then doubled up her body and, shooting her feet to the wall, pushed off against it. She had seen people do flip turns at meets, but she hadn't yet learned how. In the shallow end, the sun shining through the water made the bottom of the pool look broken, like a giant mirror with golden cracks all through it.

One more, she kept telling herself, to keep going. One more and I'll quit.

On her twentieth lap, she remembered the dream about Jack.

He was playing a small organ, pumping the pedals with his feet. He had bought Mavis such an organ for Christmas the year before, reminding her as she took the ribbon off how she used to play the piano when they were dating. Mavis looked dubious, as if she remembered no such thing.

Mavis had never played the organ that Pauline knew of, but Jack had learned a few chords. He could play two songs, "My Blue Heaven" and "Sleepy Time Gal." He sang along as he played, moving his hands from chord to chord, keeping his fingers spread in a chord-playing position. He was always giving Mavis gifts he wanted for himself.

In the dream, Jack's fingers were going up and down the keyboard, top to bottom, up and down, up, down. Cascades of notes flowed into one other like streams of water. He looked like a professional. Like that piano player from Paris, France.

As he played he looked over his shoulder, flashing Pauline a wide smile.

"What do you want to hear, my sweet baby girl?" he said, the light from above making his teeth shine. "I know everything you want to hear," he said, and he winked. "My sweet potato pie. My juicy apple dumpling. Your daddy knows all the songs."

Her father looked deep into Pauline's eyes, as if he knew her secrets.

Pauline stopped swimming. Other people had gathered at the pool. A child in a plastic inner tube shaped like a duck was crying to get out. Men and women were greasing each other's bodies with oil.

Pauline hoisted herself out of the water and wrung out her pigtails. She looked up at the windows of the hotel and wondered if Jack and Mavis were watching.

Her friend came. They dived for pennies. Pauline forgot about her dream. She forgot about having to call the pool hall. At ten, Mavis showed up in one of her Carmen Miranda outfits, wide-legged shorts and straw wedge-heeled shoes, a flouncy blouse and bright chunky jewelry.

Seeing her, Pauline dove into the water. When she came up, Mavis was waving her arms.

Pauline went back under.

When she came up again, the lifeguard was blowing his whistle at her and Mavis was standing beside his chair. Her lipstick—orange as tangerine rind—was crooked. Feeling betrayed, Pauline obeyed the lifeguard and swam over. At the bank she deliberately splashed water on Mavis's feet.

"Come on, honey," Mavis said, placing her hand to the side of her mouth as if she were telling a big secret. "Your daddy's packed up. We're ready to go."

"Go where?"

Mavis looked behind her. "Please, honey."

They were supposed to have stayed three more days, then gone on to the Blue Ridge Mountains to see if the horizon was really blue. Pauline did not protest. She did not even say good-bye to the lifeguard or her friend. She liked the boy so much, but except for the snapshot, she never saw him again.

Refusing Mavis's hand, she went to the basket room, got her clothes, put the basket and safety pin back and left the pool. The lifeguard called out to her, but Pauline didn't turn around. She knew what he wanted. She'd left her pennies. She had wanted to take them home for a keepsake but suddenly they didn't matter any more. Everybody was watching. Everybody could see how she felt. And besides, so what? It was over.

The three of them said practically nothing on the way home. Trying to find a way to fold her long legs in a comfortable position in the backseat of the Thunderbird, Pauline read one entire Nancy Drew mystery book before they got out of Arkansas. She was halfway through another when darkness forced her to quit.

Jack drove through the night, refusing to stop. They got home in the early hours of morning, just before dawn. When they woke her up, one pigtail was across Pauline's face. Her hair smelled of chlorine.

They had never seen a rainstorm quite like it. One minute there were forecasts, predictions; the next, a wall of water fell in a vertical sheet: drops as big as fat men's fingers splattering noisily on the wooden boards of the deck, battering the leaves of Will's potted plants, driving streaks of water down into the dirt.

They rinsed and stacked the lunch dishes. While Will made coffee, Pauline went into the living room and, sitting on the wagon-wheel couch, watched the deck turn dark and slick. A salmon-colored bougainvillea, the arms of which Will had wound around the porch railings, nodded and drooped, its bright tissue-thin blossoms fluttering and listless. Lotto sat beneath the overhang, paws together, watching. From somewhere, she heard Eggs crying. Pauline cracked the sliding door and called her.

"She'll be all right," Will said. "She's an outdoor cat."

Deeper thunder rolled. Pauline closed the door. The sky behind turned briefly bright, then darkened again. The rain was a steady wall of water. There were the other, familiar trappings of a storm, but mostly there was just the rain, like a stage curtain dropped from above, separating them from the rest of the world. Will brought mugs of hot coffee, black as oil. They sat in the dark together on the Western-style couch, pressed close, saying nothing. Darkness wrapped around the small house. Distracted, Pauline burned her tongue on the coffee. She tucked her feet up under her and curled her long arms around her chest, leaning against Will's arm. He stroked her hair. On the couch, they made love again.

By six, despite daylight savings time, the light had failed. The rain fell without letup. Will suggested she think about going back to Austin before it got worse.

"It's sure to flood," he said.

Pauline refused. "It's too late to go back now," she said. Will didn't press her.

They talked, watched the rain. Will brought out a bottle of vodka. He drank his on ice with a twist. Pauline mixed hers with orange juice. They walked about in the living room looking out the window, read a bit and finally—she didn't know what time it was, it might have been eight o'clock or ten—turned out the lights and, in matching white J. C. Penney's T-shirts, went to bed.

Will slept on his side, turned toward the wall away from her. As she began to doze off, Pauline pressed herself against his back, curling her long midsection around him, spoon fashion. Gradually, Will moved away. The bed was large. With so much space between them, they might have been on separate mattresses.

During the night she had her dream, the man in the street after her, this time not on a sidewalk but a gravel road. Pauline woke up and, listening to her heart thump, thought of Jack, with tubes and wires coming out of him.

She should have left when Will suggested it. It was heartless to leave Mavis in that situation. But *should* was a remote voice in her brain. She could not have left then and now it was too late.

She hated it when people told her the man in the dream was her father. She hated it when people interpreted dreams at all.

She felt on the other side of the bed. Will was gone. Pauline called but he didn't answer.

In sense-memory class, actors were encouraged to evoke concrete details of memories: tastes, smells, sounds, weather, clothes; real things, not abstract feelings. Working on the bear memory, Pauline brought a small jar of Clorox and another of bourbon, a cold fried shrimp and a record of Rudy Vallee singing "Sleepy Time Gal." She wore a bathing suit and, sitting before a mirror, braided her hair.

Eggs meowed, her plaintive, high-pitched voice a soprano counterpoint to the mumbling thunder and the dark, pounding rain.

The past was like a poem committed to memory. Onstage, she could go in and out, like a rabbit dodging headlights.

Will must have gone to see about something. In this rain, he couldn't have gone far.

"Pauline."

She thought she was in New York listening to the rush of traffic from outside on Tenth Avenue, cars and buses going endlessly uptown.

The radio was on, low. The faint glow of its numbers cast a golden light on Will's gray hair. Bulletins were coming on, warnings and announcements, roads closed, locations of emergency shelters. The rain still pounded. But the hail-like sound of one drop falling after another had changed to the endless, spiky splattering of water on water. And there was the other, new and more persistent, a steadily rolling rush.

Pauline turned on her side to face Will. She closed her eyes.

"Pauline. Don't go back to sleep. I think you should try to get to Austin."

"Let's wait until it slacks up. What time is it?"

"Four something. Nearly five."

"In the morning."

"Yes."

"Not yet, Uncle Will. Come join me."

His voice changed. "Pauline," he said in the same tone of voice he used giving Lotto commands.

She opened her eyes.

He was wearing his jeans. The room felt cold. He cradled her face in his hand.

"The rain, Missy. It hasn't stopped. Come look."

"Wait." She pulled the cowboy shirt from the bedpost and put it on. In the background, the new sound continued.

Will led her to the sliding doors and opened them. It was like walking straight into the workings of an electric motor.

"What is it?" She had to yell.

"Water."

"Rain?"

"The creek."

Pauline put her hand over her eyes as if to shade them from glare. She could see nothing beyond the porch railings. The deck looked as slick as if it had been shellacked. Will had dragged his plants from the edge of the deck back into the overhang. Lotto was gone. Eggs still lamented her fate. He pulled her back into the house.

"That sound is Snake Creek?"

Will kept looking out the door, as if looking hard enough might change what he saw.

"It's out of banks. In ten hours, we've had thirteen inches. A storm has stalled straight over us, not moving. In Lockhart, they've had summer showers. In Cuero, it's not raining at all."

"Impossible. The creek was only inches deep."

"Now it's probably twenty feet. It happens fast. It doesn't take much."

Will slid the door shut.

"Do you think it's a sign?"

"Sign?" He frowned, impatient.

"I don't know. Of you, me, us, something."

"Best not to get esoteric," Will snapped. "There are too many problems at hand to deal with. You need to think about leaving. I moved both trucks up to the highway. Eventually, my road will wash out. I should have sent you on home earlier. I don't know what I was thinking of."

"You've been busy."

"You sleep deep."

Will went back into the bedroom to listen to a new bulletin.

Pauline slid the glass door back open a little and went outside again, to stand beneath the overhang next to the bougainvillea. Will had attached the vine to the screen door, winding its arms around the edge, so that the flowers would not drag or fall.

In New York, she and Michael lived in a floor-through apartment rented with her first paycheck from the water ballet. The job had been union and so the pay, while minimum scale, was decent. The water ballet hadn't lasted long, but once they were in, Pauline managed to continue making enough money to keep the apartment. Five flights up, midtown on Tenth Avenue, the apartment had rats. The bathtub was in the kitchen, but at least they had hot water, a bathroom inside the apartment, more room than she'd had since she left Texas. Pauline had gone to city hall for rat poison. The rats went somewhere else. Handy with tools, Michael built a windowseat in the living room beneath the windows overlooking Tenth Avenue then put in a shower stall in the kitchen next to the sink. Together, the two of them had worked long nights laying large black and white tiles over the undulating, ugly floor. The water pressure in the shower wasn't great. Water sprayed out onto the kitchen floor when you showered . . . but it was better than lying in a tub of water next to the stove when beans were boiling and anybody was likely to come to the front door.

Michael had conceived the plans while Pauline assisted, held tools, went to the store with lists. Their apartment was now quite stylish, with a clean, squared-away look. Pauline felt proud and fashionable every time she opened the front door. She liked being able to stand in the living room by the windows and see clear through to the back wall. She liked the emptiness. Little furniture, white walls. All angles and slickness.

Tenth Avenue was home. Dave at the candy store gave her free coffee in a Styrofoam cup every morning when she went for the *Times*. White-haired Mrs. Poshkosh from downstairs— a golden-skinned Czech, grumpy but dependable—swept the sidewalk outside their building the way black people in the south swept their yards. Ed the produce man picked out the kind of bananas Pauline liked, barely ripe with no brown spots. At night, with all the lights switched off, Pauline could make her way through the apartment without bumping into anything. She often tested herself. She never missed. She knew exactly where everything was.

The out-of-banks creek was Pauline's sleeping pill. Ordinarily in the country the pure black quietness of night felt like a steel bar in her head, pressing from one ear to the other. The roaring creek made her think she was at home, kept company by the sounds of traffic, cars and cabs and trucks, honking horns no matter the time of night.

Will touched her shoulder. Pauline came back into the house, closing the door behind her. Will was buttoning a long-sleeved plaid shirt.

"The highway's still open. I think we should try it. This is all from the San Marcos. Once the Blanco comes in from the west, you won't be able to get out at all. I'll follow you as far as the interstate to make sure you get on it. Once you're that high, you'll be fine."

"I don't want to go."

He gathered her to him, both arms across her back. "And I don't want you to, Missy, but we have to think beyond what we want."

He let her go.

"Maybe I could come back."

"First things first. Your clothes aren't dry but they'll be soaked anyway, once you take the first step outside."

She put on her damp clothes and laced up some hunting boots Will gave her, put on his yellow rain slicker. Around her head she tied a bandanna. She had not gone down two steps from the house when the bandanna was soaked. She took the scarf off, wadded it up and stuffed it into the pocket of the slicker.

She stepped from the stairs to the ground, lifting her feet like a drum major. The field next to Will's house looked like a lake. There was an industrial plant of some kind to the north. Its orange lights cast a glow across the horizon like an artificial sunset.

The pickup trucks looked like obedient animals. Lotto appeared from somewhere, his hair a soggy mop over his eyes. He looked pathetic but game. Will opened the door to Pauline's truck. Lotto started to jump in.

"Down, Lotto. Goddammit, down." Will said, and he smacked the dog on his nose.

Lotto whimpered and lowered his tail between his legs. Pauline got into the truck.

Will held the door. He shouted over the sound of the creek. "I'll follow you across the bridge. There's a store on the right about three miles down."

"That's where I called. I know where it is."

"What?"

"Never mind."

"They'll be open." He frowned. "Or they should be. We'll stop there to see what's what." Pauline wanted to reach out for him, but Will stepped back, still shouting over the sound of the flooded creek. "Be careful. You're better off with your lights on low beam." He closed the door.

The cab of the truck smelled like oil. The engine turned over immediately. Pauline put the truck in gear and pressed gradually on the accelerator. Her father had taught her how to drive in mud so she knew what to do. No spurts, no quick releases, slow and steady pressure, never letting up. Will's headlights came on behind her. Water ran down her head and neck, into her shirt and down her back. She shivered.

The highway was deserted and black. There was nothing to see. The tires spun, then caught. Turning left with no notion what was out there, she pulled onto the asphalt, leaning forward, hands together at the top of the steering wheel, her face so close to her hands she might have rested her chin on them.

Against the flow of so much water, the wipers were of little help. The minute the blades pushed the water away, a new wave covered the glass. She could see only the orange glow of the industrial plant to her right and ahead of her, in the distance, the lights of San Marcos. The rain fell without compromise. The world all around her was black.

She shook her head to dislodge drops of water from her eyelashes, not wanting to blink, or miss the few seconds when the wiper blades smeared at the water. She hummed to herself, a country tune she'd heard on the radio coming into town. She wished for company, Will, even Lotto or Eggs.

To concentrate, Michael needed total quiet from nine in the morning until three in the afternoon, as well as a certain brand of pencils—Dixon Ticonderoga only, even Eagle would not do —an expensive desk lamp—Luxor, no substitutes—which emitted perfect nonglare light, a brand of canary-yellow second-sheet paper carried only by a store crosstown on Twenty-third Street. Just the right yellow. Precise not only about his art but every facet of his life, he got his hair cut at a midtown hotel on the East Side, the only barber he'd ever been to who understood his straight, slippery hair. He took his shirts to a particular laundry which did the collars just so, and summers had his wool things stored, no matter how broke they were. Fearing shrinkage, he washed his bluejeans by hand and asked Pauline to do his wool socks in cold water and then hang them on stretchers to dry. "You know how I am," he said. "One sock after the other drives me nuts."

By example and rebuke, Michael taught her.

"Care, Pauline, care," he said to her when after doing her face she left a film of powder on the sink. "I hate to see this." He ran his finger across the sink. It left a wormlike track in the powder. "See?" The fingertip he held up was smudged.

In the water ballet she'd had to learn to do a ripple dive. The dive was supposed to cascade, one swimmer to the next like a deck of cards being shuffled. Other swimmers got the idea fast; not Pauline. In line, awaiting her turn, she concentrated, trying to figure out a counting system. But logic failed her. Her dive was always a beat too late. "You think too much," the director shouted. "Don't think. Just do."

They came to the bridge crossing the Blanco. The river was high but still in banks. Just beyond the bridge there was a curve in the road. Pauline had no idea which side of the road she was on. But when she made her way around the curve, she could see again. Streetlamps, cars, flashing yellow lights.

She finally had got the dive, a triumph. The secret was in knowing when to let go, the same as on a rope swing.

The grocery store was wildly lit up. In the parking lot, five or six cars had been pulled up so close to the edge of the front porch they seemed on the verge of driving on in. Some men stood on the porch, drinking soft drinks and coffee, looking toward town. Past the store, she could see blinking lights, warning signs, barriers, stalled cars. No grass, no access road. From the underpass beneath the interstate and beyond, there was only water.

Pauline pulled into the parking lot next to a maroon and white Pontiac. Will parked a few slots away. The men on the porch didn't seem to be talking. They stood toying with their drinks, looking out. Pauline stayed in the truck. Will came over and got in on the passenger side.

"Damn," he said.

"Well?"

He looked at the flooded underpass. "I knew better."

She waited.

"Well," he sighed. "There's nothing to do about it now except wait it out. We need milk. Let's go in and stock up in case the Blanco washes out the bridge. Also dog food."

He got out of the truck. Pauline followed.

Her presence on the porch of the grocery store in the middle of the night with Will went unremarked upon by the men gathered there, but certainly not unnoticed. One of the men nodded at Will. Another tipped his hat. As she walked past, Pauline felt the heat of their sidelong glances. The men drank coffee and shifted their feet.

Will held open the door for her.

An old man in a grease-darkened felt fedora, a white shirt open at the throat, and brown suit pants with no belt, was behind the cash register.

"Phone's out," he said the minute Pauline stepped into the store. His voice was flat and unfriendly. "Been out a hour."

She turned around to speak to Will but instead of Will encountered a thin young man with long blond hair pulled back in a ponytail. Will held the door. The boy flew past. He wore blue jeans and a sleeveless black concert T-shirt saying CHEAP TRICK three times in white. The sleeves of the T-shirt had been ripped off, the bottom half torn away at the boy's rib cage. The blue jeans hung low on his cliffhanger hipbones, exposing his navel. His waist caved in as if headed toward his spinal column. He had tattoos down the length of his arms. The bottoms of his jeans were rolled, his feet bare.

Pauline stepped out of the boy's way. He went straight to the back of the store to the refrigerator case, got something and turned around. His ear and cheekbone were black with crusted blood.

There was a gash on that side of his head just above his ear. Blood had run from the wound down into his ear and over his neck. When the boy came to the cash register, the old man behind it nodded and rang up his purchases, two half-gallons of milk, two six-packs of Miller Lite, a green tin of Copenhagen chewing tobacco. The old man glanced at the boy's wound then looked away, saying nothing.

The bleeding boy paid and, turning around, saw Pauline. He stopped and stared, as if he might know her, and then went on.

"Let's get our stuff, Missy," Will said from behind her, ushering Pauline into the store.

A bulletin came on the radio. The old man turned it up. More rain was predicted, more flooding. Schools closed, roads blocked off. Warnings of flooded low-water crossings. Admonishments to stay at home.

"I repeat," the announcer said, "if you have no reason to be out in this then please . . ."

The announcer was beginning to beg. He sounded like a child.

They bought party food. Oreos and ice cream, Fritos and cheese, pork skins, beer, peanuts. Dog chow, batteries. Milk and candles. Will picked up a cluster of bananas and a loaf of white bread.

When they passed the group on the porch, the men were talking about floods in previous years. One of the men said while this one looked to be a decent sort of flood, it couldn't compete with another one fifty years ago. Another man laughed at how easily people were frightened by a little water these days. Will pretended to take no notice.

Pauline sighed. She would never get it. If she worked her whole life, she would be no closer than she was now to decoding the curious rituals of men. There was something between Will and the other men, some old argument which had gone beyond the need for speaking. Possibly the men didn't know what it was themselves. Whether they knew or not, it wasn't going to stop: the judgments, the competition, the need each felt to declare the unqualified rightness of his own life, each the center of his own closed world.

She cranked her truck and put it in reverse. At least she knew better than to say anything.

As they drove back east down the highway, the light in the sky began to change. The rain slackened slightly. And in the east, the first soft spikes of morning light pushed their way into the darkness.

At Will's house, they sloshed back through the mud. Will held the bag of groceries beneath his slicker. By the time they put up their food, the light in the sky had intensified. They could see where the water was.

14

From the knee-deep stream of the day before, the creek had risen some thirty feet. The place where they had stood the day before looking down at crawfish was now a torrent of swollen, hurried water. The water was not yet up to the stilts of the house, but it had crested the banks and occasionally went higher still, lapping out beyond itself to grab things, trees and bushes and whatever else was in its way. On the other side of the creek, the topmost branch of the lush red buckeye lifted its head from the creek's grasp like a drowning swimmer, down to one thrashing arm. Atop the branch, one last red blossom bobbed and shuddered.

Shoes floated by. Tree limbs. Clorox bottles, aerosol cans, plastic milk jugs, old Styrofoam ice chests, garbage cans, paddles; a large wooden box, its lid hanging on by one hinge.

"Somebody's feed box," Will said.

Like the men on the front porch of the grocery store, Will and Pauline stood silently. They couldn't get enough of looking.

"I can't believe it," Pauline said. "I'm standing here looking at it, and I still can't believe it."

She felt her skin crawl at the tops of her thighs just beneath the curve of her buttocks. She reached down inside her jeans and brushed at the skin there. When she touched herself, her skin came alive.

The poison ivy. She took her hand away and tried to concentrate. If she could remove herself from the feeling, she might float above it and leave the itch behind. She closed her eyes and took a deep yogic breath, letting the air seep slowly out through her nose.

When she looked back for the buckeye, it was gone.

"What if it keeps rising? When will it be over?"

A fence Will had built had been ripped apart like a toy. Pieces of the fence floated by. In the distance, trees cracked and snapped in two. Lotto's makeshift doghouse floated by.

"It was folly to build those things," Will said. "I knew it at the time."

"What about the house?"

"Not that foolish. The house is safe."

An entire cottonwood tree came by, roots to treetop. The cottonwood, tall and slim, looked like a ballet swimmer sculling, feet first. The cottonwood passed them the same way the snake had, with elegant indifference, making its swift, mindless passage down the creek.

Yoga was not working. The burning across the back of Pauline's thighs intensified.

"Will," she said.

He didn't answer.

She put her hand on his shoulder.

He turned to her, focusing on her face with his good eye. He had his black-rimmed reading glasses on, cockeyed, one lens higher than the other. The fake eye did not move. He peered up over the top of his glasses, looking worried, angry with himself.

"Mr. Poison Ivy," Pauline said. "I think he got me." She pulled down her pants to show him.

Will positioned her in the light so that he could see. "By God," he said, "he did." He laughed. "I warned you."

"Too late."

"Come," he said. "I can help you."

He told her to take her clothes off and to get in the bed and lie on her stomach. Pauline obeyed. Will went out of the room. He came back carrying a plant.

"What is it?"

"Aloe vera. It will keep the rash from spreading and soothe

the itch." The plant, pale green, looked like a soft, unspined cactus.

Will snapped off an arm of the plant and broke it open. "Look," he said.

Inside, the plant ran with sticky juices. Will told her to lie back down. He dribbled the juice onto her rash then smeared it directly from the plant. The juice felt cool and sticky. With his fingers, he spread it across the rash.

"Allergic or not," Will said. "It got you."

She tried to turn over, to raise up to him again, but Will held her, pushing against the small of her back with his wide strong palm.

"Lie still, Missy," he said. "Let the aloe do its work."

The sensation of his fingers spreading plant juice over the raw place was barely tolerable, like unthinking fingers on an open wound. She shuddered, and felt it to her teeth.

Will explained what a succulent was and what the aloe had in it and how it healed. And then he gave her a back rub.

She slept. When she wakened, it was daytime. The rain had stopped.

Will had made coffee and pancakes. They had skipped dinner and Pauline was starving. They ate, looking out the glass. The world outside was all water and slickness, everything in constant, hurried motion. The air was faintly pink, bright and misty with leftover dampness. Will asked about her rash. It still itched but no longer with urgency. She sat on the edge of her chair so as not to rouse it. The aloe, Will explained, was only temporary. They would treat the rash again after breakfast.

The radio was still on. The same announcer who had begged people not to leave their homes said the flooding would not be over, nor would the water start to recede, until the Blanco had brought in its share of water from the north and west as well, which would come later in the day. Rains in other parts of the state had been nothing like those in San Marcos, but more water only meant more flooding. The announcer seemed proud of the statistics, as if he were responsible for the fact that San Marcos had received a record thirteen inches of rain in six hours.

"He sounds young."

"He is. He's a high school student who happened to be doing the late-night show when this thing hit. He's been on the air the whole time."

"Probably make him famous."

"For a while."

"But not rich."

"No. Not rich."

Pauline poured syrup over her pancakes.

Will had cleaned yesterday's dishes and put them away. Now there was a new mess. He had spilled coffee grounds. On the sinkboard, he had left out his pancake ingredients, flour, buttermilk, baking soda. The pancakes were soft and high.

"I'm not used to eating so much," Pauline said. "If I stay much longer, I won't be able to do my underwater act. I'll be so fat, I'll bob to the top like a cork."

Will nodded, ate.

After breakfast, he put more aloe juice on her rash.

The first drop in the water level came dramatically, four or five inches in less than an hour. After that, the receding went more slowly, but from the moment the rain stopped and the sun came out, a feeling of quiet settled over the landscape. All the trees were bent in one direction, but it was over. The flood had gone as far as it had to.

Midmorning, Pauline went to town and called information and got the number of the pay telephone in the ICU waiting room. Someone called Mavis to the telephone. In the background, the hospital PA system paged a doctor.

"Honey," Mavis said, "we were worried sick. Wanda's at the motel in case you called us over there."

Pauline told Mavis about the flood.

"Oh, honey, we already knew about that. Wanda warned you, you know. Her hip."

There was no change in her father's condition. Pauline said

she thought sure she'd be able to come back to Austin the next day.

"What's your phone number there?" Mavis asked. And she cupped the receiver beneath her chin and called out for a pencil.

"What?" Pauline asked.

Mavis raised her voice. "Your phone number, honey. Your number. In case I need to call. Oh, there's so much noise here. All right, now I have a pencil."

"There isn't one."

"No phone?" She was incredulous.

"No."

"Then how are you calling?"

"The telephone where I'm staying is out. The lines are down. I'm at a pay phone. These people don't know me from Adam."

"Oh, Paulie." Mavis was on the verge of tears.

"Mama, I'll be all right. Please don't cry. I'll be home as soon as I can get away in the morning. All right?"

"Oh, I guess. I just wish . . ."

"You and Wanda figure out what you want to eat tomorrow night and we'll go out and have a grand dinner to celebrate my return. Anything you want. All right?"

The mention of food brightened Mavis's spirits. She said all right and Pauline told her mother she loved her.

Mavis said, "As long as you're safe."

Will and Pauline spent the morning watching the water, reading, listening to the radio. Will thawed a chicken for lunch. Later they ate cookies and ice cream in bed. They made love again, but Will seemed distracted, less patient, more in a hurry. Pauline went through the motions. The edge was off. There was a feeling of performing about their lovemaking, each doing an act for the other. It was time for Pauline to go.

She put more aloe juice on her rash. With her fingertip, she explored the ulcerated place on her tongue burned by the coffee.

She'd finally convinced Will to let Eggs in the house. Eggs lay curled and purring at the foot of the bed, never happier. Pauline invited Eggs to come live with her in New York, but Will said she couldn't go. "I'm used to her," he explained.

After lunch, they cleaned the kitchen together. When Pauline went to do the dishes, Will came up behind her and began kissing her neck. She pulled away. "Let me do this," she said, like a housewife. He went out on the deck.

His professorial distance was beginning to get on her nerves, as was all the talk about nature and symbolism: lessons to be learned from the example of the universe. Wasn't that old news, really? Pauline nodded, but did not listen. He was beginning to sound like Serebryakov.

Housebound, they paced and tapped their fingers. Small inconsequential annoyances grew in importance. After he ate, Will sucked his teeth. He was overprotective and possessive, like a nested mother hen. The house was so small, there was no place to go.

Early the next morning, Pauline washed her hair, then gathered up the few things she had taken from her purse. She tucked her nearly dry black T-shirt into her blue jeans, squared her shoulders and turned to Will. The water was low enough for her to leave, and she was ready. She actually looked forward to seeing Mavis again.

Nothing was ever easy. As soon as she had made the first move toward leaving. Will held on. He knew she had to go, but now that she was on her way, he mourned the loss of her in advance. She could see it in his eyes. He wanted to talk about what-ifs, and create an imaginary, impossible future together.

He came closer. "I wish . . ."

"What?"

He started over. "If you ever . . ."

When she started to object, he placed two fingers gently over her mouth. "Leave it," he said. "Let it go."

He drew her to him and held her. When Pauline pulled away, she was surprised to find his dark eyes turning misty with tears. The good one looked away. He pulled his bottom lip inside his teeth and held it.

She wasn't sure what she was leaving behind. She only knew she had to go. She kissed him and left.

On the road, she thought of what she knew she should have thought of before, boring matters, the crux of every grown woman's love life. Because of an inclination toward circulation problems, she could not take birth-control pills. Knowing Michael would check, she had left her diaphragm at home. She was sure she was safe. It was the wrong time of the month. She'd just had her period. And there was narrative improbability to consider, the sheer weight of historical cliché, to which Pauline had convinced herself she was invulnerable. That she should get pregnant now, because of the flood, because of being with her uncle who wanted her to do Chekhov on the banks of his creek, that life should do that to her, seemed too pat and old-fashioned a plot device to take seriously. And if in the wildest off chance it did happen, she would take the necessary steps.

When she was safely on the interstate, she reached for her purse. Something was on the seat beside it, wrapped in newspaper. Pauline opened the newspaper. Inside were offshoots of the aloe vera plant and a note. *Put it in dirt,* Will had written in his spidery hand. *It will take root on its own. Water infrequently. Watch for weather reports from West Texas.*

Pauline rewrapped the plant.

She was barely past halfway to Austin when the watery landscape began to turn green again. As if no flood had happened.

Beyond Buda, she thought of her father. His death might be slow, but it would not be hard. He was gone already . . . a thought which gave her a wild rush, as if she'd left her truck and gone floating, the way she had tried and failed to do with the poison-ivy itch. From up there, she saw the whole picture, Will at his house, her in her father's pickup driving north on the interstate back to the hospital where her father lay dying and her mother and aunt anxiously waited. Michael in New York. From the larger perspective of the clouds, it was an amazing picture.

I'm glad, she said to herself. On the radio, a bass guitar plucked a low mournful sound. A harmonica tuned up.

"Glad," she said out loud.

At the motel, she changed her clothes and went to Brackenridge. Wanda and Mavis greeted Pauline with exuberant expressions of welcome and relief, as if she had been gone years instead of two nights.

They ate that night at Green Pastures, a beautiful Victorian home turned into a restaurant. The meal was expensive but good, roast beef and fish with delicate sauces, soft rolls, a nice, if sweet, salad. The dessert selection was too tempting to resist. Mavis ordered two, raspberry mousse and peach cobbler. Pauline had a Texas Pecan Ball, a scoop of vanilla ice cream rolled in toasted pecans and topped with chocolate sauce. Mavis said the mousse was all egg whites. No calories. The pecan ball was excellent.

Two days later, an ambulance took Jack to Houston. The three women followed. Wanda drove the Cadillac, Pauline the truck. Once Jack was settled in a nursing home, Pauline went back to New York. Wanda agreed to stay with Mavis until she seemed strong enough to have her go.

Michael welcomed Pauline home with a feast: hamburgers, steamed artichokes, fresh pineapple slices. They spent the afternoon in bed. He read her some new dialogue he'd written. That night she swam at the Shipwreck. Turning flips, she felt almost happy.

In Austin, she had quickly used up the aloe vera on her rash. By the time she left, the pieces were shriveling and brown. She left them on the dressing table by the bathroom sink. It was just as well. Pauline had no luck raising plants. For a special treat of green, she sometimes bought magnolia leaves and put them in a basket. When the leaves died, she threw them out.

When Michael asked about the books, she said she'd been so busy—talking to doctors, taking care of Mavis, arranging the ambulance ride—she'd had no time even to think about them. She wasn't even sure, she said, where Will Hand was.

Her lies often went a step too far. She had the feeling Michael knew. Not exactly what, but something.

Once, finding Pauline sitting on the windowseat staring out at traffic—she was thinking of Will, hearing his voice, remembering the sound of the out-of-banks Snake Creek—Michael asked her what she was thinking.

"Nothing," she said, coming to. She focused her eyes. "Nothing."

"Nobody thinks about nothing," Michael replied. "Everybody knows everything, all the time."

She thought he was probably right.

III

15

The same dream again, the baby midair, falling, Pauline with him, he and she the same slowly dropping creature, going down.

With is wrong. She is not with but *as* him, both—each—going down as if down will never end.

In dreams falling does not stop or come to anything, there is no crash, no earth to fall to, the descent is slow and endless and pure tedium: the terror of sensation without gain or accumulation, that ticklish, unbearable *whoosh* . . .

Until she wakens, arms out, palms flat against the mattress like an infant grasping at the air for help.

She shook her head. Her long hair whipped at her cheeks and streaked into her eyes.

In the dream the baby is always a boy, a fact not stated but somehow known, background information, like an atmospheric condition.

Outside the windows, east-west traffic, released by a green light, roared up again. A blade of yellow made its jagged way across the bedroom wall. In the kitchen, Kathleen pawed at the blue bits of rock in her litter box.

Pauline pulled the covers up. For hastily improvised warmth, she had thrown two sheets over her, afraid if she spent too much time getting ready she'd be awake for the night. She bunched up her legs. Spring had stalled, forever it seemed. April, and nights were still freezing.

She had begun sleeping on the windowseat again. The bedroom felt too isolated, the bed too large and lonely. The windowseat was narrow and, divided into seamed cushions, un-comfortable. But she felt safer there, closer to the comfort of other people out on the streets going places. When the wind blew, she could lay her hand on the windowpane and feel it rattle the glass.

Four years Michael had been gone. Four years since she saw Will. And here she was, still crazed.

She reached for her notebook, which she had left on the floor, having planned to jot down some notes before she went to sleep, having gone—fallen—mercifully to sleep instead. By the light of the streetlights outside her window, she wrote down the dream.

Sunday, April 7. Middle of the night. The baby dream again, version #1: falling.

The traffic light at the corner cast a red glow on the pale green unlined page.

There were three versions of the same dream, all of which she had catalogued:

1. The dream of slow falling: no finish, the endless fall.
2. The dream of impossible rescue: she (turning time backward) saves him.
3. The dream beyond: no options.

Actually by now it was Monday. In her notebook, Pauline noted the fact in parentheses:

(Monday a.m. to be exact.)

Dates were important, exact times of day, precisely what was worn, seen, said, the exact circumstances of every dream. Attention to details gave life its necessary order. Structure, that was it. She wrote down not just dreams but everything. Where she went, what she ate. Structure was glue.

Her pillow had fallen to the floor. In the dark Pauline felt for it. She doubled the pillow to raise her head and pulled her T-shirt down over her stomach. She slept in socks, underwear, that day's shirt. Her jeans were down there somewhere, lost in bedclothes.

This after a lifetime of letting loose ends take care of themselves. After a lifetime of . . . sometimes she wondered, if she was the same person.

"We always thought," she heard herself saying just last week, speaking of her family, including, surprisingly, herself, "that things would come around again. That if *we* stayed the same, so would the world. Possibly an ingrained Christian response, believing in the eternal return. I knew my mother thought that. I didn't realize I did."

A fantasy: Look to the verbs. Thinking, believing, knowing, realizing were actions of the mind only, and loss created its own deep pit, which neither mind nor the imagination could picture the exact nature or location of before the feet stumbled and the poor dumb body fell in. There were no analogies to be made, nothing compared. The thing had to happen, an arm torn from its socket, the wind socked straight out of your gut. Then you, what is called, *knew*.

Looking back several pages in the notebook, Pauline came across another night's dream in which, swimming in a clear, narrow channel of water, she had seen beneath her the body of a pale, obviously dead woman. The woman's mouth was open, as were her large blue unseeing eyes. Her blond hair pulsed and her torn and flowery V-necked dress floated up around her, drifting with the current like sea grass. Terrified, Pauline swam faster. She knew she should do something, offer help, tell someone. She only wanted to get away.

The dead woman could be Sonya, Russell Loving had suggested, the dream a wishful one, indicating Pauline's desire to bury Sonya and go on to something else. Back to acting, another role. He didn't say so but Pauline knew Loving thought she should make some effort to get back to work again. Real work, not just a job. Loving quoted Freud on the subject—work the closest we come to sanity; quoted Chekhov. Pauline disagreed. She liked sitting, stroking Kathleen. Now that she was getting Mavis's monthly allotment checks, she didn't need the money. And so, why bother?

Kathleen finished her business in the litterbox. The smell drifted in from the kitchen.

"Pee-you, Kathleen."

At the mention of her name, Kathleen responded with her special "Oh, yeah?" meow and then began to wash herself, licking her paws, digging with her teeth between her toes.

Pauline patted the windowseat. "When you finish, glamour girl," she said into the darkness, "come sleep with me." Kathleen said nothing. A silvery part-Siamese beauty queen who on her best days looked like Marilyn Monroe, Kathleen was choosy; she did as she pleased.

Pauline hadn't asked—wouldn't—but she had the feeling that if he knew, Russell Loving would not approve of this particular activity of hers, scribe to the subconscious, writing down dreams for herself before bringing them to him.

There was no way to be sure, of course, but she'd been with him a year, in which time she'd gotten pretty much up on his thinking. Loving liked spontaneity. He said she shouldn't try to second-guess him but she couldn't help it, even though sometimes—usually—it didn't work. He always managed to save back surprises to keep himself in the driver's seat.

Traffic on Tenth Avenue came to a quick halt. From farther away, a crosstown bus strained and groaned. Traffic was the great sleeping partner. Husbands left, lovers moved on. Even pedestrians gave up and went home. Loyal as sunrise, traffic never stopped. She closed the notebook and laid it on her stomach, then reached beneath the cushions and slid open a built-in drawer. From inside, she took out a wavy-patterned afghan Wanda had given her for Christmas. Outside, another shift. The moving cars were just beneath the windows again, closer, louder. She spread the afghan over her legs.

Another possibility was that—having heard so many—Loving already knew. Maybe he could tell the difference between a dream being spontaneously recreated and one that was a second-hand rehash, like a rehearsed speech in a play. And then again, maybe all of this was wishful thinking on her part; vanity only, wanting Loving to want her to be all his. After all, what was she to him? Only a patient, one of many. But in truth, he was a demanding master. His room, his couch. The way, in the beginning, he pushed her around.

Well, no matter Russell Loving's wishes. Translating a dream from the mostly visual and always disorderly into the rationale of language was a corruptive act in and of itself, written or recited. And Pauline valued her notebooks—went out of the way to find ones that pleased her, nicely sewn, imported from Florence with bright swirly covers and pale green pages. She would not give them up. In the past two years she had filled five, one in flamey shades of red and orange, two in purples, one in grays, another in pinks. The latest one was bright turquoise.

She doodled in the margin, a five-pointed star, with curlicues.

She stored the notebooks, labeled by season and year, on the shelf Michael once used for play scripts. Michael's office was hers, and the apartment. Her notebooks, life, the shelves, everything.

Self, she wrote. *An illusion. Self is a dream, like the dead Sonya.*

The point of course was not that she wrote down her dreams—her life after all was her own—but that she felt a need to keep the fact of those records to herself. Keeping secrets was an old habit she was trying to break, but it was hard. She was afraid that if she told Russell Loving everything, he might convince her to do things she didn't want to.

From down on the street, she heard voices, loud, animated, raised either in anger or in fun. She sat up and looked out.

A group of people, two men and a woman, were just coming out of Al's Bar, across the street on the corner. The woman's hair was so blond it glowed like glitter in the streetlights. One of the men locked the door to the bar, put the keys in his pocket and turned to the others. The trio crossed Tenth, one man on either side of the woman. The woman wore high heels. Her ankles wobbled. Across the woman, the men were arguing. One raised his arms high in the air, palms toward his face. Head turned toward the other man, he pressed the backs of his hands against the night air to make his point. The Al's Bar sign was off. The three people were going east, of course. There was no reason to go west except the Hudson. The man lowered his arms. When the trio got close to Pauline's side of the street, they vanished.

Pauline made mental notes, how they walked, what the angry man's gestures were like, the pitch of his voice, the glow of her hair.

It was Sunday. Bars were closed. No telling what they had been up to in there.

Pauline lay back on her pillow and stared at the ceiling. The plaster just over her head was puckered and saggy from a burst water pipe. She wondered if the plaster might ever just fall. Some unusually dark nights, she could see a reflection of the traffic lights from the street on the ceiling as they switched colors. Not tonight.

In a year's time she still had not yet settled up with what she wanted call her new adviser, dream interpreter, the improbably named Russell Loving, her what? Psychiatrist, therapist, doctor? Or could she all of a sudden become an old hand and, like all the others she knew, call him shrink?

She ran her tongue back and forth along the inner surface of her bottom teeth, in and out of the crevice made by the crooked one in the middle. She had not taken time to Vaseline the mascara from her eyes. With thumb and forefinger, she slid clots of the black stuff from her eyelashes and flicked them into the air. Traffic changed directions again.

No. She had gone far enough toward joining the modern world, seeing him at all. She held the line on jargon. Let others yield to slang and first names. He was her doctor. Speaking— thinking—of him, she called him Dr. Loving. Or simply Loving.

In version two of the dream, the baby is on the window ledge looking out. (The window is always the same, the one in her kitchen. There is nothing to see out the window except the airshaft, other grimy windows and walls, nothing at the bottom except, four flights down, a triangular patch of blackened concrete, one beat-up metal garbage can, usually a plastic bag or two, maybe some rotting food, whatever people have seen fit to toss out the window.)

In this dream, Pauline comes up from behind the baby, holding her breath to keep from making the slightest sound. She is so afraid, her heart feels frozen in her chest. If she makes a noise, the baby goes. But she can't move. Her feet feel glued. It is as if she is trying to run the hundred-yard dash underwater. And then (although there is no narrative *and then*, it only happens), not because speed has come to her, not because of anything, she has him. She grabs a foot and pulls him to her. She has done the trick, become the hero, saved him. Against her chest the baby feels like a willing sack of potatoes.

Flying is sexual, falling is not. Falling means the primal drop in both directions, birth and death at once, the concurrent *whoosh*. Fear in either instance, also high arousal, the irresistible push-pull.

She had let her hair grow, to the middle of the back. She pulled it out from under her neck and gathered it to one side. No haircut, no style, just long. She wore it caught back in a clasp or pulled to one side braided in a single thick plait down her chest. In the past four years the few gray hairs she had in the front had widened to narrow streak. Pauline liked the gray. Arlene objected. "You're an actress," she said. "You're too young to play gray hair. It goes."

In dream three, Pauline looks out the window and there he is, a pitiful wreck of small useless life on the concrete beside the garbage can, an incomplete baby, soft and translucent and full of veins. A horror baby, like the pictures in pamphlets handed out by furious women picketing hospitals and birth control centers, those babies pickled in jars. Guilt, regret, recriminations; miscarriages of dead hopes flushed down the dark bottomless air shaft.

About the abortion she had nothing to apologize for. She

had shouldered her way past the self-righteous women and had it done. What the furious women did not understand was that the abortion was not, had not been, would never be easy, nor was it lightly decided upon. All that was one thing. The abortion also was not wrong. Right and wrong were not at issue, she had no problem with right and wrong. Wrong was mental and mental was nothing, a socialized response applicable to symptoms only. Compared to sadness wrong was nothing. Compared to dreams wrong was a snap. Compared to loss and sorrow and inexplicable grief, the fall, the jump, wrong went down sweet and fast, like a cookie.

What did they know, those women. She hated them all.

Dream two was the worst. She woke up thinking it had happened, that like a lifeguard she had dived in in time and, cupping their chins to float their heads above the surface of the water, stroked them all safely to shore.

She felt happy those mornings. Like Mavis. Thinking it had all been somehow fixed and nothing had been lost. Thinking Will was within reach, so that she didn't have to miss him any more. Thinking the baby was saved, so she would not have to sleep alone.

In her notebook, by the light of the streetlamps, she wrote, *Helplessness is progressive, a disease. Once admitted to, it never eases up but only grows. The reason people come to think of themselves as victims and never get beyond. Once it starts.*

16

When she got home from Texas, it took her six weeks to admit what she basically already knew: that organs, being dull-witted, had no fear of historical clichés. Narrative improbability had failed her. She was pregnant. Having spent those six weeks finding ways not to believe, she had no time to waste once she owned up to the truth. First, Michael.

It was late afternoon. She was fixing soup before going to work. "Well," she said—having rehearsed her speech many times, she was able to affect extreme casualness—"I've slipped up. I guess I'm pregnant." Before she could go on, Michael began to laugh, not sardonically but outright.

She turned from the soup. Dark eyes never shined brighter.

"Terrific," Michael said. "We've been in a slump, couldn't you feel it? We need a boost." He didn't wait for corroboration. "I didn't expect this of course, but now that it's here"—he raised his hands palms-up as if to the heavens—"it must be right."

Carefully, Pauline set down her spoon, covered the soup and turned off the fire.

"Michael, we agreed," she said with great deliberation. "No children."

Thinking there was no fixed point upon which she would stand and refuse to budge, Michael waggled his finger. "We never said never. We said not right away. Now that it's happened"—he shrugged his shoulders—"how can we not? It's destiny, Pauline. Fate. I hope it's a girl. We can call her Destiny Caproselli." He threw back his head and laughed, then abruptly went quiet. "Joke," he said, pushing his hands out in a stopping motion. "Destiny as a name is a joke."

Pauline's throat went dry. Something beyond sense was in motion here, a subtext beyond words. Michael looked like instant "Father Knows Best." But there was no use trying to figure it out, she was in too deep herself.

"Michael," she said. "I'm not having this baby." Her voice wavered a bit, but she felt strong. For once she knew what she wanted. If she could have reached up inside and pulled the baby out with her hands, she'd have done it then and there.

Michael looked baffled, hurt. But there was no reason to expect Michael to understand. The implacability of her stance had nothing to do with Michael . . . or with Will. The decision —commitment, discomfort, urge, responsibility (dreams, baby) —was hers.

He ducked his chin.

"Pauline," he said with boyish charm. "Don't take this life." He sounded like the pamphlets.

Frantic, Pauline grabbed at a silly straw. "I'll lose my job."

"We'll think of something."

"And afterward, what? Who'd take care of it, you? Who won't put your hand in the john when you drop your razor? What about diapers, where would we put it, where would you work, how could I? What are you thinking of?"

He had lured the argument into secondary issues. Pauline put her hands over her face.

"What am I saying? You're baiting me. I'm not going to have it."

He moved toward her. Pauline backed away. She didn't think he would hurt her—he never had—but he looked dangerous. Of all the churchly virtues, surely self-righteousness was the most shameless.

She backed into the wall.

"I'm going to have an abortion, Michael, with your help or without it. I swear, this is not going to happen. I am not going to have it."

Michael bent his head charmingly to one side and kept coming. He smiled sweetly. "Pauline . . ." he began.

"It's not yours."

He stopped abruptly. She had not meant to tell him. She meant for no one ever to know, but he had pushed too far.

"Don't ask whose, but I know. I'm not guessing."

One eye might have twitched and then his face went slack. "The woman's revenge," he whispered. "Pure Strindberg."

"I'm positive, Michael. I know." Her mind began to clear. With her back against the wall, she felt calm.

Michael took a step closer. A strand of his dark hair fell into his eyes. She could smell his breath.

"We had a deal, Pauline. I knew you'd be the one to break it. You never really committed. Always floating, two feet off the ground. I never lied to you, Pauline. Not once."

It took all her strength not to turn away.

"So what?" she said. "What difference does it make?"

He took her face and placing his hands around her jaws, his fingertips pressing against that soft spot just beneath the ears, began to rock her head, slapping it against the wall. Not hard. But she felt humiliated and afraid. He *could* hurt her, which was the point. He was making use of his strength to let her know it . . . keeping her, as Jack used to say about women and dogs, in line.

Gathering her courage, Pauline put her hands on his shoulders and pushed against him. Michael stopped rocking her head. He punched his fingers in harder and held her head flat against the wall. For a few seconds, he seemed on the verge of either kissing or slapping her. And then he let her go.

Pauline went to the Shipwreck, swam. When she came back Michael was gone. He had dumped the soup in the middle of the kitchen floor, poured milk on all the furniture and burned his plays in a metal garbage can. (Xeroxes? Pauline wondered. Had his gesture been only that? Or had he actually burned the only copies? She never knew.) Later, one night while she was at work, he came for his things.

The smell of sour milk died hard. She had used every brand of disinfectant and deodorizing spray, but the odor was still there. If she buried her face in the pillows of the windowseat Pauline could still detect the presence of leftover clabber.

And now? She missed him. His mood swings and wise-cracks, the way they slept together, so close. Married to Michael she had known where she stood. Within the tight circle he drew, she could dream and plan.

Delayed reactions were one of life's crueler tricks. Before it was out, she had thought of the baby as an *it,* a *thing,* a problem to be solved. As soon as she had the abortion, the thing changed from a convenient *it* to a baby. Suddenly she cared.

She wanted life to make sense and it never seemed to. She wanted to value things—people—in advance instead of under-standing after they'd whirled through the revolving door and were gone how much they had meant.

How could she dream about a baby she had never had, how remember the *whoosh* of birth when she'd never done it? Every-body knows everything, as Michael used to say. Somewhere back in the cobwebs she'd felt it, beyond mind and memory, like the tree in the forest, complete within itself, needing no ears.

Enough. The doctor who performed the abortion said that Pauline in all likelihood would not have been able to carry the baby to full term anyway. She had gynecological problems which, if she ever decided to have a baby, she would have to see to first.

"It's in my family," Pauline told the doctor, a slim, polite, blue-eyed young man. "A lot of the women in my family have had trouble having children."

I'm afraid, Pauline wanted to say to him—and the words forced their way up all the way to her throat, but she stopped them. Didn't he understand? Just because she looked so strong, didn't mean she was.

The doctor kept writing, his arm curved over on top of the paper he was writing on, in that backhand slant peculiar to left-handed people.

She bled for weeks, massive black clots and strings, a gushing flow. Her uterus cramped in simulated labor, turning her stomach into a rock of pain. She stayed in the apartment day and night, the four flights down and up an unthinkable climb. Coco brought food. Knowing nothing about the abortion, Mrs. Poshkosh, thinking Pauline had been abandoned, came one day with Kathleen, the runt of a litter born to the candy-store cat. Kathleen became Pauline's instant roommate, pal and heating pad, warm against her disappointed belly.

She drew a line underneath the last paragraph and then wrote in all capitals, *If only emotion was still an acting tool. Once it gets this far, Pandora's box. No telling.*

She set the notebook on the floor.

Loving said (and hadn't she become like her friends, always quoting?) there was no way to prepare or plan when the emotions were drastically involved, that all she could do was think and reflect and listen to herself and to try, in time, to detect patterns with enough accuracy that she could incorporate the patterns in her life and make plans around them.

Refusing to accept this brutal assessment, she had protested.

"No control," Loving had repeated, his voice drifting from behind her. Loving's voice was strong. He had a light but emphatic—never tentative—therapeutic touch.

Kathleen had found her spot for the night, behind the rocking chair on the silk kimono Pauline had dropped and forgotten about. Kathleen liked to experience new places.

The digital clock on the coffee machine announced the time in broken green dashes, two twelve.

Mavis had sent the coffee machine. When Jack went into the nursing home, Mavis had begun sending lavish presents ordered from expensive catalogues. A digital weight scale, an electric wok, a microwave oven, linen napkins, personalized stationery, a fish-poaching machine.

As Jack lived on in a vegetable state for a year, the gifts had piled up. Pauline and the UPS delivery man were on first-name terms. Most of the things were still in boxes in the back room.

Pauline had meant to sell or donate them. Then when Mavis died, she couldn't. The gifts seemed like small messages from the grave. There wasn't much back there she cared about—what in the world was she supposed to do with a fish-poaching machine? —but when she dropped her old Chemex, she did uncrate the electric coffeemaker. German, white and very stylish, the new machine did everything, ground the beans, dripped the coffee, told time. You could set it at night and wake up to brewed coffee. Pauline hadn't thought herself up to such luxury. Now she loved it.

Time moved. Two thirteen. Two was endless, the longest hour.

After languishing on the market for a year and a half, the condominium Jack and Mavis had owned in Houston had finally sold . . . at a loss, but Houston real estate was a swamp; Pauline was happy to be rid of the thing. In twenty-four hours' time— less—she was going to Houston to sign the closing papers. She and Wanda were having dinner. The day after the closing, Pauline would see Will. She'd written. Will had responded with a formal note.

The black and white tile floor she and Michael had installed had remained in remarkably good shape. This past winter, Pauline had added a thick coat of high-gloss polyurethane wax. The indestructible shine pleased her enormously. Even in the night, the floor glowed. Michael, on a visit, had seen the new floor. The cold blast of his disapproval had chilled her bones.

Loving had never actually said she had to tell him everything—he in fact had not suggested much at all—but the process couldn't be worth much if she purposefully held back important information. Didn't he save his sharpest inquiry for the times he suspected her of meaningful concealment? Wasn't there comfort in knowing there was one person whom you could safely tell absolutely anything? She even knew what he would say if he knew she was holding out: that what was important was not what she was keeping from him, but that she felt it necessary to do so at all. Loving of course knew she was going to Texas—

she would miss a week of sessions—but not what she had in mind.

On the street below, a large truck lumbered by, a produce truck, she thought, delivering lettuce, oranges, kiwi to the markets on Eighth Avenue.

The apartment smelled of Mexican food: grease, garlic, red spices. She and Coco had fixed a fabulously hot going-away dinner. Beans, tostadas, guacamole, chicken enchiladas with sour cream and green salsa. Coco had brought fancy ice cream, and San Miguel beer in brown bottles . . . not the right country but cold and good. They'd downed the entire six-pack.

She wasn't sure what she wanted or expected from Will Hand. She'd have to improvise. Will lived in a new town. He was married again. Or had been. He never stayed married long. Maybe if she felt flippant—brave—enough, Pauline would propose.

Married to Will, what an idea. No more acting, no substitutions. She would not even need Loving. The circle would be drawn tight once again.

Staring at the ceiling like a doll with no mechanism for blinking, Pauline switched to the other eye, combing the mascara from her lashes.

For warmth, she put one foot on top of the other. Freezing cold in April was ridiculous. In the East, winter did not ever know when to quit.

"Kathleen," she begged. "Please."

Curled on the silk kimono, Kathleen loudly purred. Kathleen would come in her own sweet time.

17

By the time Mavis went to the doctor it was too late. The warts and moles on her face and arms turned out to have long, unforgiving roots reaching into vital organs. The doctor had decided not to operate. Pauline imagined the roots looking like long, black deadly threads, hanging down like the legs of jellyfish, swinging from one organ to the next.

It was early spring, a year after Jack died. Wanda and Pauline stayed at the Houston Medical Center Holiday Inn for six weeks. In that time, they made a kind of temporary life together, taking what pleasure they could.

At night after visiting hours they went to movies at the nearby Shamrock Five, to Ninfa's for Mexican food, James' Coney Island for chili and hot dogs, the Goode Company for barbecue. For raw and fried oysters—also fried whole catfish—they stood at the bar at Cap'n Benny's on South Main and ate until they couldn't move. Tuesdays, they went to Ouisie's for chicken-fried steak, Sundays tried various buffet brunches, all you could eat for a set amount. Some mornings Pauline sneaked into her former place of employment, the Shamrock Hilton pool. Surrounded by palm trees, the pool—fifty meters of glassy green water—created its own world, tropical as a Caribbean island. That early in the spring, Pauline was usually the lone swimmer. A mile came back to her easily enough. In two weeks' time she felt her stroke grow powerful again, the old rhythm returning. Afternoons, she jogged on broken sidewalks around Rice University and one night went to a play at the Alley. Their motel room had cable. Pauline and Wanda watched movies. Daytimes they visited Mavis or sat together in the waiting room telling stories while Mavis slept. They took turns feeding Mavis. In a medicated daze, Mavis sometimes knew who they were, but more often than not had no idea. She called for Jack.

Questioning Wanda, Pauline asked what her and Mavis's childhood had been like and when it was that Mavis seemed to have lost her hold on reality, and what all those trips to the Houston sanitarium were really about.

"Nervous breakdowns," Wanda said flatly. "Mavis was born small and sickly and she never got over it. The first month of that baby's life, she was so agitated she didn't sleep more than an hour at a time day or night. They gave her what we used to call sugar tits, they held her, they gave her aspirin and sugar, they boiled humidifiers by her bed night and day, they wrapped her in mentholated blankets. Nothing worked. Everybody took turns rocking Mavis. Lap to lap she went. Lap to lap. I bet her feet didn't touch the floor more than five minutes a day the first three years of that baby's life. Then there was Daddy. Mavis doted on Daddy. He died when Mavis was five. Some children, you know. I don't think poor Mavis ever got over it." She paused, stared at the wall. "Mama was too old to have a baby by then anyway. She was nearly forty, and forty was a lot older then than it is now. Daddy was fifty-five. I think that's too old for a man, don't you?"

"Did you rock Mama?"

"Oh, no, honey, I was just a baby."

"That's what I thought."

"But I heard the stories."

Loving pressed at her to remember, remember. *What does this remind you of?*

Her earliest memory was of an afternoon, hot, no air conditioning, Mavis asleep, Pauline antsy to leave. Mavis liked naps. Her breath smelled of bourbon. The room was dark. Inch by inch, Pauline crept off the bed and went down the hall, out the front door and down the steps, running as if someone were after her, to a secret place behind a brake of scrub oaks she called her cave but which was really only a mound of brown dirt she could sit beneath. She liked to move her bowels there. Liked the special feeling when the snake came out and curled in her lacy underpants. Mavis woke up from her naps slowly, like some long-frozen Frankenstein thawing back to life. Pauline waited for Mavis to come looking for her. No one did. Finally she went back on her own. No one seemed worried. Someone cleaned her up. That was all.

Lying on Russell Loving's couch, she closed her eyes and saw the picture—the light, a shadow across Mavis's face— clearly. Felt the exhilaration, running away. The shameful pleasure at the moment when her bowels let go. She might have been two, three. But was she remembering or only imagining, from having heard the stories? She wasn't sure she knew the difference between memory and imagination.

One night about two weeks into the Houston stay, after a so-so meal at Fred's Italian Corner, Pauline and Wanda got mildly drunk on beer. Eating her last meatball, pretending she'd just thought of it, Pauline asked Wanda about Will.

"You mean you didn't hear?"

Pauline said no. Wanda settled her shoulders and took a swallow of beer.

"Girl, he got married again. Myself I couldn't believe it. I thought he was going to live on Snake Creek by his own true-love self forever."

Pauline set down her empty beer glass and ordered another. Her head shook slightly and a place in her chest opened up, a hairline crack, narrow as the slice of a razorblade. She had no right to be disappointed, but she had planned to drive to see him . . . expecting, foolishly, everything to have remained the same, him, the dog, the house, Snake Creek, having held on to his "If you ever . . ." as if it were an oath.

"Who did he marry?" The waiter set a new mug of beer on the table. Foam sloshed. "Anyone we know?" She mopped at the table with a paper napkin.

Wanda ran her finger around the rim of her glass. "Your uncle," she said, "which there is no way for you to know, has always had an eye for the girls. And a yen for dark and flashy women. I think when he was in Spain that time he must have had a girlfriend there, one of those"—Wanda snapped her fingers together and clicked her heel against the floor—"Spanish fancy dancers. You get me?"

Pauline nodded, drank beer, took deep breaths.

"So he found himself the next best thing. A Mexican. Ha!"

Wanda turned up her mug. Foam clung to her upper lip. She licked it off. In the low, pale yellowish lights of the restaurant she looked beautiful: her forehead pale and smooth, her blue eyes shining.

"Not an ordinary Mexican, no. A rich one. The conquistadoress, I call her. Well, I have one thing to say to the conquistadoress and that is, good luck on your new job. She's going to need it."

"Does she . . . what's her name?"

"Isabel. Isabella? No, Isabel. Isabella's the one who gave Columbus the money. Plain Isabel."

"Does Isabel live in that tiny house?" Pauline caught herself. "The one you told me about? On the creek?"

Wanda frowned. A flash of new information rolled across her intelligent blue eyes. She looked down into her empty glass, thinking back. Pauline held her breath. When Wanda spoke again, her voice had lowered.

"No," Wanda said. "They moved. He sold the San Marcos land and bought a place near the Edwards Plateau. Up past Waco, a town called Eulogy. Four hundred acres, I heard, nothing but limestone, rattlesnakes and rocks. Which is just about his hardheaded style, I don't know about her."

Wanda picked a breadstick from the basket on the table and broke it apart.

She shook her head and held one piece of the breadstick up,

as if proposing a toast. "Good luck on your new job, Queen Isabel."

She set the broken breadstick on the table mug and said she was tired, she wanted to go back to the motel.

Wanda was on a biographies kick that spring. There was a secondhand bookstore a few blocks from the hospital where she could make trades, buying a used paperback for half price then trading it back in for one-fourth down on another. That winter, she had read the life stories of Joe Namath and Malcolm X, Queen Elizabeth I, Shelley Winters, Eleanor of Aquitaine, Flaubert. At the hospital, she read Harry Truman and Marilyn Monroe and a Jackie Robinson written for young people.

"I love history," Wanda said. "And other people's lives." She had just traded Harry Truman for Edith Wharton when Mavis died. "I knew this was too long when I got it," Wanda said.

Mavis, for whom relinquishment was an old habit, gave in quickly to her disease. In six weeks' time Pauline watched her mother shrivel to threads and shadows, her hold on life as fragile as the dew-laden strings of a spiderweb. Pauline held her mother's hand, fed her, talked to her, took care of her. Mavis looked blank. Pauline could have been anybody.

Wanda and Pauline were in the waiting room watching the news when she died. A nurse appeared. They looked up. "Your mother," the nurse said to Pauline, "has passed." Pauline felt strangely woozy, then nothing. The loss of Mavis at that moment touched her lightly, as if she'd suddenly let fly free a bird she'd kept cupped in her hand.

"If you'd like to see her . . ." the nurse said.

The nurse had closed Mavis's eyes and folded her hands. Wanda went over and kissed her. Pauline hung back near the door. Wanda rearranged a lock of Mavis's hair. "I guess it's just you and me now, Pauline," she said.

When Wanda turned around, Pauline held out her arms. Wanda came to her. They dropped their heads on one another's shoulders and, holding one another, cried aloud, not for their own loss—about which they still had no real information—but for the waste.

"Poor Mavis," Wanda said. "Poor, poor little old thing."

Pauline flicked her tongue across the backside of her teeth.

Another incident occurred during the trip to Arkansas, one which Pauline often set aside in her mind and chose not to remember. She thought of it when Wanda said "Poor Mavis." And again when she got back to New York after the funeral.

After her parents left her in bed to go down and hear the piano player from Paris, Pauline slept a while and then at some point abruptly wakened. Without checking the time, she dressed, took her key and went down to the ballroom. The maitre d', stiffly attired, asked if he could help, but Pauline, drawing herself up as tall as possible, told him her parents were inside and she wanted to join them. The piano player was banging out a jump number. A large band backed him up. The room was huge, with droopy chandeliers and enormous potted palms, but the dance floor was tiny. People were bumping into one another. Pauline spotted her parents right away. Hiding behind a post near the dance floor, she watched them. Jack twirled Mavis out, held up his arm for her to go under, brought her close, then whirled her away from him once again. Mavis's breasts bounced in Pauline's blouse, rising up out of the sweetheart neckline, shivering like pudding. Her tiny feet made quick, mincing movements, sending her broad hips in one direction and then the other. Her dyed blond hair lay in wet ringlets about her face. Mavis didn't care how she looked or how fat she was. She didn't care about anything. She raised her arm and pointed her finger to the sky, closed her eyes, opened her red-orange mouth, let her breasts go where they would. Jack pulled her to him hard, banging her stomach and breasts against his flat midsection, then twirling her out again, watching her fat jiggle. Jack said he didn't like for her to get fat but Pauline could tell by the look in his eyes; he loved seeing her white flesh shiver. And Mavis was in heaven.

Pauline hated them both. She felt as scared of them dancing together as she had been of the bear. She went back upstairs to bed and buried her head under her pillow so that she would not hear them when they came in. The next thing she knew it was morning and there they lay in the bed beside her, their loud boozy orchestrated breath filling the room.

It took months for Mavis's death to have its effect, long enough that when Pauline tried to get up one morning and could not, when she suddenly felt as if someone had smacked her on the back of the head so hard she could not think straight, much less move, she had no idea what caused it. At the time, there had been distractions: the funeral, the family, Mavis's will, the condominium to put up for sale, transfer of the gas allot-ments into Pauline's name, the decision what to do with Mavis's Cadillac. Pauline went back to New York feeling tired and essentially dulled but not overcome.

Dreams hinted at a more complicated response, the one about cloth unraveling at her touch, another about making love to a slim-hipped stranger while Will Hand sat in a chair at the foot of the bed and from between Pauline's spread knees watched, smiling. The one about Mavis in the casket trying to hold on to her. Pauline dismissed these warnings as insignificant. Dreams, she said to herself. Only dreams.

She had thought trouble announced itself, if not immedi-ately then with examination, and that there was always a way to stand far enough back from trouble to get a bead on it. Suddenly exhaustion flattened her. Faced with decisions, she panicked and could not breathe. She felt so tired she could not get up out of her chair. Then never got tired and did not sleep. There seemed to be no reasons, no cause, she could make no connections between motivation and response. She was so much in the soup she could not feel its hot presence all around her.

She gave up socializing, went out only when she had to, to shop or do the wash. When she did go out, she was usually sorry.

Faithful as a lapdog, Arlene called regularly to tell her of auditions, new plays, commercials being shot. When Pauline declined, Arlene was never discouraged. "Just checking, sweet pea," she said. "Just checking."

Too much had been snatched away in too short a period of time. Pauline sat for hours stroking Kathleen, not realizing how long she'd been there until she looked up and found long shadows streaking across the tile floor, the day grown dark. Nothing seemed to matter. She went to a doctor. He suggested vitamins. She was exhausted and could not sleep.

My mother? she said when someone suggested it. I was never close to my mother.

Focusing on the concrete, she went on eating cures, no food then everything in sight, white food, yellow food, high-protein cereal six times a day, megadoses of vitamins until her throat clogged. Ate for love, for replacement. For life. For something to do. Arlene protested. Dye the gray, she said, go to auditions. Pauline was thinking of turning to a more useful profession. She was considering becoming a nurse.

She had not slept with a man in almost a year. Once she had unstocked her life of confusion, then—perhaps—she might be up to the unpredictability of complicated relationships. Until then, no. Coco had become a pal, the best. They no longer made love.

After Mavis died, Wanda finally went on to the next thing. In two years' time she had been all over the world. India, Nepal, Iceland. She liked the unusual. "Any fool can go to Paris," she said. Wanda went to Dakar and an island called Timor where she stayed in the home of a local fisherman and ate raw octopus. She bought a thirty-five-millimeter camera and took pictures.

The muscles in Wanda's calves were as thin and wiry as coat hangers from all the walking. Her skin was tan, her bags perpetually packed.

Pauline made Wanda promise to call once a month no

matter where she was. "I need to know you're still out there," she said.

In the kitchen window a familiar red light from far out on the Hudson jabbered on and off. Careful not to uncover her feet, Pauline pulled up the afghan then turned on her other side, away from the windows.

Sleep, where was it? She used to be such an expert, used to get her childish eight hours no matter what, could close her eyes and simply go there, as if sleep were a town to drive to. Her talent was one she had never boasted of. Her friends took pills, walked the floor. How could she sleep eight hours and call herself artist? Their insomnia had seemed fashionable; the big romance.

Now sleep was. Her wish was simple: not to work on it or think about it, to fall, as in her dream.

18

"Fifty-minute sessions, psychotherapy. Treatment continues. No drugs." Russell Loving typed this explanatory note at the bottom of her statement every month.

"No drugs" was for the union insurance company. She had never asked for any, not from him or her friends. No drugs was accurate.

Or, no pills. She kept marijuana in the apartment but the weed had turned on her. Instead of easing her into sleep, it woke her up like black coffee. Wine too, and gin. Whatever she tried had the same effect, stunning her mind into awareness, her eyelids into constant vigilance. She had given up even regular morning coffee, having switched to a decaffeinated blend of dark- and medium-roast beans. To tire herself, she lifted weights, ran. Nothing worked. She was never tired. A book on depression said that never being tired was a symptom of a certain kind of depression.

She arranged a corner of the sheet over her eye so that she could not see the green numbers on the clock. On the street someone honked a horn long and hard. From far away an ambulance siren screamed.

The menacing man in the street, the falling baby. The dead Sonya. No telling what new shapes horror might come in.

She closed her eyes and tried to think of nothing.

Resignation, negotiation, acknowledgment of her own complexity. She had always found all that such a bore. Yet when she looked back, she had to shake her head to see what a smiling stick-figure fool she had been, expecting life to go on the same forever, as if tomorrows were only stepping stones ahead, to maneuver her way across by jumping. As if all she had to do was move her feet.

She could not figure what the payoff in such a life was supposed to have been. You do it all your life and then you die?

"Kathleen, please," she begged. Kathleen said nothing.

Russell Loving was an ordinary white man, not Jewish, nothing exotic. Except for the accent, he might have been from Baytown. The first time Pauline went to his office and saw that not only was he probably not even city-born but more than likely Midwestern—like a Methodist—and also graying and—not as small as Jack, he did not have that perfect soldier-doll look but was trim instead, someone who is not worried about size, nonetheless, the fact was, small—a small man, she wanted to walk back out again. Not to mention the mustache. It wasn't fair.

All her friends except one had Jewish psychiatrists, and hers was an Argentinian whom she called by his first name, Jorge. Those first weeks, months, Pauline railed and complained—to Coco, not to Loving. I need someone else, she whined, at the very least a woman. A woman would understand. I don't like his shoes.

Coco had worked at finding Russell Loving for her. In New York psychiatrists were a dime a dozen. This one, he insisted, came highly recommended, the highest credentials. She should not judge too quickly.

"If he's such hot stuff," Pauline said, "you go."

"I'm operating," Coco explained. "You're not. It's not supposed to be easy, Pauline. Just do yourself a favor and don't leave."

Pauline had held on to Coco's advice. For a year she had stuck with Russell Loving, for a year traipsed crosstown to lie on his couch and confess things she'd never dreamed of uttering aloud to anyone.

Not that it had been easy. Not that she hadn't quit once and threatened to many more times. They had started out sitting face to face. When he suggested the couch—"I suspect," he said, "you know about free association?"—she'd been glib. "Of course," she snapped.

"It's not for everyone," he warned, "but perhaps you'd like to try."

"Why not?" she said with the arrogance of the ignorant.

The couch of course had been there all along, but until that moment Pauline had managed not to look at it, in the same way patients in dentists' offices manage never to look at the drill.

When she went to her next session, hoping he'd forgotten, she made a move as if toward her usual chair. But with a downward gesture, Loving motioned her toward the couch. A daredevil kind of girl, afraid of nothing, Pauline had no choice but to do it. She went to the couch, sat—as he took a seat behind her, waited—set her purse down, sat a minute with her feet on the floor, then swung them up and there she was. She could think of nothing to say.

"Are you," he asked after what seemed like a very long time, "having trouble getting started?" As if the whole thing had been her idea.

When she did begin to talk, she could not stop. Like the dream of the baby's falling, the talking seemed to have no gravitational pull, no earth at the bottom to crash to. Without purpose or direction, it simply went on. Until her time was up.

The second week of the couch, she came in, lay down, felt the fury rise up in her. Lying down felt like yielding, she the not-quite dead insect, he the professor with corkboard and pin. Like the menacing man in the dream, he had skewered her, having asked her to submit in the most primitive fashion, she on her back, him in control: *his* office, him sitting up in his chair behind her where she could not see what he was up to, he the one taking notes.

She did not, however, tell him of her anger but talked on, without direction, one thing and then another. Away from him, she raged against him, rehearsing in her mind speeches explaining her wish—demand—to sit back up again. Then the next week she went back and lay down for him again. And then quit. Missed a week, went back the next.

She was not in real analysis, she only went twice a week but on your back was on your back, and whatever she had read about it—jokes, movies, cartoons—had no effect, did not diminish the effect of the real thing. When after missing two sessions she went back again, she finally voiced her anger—fury—at him, as well as her discomfort at yielding to him.

"I suppose," Loving suggested, "it may feel something like rape?"

No. Rape was brute strength, a subversion of the will. This was voluntary. The rules of the game were obvious: the only way she could win was to lose, willingly to submit to him.

Loving said well, yes, that was so.

That was last year. She felt more settled in with him now. Not that she didn't still make her plans. I feel better, she told herself. Next month I'll cut back to once a week, the month after I'll quit.

All that was one thing. Her dislike, fear, distrust. And his voracity, wanting more. No matter what she brought him— tidbits of her life wrapped in perfectly wrought description like drops of homemade candy hand-wrapped in cellophane—it was never enough. *Yes,* he said, *but.*

She dreamed of him constantly, at home in polka-dot pajamas, with his wife giving a party—close-up dreams, like shots in a movie. Once he was a mouth, all molars, a mouth designed not for talking but for eating only. Another time he was dressed in a hospital smock: naked from the waist down. And then the dream-camera focused in on him and the man Russell Loving became genitals only: hair and penis, balls, filling the screen of her dream.

Every time she dreamed about him he said she was dreaming of someone else. Many times when she dreamed of some other man he said the other man was himself disguised. And so he kept her in his thrall, on edge, uncertain. There were no final revelations, no rats back in her past gnawing away. There was only the one day at a time unraveling, sometimes meaningful, often not. Just this one-foot-and-then-the-other tedium.

Well, and so?

So she could take all that. The demands, the unpredictability: these were familiar. What she could not stand was for Russell Loving to be kind to her. She wanted him there for her but not soppy. Firm and unyielding like a real doctor.

Recently she suggested she cut back to one session a week. Loving's response was immediate. He said only, "It's not a good idea, no." That night she dreamed his office was in a hospital in which psychiatrists were expected also to be trained butchers. From behind a glass, as if looking into a hospital nursery, she watched the white-garbed butcher-psychiatrists as they expertly sliced meat with razor-sharp cleavers. She wondered how the hospital found psychiatrists who could also carve and what kind of audition they had to perform, in order to qualify. In a white unbloodied butcher's suit, Loving came up and asked her what cut she preferred, then without waiting for her answer went to get her a thin slice of rare tenderloin.

Pipes inside the walls clanged, as if someone were inside the walls shaking them.

Pauline's building was one of only three left standing on this side of the block, the others having been turned into heaps of rubble by whacks of the wrecking ball. Word on the street was, condominiums were coming. Her landlord was holding out for a better price . . . or so she had heard; nobody in the building had ever laid eyes on the landlord.

The candy store was gone, the produce stand, the washateria. Mrs. Poshkosh had moved to Staten Island. It was like living in a war zone. There was no reason for Pauline to think she would ever see any of her neighbors again. They were as gone as if they had died.

The pipes banged again. Someone in the bulding was up, running water, flushing a toilet. In an old building no one was ever entirely alone.

Robert and Dennis had moved to California. In no time at

all, Robert had done two HBO movies, several television spots and a mini-series. Dennis was growing his own vegetables and cooking like crazy, up to his elbows, he swore, in cilantro. They begged Pauline to come.

She made a space for Kathleen and patted it until Kathleen jumped up beside her, making soft gurgling cat noises, kneading the spot until it was perfect.

Pauline drew the cat into the curve of her midsection. This would not last long.

"Ah, Kathleen," Pauline said, hugging her close. "Light of my life. Kathleen the queen."

Thinking of Russell Loving was a useful distraction. In quiet moments Pauline restaged sessions, listening as his chair squeaked, his feet moved, heard him say "Yes" when she got something right. Saw him at his door, heard the tone of his voice when he said, "Good morning, won't you come in." The hum of his ceiling fans.

Unlike everybody else, he never changed.

Kathleen squirmed. Traffic changed directions.

What she secretly yearned for was to be able, once in her life, truthfully to voice Desdemona's sentiment. "If it were now to die, 'twere now to be most happy."

Words. More than likely, a dream. And then again, maybe not.

Dream or not, she had to find out.

It had been a mistake to let the kitchen go until morning. The apartment smelled like Taco Bell.

In her T-shirt, underwear and socks, Pauline sped through the mess. In the bedroom, she rubbed her feet on the small throw rug beside the bed to clean them. Bits of lettuce and tortilla came free. Her suitcase, a navy blue nylon duffel, lay unzipped on the bed, empty. Mavis had sent a set of Louis Vuitton, but Pauline was embarrassed to use it.

The drone of Monday-morning traffic, higher pitched and

more insistent, had begun. The coffee machine growled. Pauline went to the bathroom, locking the door behind her. The bathroom was tiny and dark with only one opaque window, sealed shut with paint. Her cocoon. She blew her nose, pulled down her underpants and, elbows on her knees, listened to the sound of her own urine.

Like Robert and Dennis, Michael had moved to California. The divorce went fast, cost eighty-five dollars. Nothing to it, the marriage vanished before their eyes. Occasionally, Michael came to New York. Sometimes they had lunch, like old pals.

She flushed the toilet, went to the sink, washed her hands and face and looked in the mirror, turning her face from side to side, trying to see if she looked as different as she felt. Except for the gray streak, she could find little change; the same old face. She brushed her teeth and went into the kitchen. The coffee machine was not finished. Interrupting its cycle, she poured a cup.

Outside, the morning was smoggy and without color. She could barely tell where the buildings ended and the sky began. Sometimes on the clearest day she could make out the barest glint of the George Washington Bridge. The Hudson was out there, but who noticed? City life had its own geography.

Pauline sipped her coffee. Rising from sleep, Kathleen stretched a back leg and came into the kitchen. Pauline shook some Kitten Chow from a box. Kathleen was too old for Kitten Chow, but she liked it better than the grown-up kind.

Pauline ran her hand down the cat's silver neck and back. Crunching down on the hard food, Kathleen closed her eyes.

"Going to Pet Hotel later on," Pauline told her. "Not going to like it. Going anyway."

Recently, she and Michael had met for lunch at a macrobiotic restaurant in the Village, Michael's choice. Michael had switched from being a New York kind of crazy man to a California one. He had quit smoking long ago and while he wasn't a purist, he liked as he said, "to hug close to the macrobiotic shore."

An old friend from Brooklyn had convinced him to come to California, and, according to Michael, the move had been strictly positive. The friend was in business for himself, making videotapes designed to help small and large corporations indoctrinate new employees. Now a vice president, Michael wrote scripts for the videotapes and oversaw the opening of new offices. He was also married, with a baby.

In the macrobiotic restaurant, Pauline felt smudged at the edges, like a line in one of Michael's plays he'd almost managed to erase. He looked straight through her—at what, she could not tell—occasionally frowning, as if thinking perhaps he recognized her but wasn't quite sure from where. No dark, mesmerizing looks, no jokes. Not a hint they'd once done all that secret, smelly exploring together, those afternoon marathons. Their marriage might have been a moment of childhood silliness Michael had once indulged in, which, now that he was older, he'd like to forget.

"I want to apologize," he said, "for my tendencies toward violence back then." He stabbed his fork into a huge mound of seaweed. "My energies," he went on, "have since been refocused."

He ran: daily, distances; marathons, recently two in one week. He'd done a 10K around the horserace track at Santa Anita and had gone to Oregon to run straight up the side of a mountain. He was saving his money to go to Greece to run the course of the first marathon. He was grizzled and bone thin, his eyes dark as caves. When he sat for very long, he had to stretch his Achilles' tendons, to keep them from drawing up on him.

Pauline toyed with her sea bass.

"How's Rose?" she asked, plying a bit of flesh away from the bones. Michael had sold the restaurant in Brooklyn and moved Rose to California.

"Great. She has an apartment near us."

"I can't imagine Rose in L.A. All that sunshine."

A ropy muscle in Michael's neck tensed. "She loves it. The sun is great for her arthritis."

"I suppose."

The muscle slackened then tensed again. He leaned forward. "It is. She does."

Pauline pushed aside the sea bass and reached for her dessert, a slice of cherry tofu cheesecake. "I tried to call her once. Before she left. She wouldn't speak to me."

Michael sipped his herb tea. "No? Well, Rose has her reasons."

"I'm sure she does."

"Don't look at me, Pauline. I don't tell Rose who she can talk to. She's Catholic, what can I tell you?"

"I wasn't."

"You—" He stopped himself. The neck muscle again. "No."

"Good."

At least she'd gotten to him.

He said he was still working on his plays, at night and on weekends. Writing better, he claimed, now that he had less time to. He'd been paid for ideas for a couple of pilots. Pauline had no idea whether any of what he said was true or not. She'd believe him when she saw something of his actually performed.

Michael's wife, Almond, was a holistic nurse from Santa Cruz. Michael showed Pauline a picture of the baby, a girl named Rosalie. Rosalie was a chunk, dark-eyed and beautiful. They fed her only home-processed food, mashed fruit, tofu, no meat. Rosalie was not yet two and Almond was pregnant again.

"This tofu cheesecake is excellent," Pauline said.

"We eat no sugar and no red meat," Michael replied. "A little fish, some chicken, but no red meat."

"You used to love it. Steaks, hamburgers. Blood-rare, remember?"

He didn't look up. "I've learned."

She drank some tea. It tasted like tree bark. She set down her cup and ran the tines of her fork down the side of the cheesecake to break off a thin, scalloped slice.

"Is Almond your wife's birth name?"

Michael took a long time to look at her. By the time he did, he'd managed to perform a trick on himself. The pupils of his deep-sunk eyes had gone blank, their usual spark dimmed by a glaze of unnatural bliss.

"You always were a skeptic, weren't you, Pauline," he said. "You should do something about that. You should learn to open up to trust."

Pauline dropped her fork. *No,* she said to herself, nearly choking on her cheesecake, *I was not always a skeptic.*

Not sleeping with men was like keeping the diary: structure, glue, quietness within herself which enabled her to hold things together. Until? She did not know, maybe Loving was right, until she went back to work.

Kathleen moved out from under Pauline's hand, around to the other side of her bowl. Made of bright yellow plastic with MEOW written in red on one side, the bowl came free with a coupon from Meow Mix.

In the living room, Pauline found her jeans among the twisted sheets. She pulled them on and buttoned them. The jeans were roomy. Tight jeans used to make her feel safe and strong. Now they only pinched.

She straightened the pillows and put her sheets and the afghan into the drawer beneath the windowseat.

"You can't go back down there," Coco—sensing what she had in mind—warned. Coco was small and wiry, with no extra body fat. When he walked, he bounced.

Pauline said nothing.

"You can't go back," he repeated. "You're an actress. New York is where you belong. You have to find yourself another apartment, that's all." Coco was a dyed-in-the-wool city dweller. And after a while, advice all sounded the same. That was one thing she liked about Russell Loving. He didn't give her advice or try to offer reassurances.

In the kitchen, she squirted liquid detergent over the enchilada pan and filled it with water. For company she turned on the radio and listened to the news. Remembering the pint of ice cream Coco had brought the night before, she went and got it out of the freezer compartment and set it on top of the refrigerator to soften. After the meal, they'd been too full to take even one bite.

When the dishes were done, she opened the ice cream carton and, standing in the open refrigerator door, began to eat it, scooping out a spoonful, turning it upside-down in her mouth, sucking the ice cream off the spoon onto her tongue, letting it melt, then slide down her throat. Plain vanilla, her favorite. White food was a comfort.

In two days, she would see Will. Even if he was single, she would not sleep with him. She was taking Russell Loving with her to be sure, tucked into her back pocket like one of those miniature stuffed animals children clutched in their fists.

She spooned up more ice cream. "One more and I'll quit," she said to herself. And with the next, "One more and I'll quit."

When the ice cream was gone, she threw the carton away, swept the floor and packed her duffel. Packing didn't take long. She liked to travel light.

At eleven, she captured the all-knowing Kathleen and, shoving her into her carrier, took the sulking beauty and her Meow Mix bowl to Pet Hotel.

19

The goats lifted their elegant heads abruptly, in a single swooping motion, like startled birds. Blinking and worried and altogether still, they waited—tense, like dancers in the wings counting out a cue—about ten of them, huddled beneath the low-hanging limb of a feathery mesquite.

Pauline swerved to miss a rut in the road. The big car went off into a shallow gully, whirling the steering wheel out of her grip. But the ground was bone dry, the car heavy enough to be easily righted; she steered the wheels back into the one-lane tire tracks and—in no hurry to arrive too quickly—took the car out of gear. With a pushbutton, she lowered the window on her side and switched off the ignition. All morning she had gone back and forth from heat to vent. Now—it was eleven—the day was warm enough for air conditioning.

She didn't know much about goats. In her part of Texas ranchers had been disdainful of goats, preferring the thick stupidity and easier marketability of cows. Goats were valued where grass was scarce, she remembered that from junior-high Texas history.

A slight wind ruffled the lacy leaves of the mesquite tree. In New York, mesquite was all the rage. Every other new restaurant featured mesquite-smoked something or the other, fish, chickens, quail. Out here the mesquite was considered a trash tree, a pesky nuisance, impossible to kill. But, to a stranger who didn't have to deal with them, they were beautiful. Low to the ground with tiny shivering leaves like fringe on a shawl, the mesquite had an almost Oriental look. Like tall bonsai.

Behind the goats, beyond a rise in the land, the sharp blue sky was dotted with thick white clouds as precisely shaped as if painted on a flat for musical comedy. In the distance, a small airplane cut into the blue. The wind drifting into the car smelled of cedar.

She tried to lower the window on the passenger side and then, remembering, turned the ignition back on and pushed the button again. The window slid noiselessly down. The wind blew harder, in one window, out the other.

She'd gone all out with the car. The rental company was featuring a special on luxury cars and so, for a treat, she picked a Lincoln Continental the color of eggnog, with matching velour seatcovers and an eggnog steering wheel. The Lincoln had automatic everything, windows, mirrors, seat and steering wheel adjusters, cruise control, an AM-FM radio with special features she had not yet figured out, a speedometer that announced the miles per hour in bold red numerals, an engine so quiet it was scary.

Big American cars were a comfort. Like tanks. Who could harm her? On the back road off the interstate, she had taken the Lincoln off of cruise control to see how fast it would go. Ninety was no trick; she could not even feel the speed. At ninety-five, she backed off. Within five miles she passed a highway patrolman. She stayed at sixty the rest of the way.

With one eye still on the goats, she recranked the car and put it in gear. But before she had time to press the accelerator, one goat, a nanny, came out from under the mesquite and stood on a sun-soaked flat white rock. For a moment the nanny stood quite still, head high, facing into the wind, and then she spread her hind feet and, keeping her delicate toes prettily pointed, gradually began to lower her haunches. When her bag touched the ground, the nanny sent a pale stream of urine onto the white rock, keeping watch as she did her business, head high, as dramatic as a diva, her attention steady on Pauline and the big car.

The other goats watched and chewed. One had a plastic bread sack in its teeth. Another made a chatty bleating sound.

The nanny looked like a queen, the top half paying no notice at all to what the lower half was up to. Pauline pressed the accelerator and turned her attention back to the road. The nanny raised her hips and rejoined the group.

Pauline had dressed casually, a Shakespeare in the Park sweatshirt and jeans, her blue and silver running shoes. Beneath the gray sweatshirt she wore a new purple T-shirt Wanda had bought her in Houston. She was warm in the sweatshirt, but sometimes the dry, steady wind had a cool turn to it. Spring in this part of Texas was chancy. Anything could happen, windstorm, flood, snow. She left the sweatshirt on.

Within seconds, beyond a rise in the landscape, a silver barn roof appeared. When the road dipped a bit, the roof vanished then quickly reappeared. Past a curve, the farmhouse came in sight. Small and squat, curled beneath post oaks and cedars like a snail in its shell, the house looked cool, settled and quietly inviting. Behind it, slaggy white limestone hills rose up in sharp unscalable jags and peaks as if in protection of the house.

Pauline drove over the cattle guard and parked the Lincoln beneath the low-hanging limb of an oak tree next to a small white pickup truck. In the bed of the pickup were ropes, chains, a bucket, a pitchfork and a shovel.

The wind rustled the tiny leaves of the oak trees. Out here, the wind never stopped.

A black Lab, standing by the front steps of the house, ran at the Lincoln, barking and wagging its tail. A sign on the iron fencepost next to the cattle guard said, DANGER! ELECTRIC FENCE. The sign was rusted and bent up along the edge. Labs were a nervous and strange breed. They drooled and jumped. Pauline waited for Will.

The house was made of reddish-orange slabs of stone held in place by a darker orange mortar. A small square screen porch jutted out from the house like a box nailed onto it. On the porch, a hammock, a wicker chair that had seen better days.

In the pasture beyond the barn, a mare in foal grazed without letup. In another fenced yard chickens bustled. From somewhere, a rooster crowed. Will, it seemed, was no longer Mr. Solitary. Animals were everywhere.

This used to be grassland. Time had done its job, and men, overgrazing, overcropping. Now the pure greens were muted, tinged with black, the browns with dark clay-red. There was the pale blowing dust, the stupendous blue sky and, wherever the eye landed, interrupting every variation of every other color, a prediction of what was to come, the dry, unyielding white.

Where there was water, the old greenness held. The map Pauline had got at a Houston service station showed small rivers running throughout the countryside around Eulogy, rivers which crossed, merged, twisted; tiny blue lines too small to name. Thinned topsoil and scarcity of water produced smaller trees. In Houston the huge live oaks with their great wide crotches were like large friendly grandfathers with large laps and loving fingers. Here, live oaks shriveled, to become the wind-gnarled blackjack and post oak. Farther west trees would turn scrubbier still and, soon after, as water dried and turned to rock and sand, all but disappear. Then came desert. Red rock. Cactus. New Mexico. Arizona.

When Pauline cut the motor, she could hear the sound of the goats' hooves, clattering against the rocks away from the sound of the barking dog.

"All right," Pauline said to the dog. "I hear you." She leaned out her window, letting her arms hang.

Just beyond the farmhouse—possibly connected to it—was a newer two-story house of unpainted, yellowish wood. Between the the two-story house and the older farmhouse sat another squat building with a roof so shiny it might have been glass.

Pauline sniffed the air. A loan officer at Mavis's bank, hearing that Pauline was headed west, had warned her to watch for signs of cedar fever, sore throat, collecting mucus, persistent headache. It was the season, he said. Some people got so sick from cedar fever they wished they were dead.

The dog protested without letup. Pauline honked the horn.

The Lincoln announced its presence with a churchlike, altogether satisfying chord.

In his note, Will had said that more than likely he would be out somewhere castrating calves and that she should follow the sounds of work. But Will wasn't working. Not with the dog sitting by the front steps.

The Lab suddenly grew quiet and turned his head toward the house, the front door opened and Will was there . . . out the front door, leaving it open, and quickly across the porch. With the flat of his hand, he slapped the screen door of the porch open and came out, letting the door slam behind him. The speed of the dog's tail-wagging increased.

He looked the same. Same walk, same jeans, same turquoise belt buckle, same slim agile hips. His stomach flat as a boy's.

The Lab turned back toward the Lincoln and barked again. Will clapped his hands.

"Hush, Jess," he said. "Now hush."

Only his hair was different. The gray had gone lighter, almost white, and like Pauline, he'd let it grow. Curls frizzed above his ears and flopped against his neck.

The dog obeyed but stood her ground, wagging her entire backside, looking from Will to the car and back.

The wind blew steadily, sending Will's curly forelock up in a spray. He came directly to the car, left shoulder leading, toward the gate and then through it. The skin of his sun-baked face was taut and his legs moved with brisk purpose. He passed the warning sign on the electric fence.

Pauline opened the car door and unfolded her long legs. The Lincoln made a soft bell-like sound to let her know the car door was open, the keys in the ignition. By the time she was on her feet, he was there.

"Hello, Missy," he said and, standing in the open car door, he drew Pauline firmly into his arms and clamped his forearms tightly across her back. Pauline buried her face in Will's neck, pressing her lips into the creases of his skin, letting her chest relax into his, her shoulders go limp.

He felt like home, his body not just bulk and weight but a declared presence, as implacable as the jagged hills behind his house. His shirt smelled of starch, his neck of bath soap. His jaw was freshly shaved. He had not been working calves. He had been waiting.

Beside them, Will's dog wailed long and low, a mournful sound from deep in its throat. The Lincoln's bell sang on.

Pauline tried to pull away but, wanting to be the one to say when it was over, Will held on. "Ah, Missy," he said, his lips so close to her ear she could feel the moisture. "I've missed you." And he let her go.

They popped apart—too far, too fast, like toy people attached to rubber bands.

The Lab beat her tail against the ground. Dust rose.

"Enough of that," Pauline said and, stepping forward, closed the car door. The bell hushed. She smoothed back her hair, pulled the waistband of her sweatshirt down, pushed her sleeves up above her elbows and started to speak. Will fixed his good eye on her. She hesitated, cleared her throat and said, "Nice place."

Will looked pointedly around, as if for the first time. "Far enough from people to suit me," he said. "Finally." He patted the hood of the Lincoln. "This is some car, Miss Pauline. Are you richer than famous these days?"

"Rented," she explained. "There was a three-day deal. It cost no more than a Cutlass."

"Lap of luxury," Will said, shaking his head.

"I love it," she declared a bit too staunchly. Then she gestured toward the dog. "What happened to Lotto?"

Will patted Jesse's head, a curiously unaffectionate up and down stroke.

"Gone," he said. "The day we moved here, old Lotto took one look around and hightailed back off in the other direction. I tried to follow him but he ran back into the hills. Like a fool, I drove all the way back to San Marcos, stopping every few miles to call him, but he never showed." Jesse thrust her head farther up into the cup of Will's palm. "A damned dog," he said. "It eats you up. I swore not to get another one. Then a neighbor gave us Jesse. Another nonserious dog."

"What do you think it was that got to Lotto? The goats?"

"I have no idea," Will said. And he rocked back on his heels. "Maybe nothing."

Pauline glanced down. Will had switched from custom-made boots to city shoes, black and pointy-toed, with shoestrings and leather soles. How like him, now that he was in cowboy country, to switch to city shoes.

The Lab sat close, her wet black nose pressed adoringly against the knee of Will's blue jeans. Drool fell, making drops in the dusty ground.

"What about the pigs?"

Slowly Will rotated his head until his good eye was on her. "Pigs?" he said. "I never had pigs."

"No," she said. "Down the road. You said to stay in the car no matter what. I looked hard, drove slow. If there were pigs, I missed them."

"You mean Shorty's pigs."

She laughed. "I don't know whose pigs. I've never been here. You said pigs. In your note, you said and I quote, mean pigs."

"Shorty's pigs, yes. I'm sorry. I forgot. Between the time I wrote you and now, Shorty got rid of them. Lord, yes, those pigs were mean as the devil. One damn near bit the muscle out of Shorty's thigh and Shorty trying to feed the silly thing at the time. I'd forgotten I'd told you. No, no pigs. Shorty's out of the pig business."

"I can't say that I blame him. After all, his leg."

Will shook his head.

"It wasn't just his leg. Shorty's wife died, his boy went to Dallas to sell computers or some damned thing. Besides which, nobody makes a living off of livestock any more. Except the big guys, of course. Otherwise, you have to be a little crazy. We all are." He seemed to enjoy the suggestion. "It's a losing proposition out here."

He sucked his bottom lip inside his teeth and either let his attention wander away or pretended to.

Pauline sighed. The wind blew. She hooked loose strands of hair behind her ears.

She nodded toward the white truck. "That yours?"

Will swiveled his head to see what she meant. His good eye brightened playfully. "A Jap truck, what a comedown."

"Everybody's doing it."

Will rubbed Jesse's ears. There was something he wanted to say and so far hadn't. He seemed either distracted or—more likely—annoyed, whether with himself or her presence she wasn't sure. Pauline, searching for a safe topic of conversation, went back to animals.

"Is Jesse a girl?"

Will nodded. "Spayed. But female."

At the mention of her name, Jesse perked up. She began to beat her tail in the dust. A long rope of drool fell from the side of her mouth onto Will's shoe and she began to rock her head from side to side. Her shoulders trembled and her chest heaved.

"What's she doing?"

"Watch."

Jesse's eyes rolled back and she drew her lips up, baring her teeth and gums, lifting the corners of her mouth in an upturned crescent. Her lips shivered with effort.

"She's smiling!" Pauline exclaimed. "Look. She's smiling."

Chin raised, Jesse's back stiffened with effort as she struggled to hold on to the smile.

"Oh, Jess," Will said, and he ruffled her ears. "You're hopeless. I've never seen such an unserious dog." His voice was warm, that special tone he saved for dogs and women. "It's her one trick."

"It's a good one. Was it for me?"

Ever hospitable, Will lied. "Of course," he said.

Jesse stood up, stretched and, like a good performer, turned and walked away.

Will turned his face into the wind and, letting his hair fly, finally said what was on his mind. "I'm married, Missy."

So there it was, his big news. But where was Isabel's car? And where was she?

"Yes. I know that. But, hey . . ." Sometimes in a tricky situation, the best thing to do was state the obvious as if it were the last thing on your mind. "I came for a visit. I'm not after anything." In imitation of him, she cocked her head. "You know?"

He blushed, a very earnest rose-red. "I didn't think you were."

"Should I not have come?"

"No, of course not. I just . . ." He faltered. "How did you know?"

Bluffing ignorance, she frowned. "What? That you were married?"

"Yes."

"Can't you guess?"

He studied the backs of his hands. "No."

She waited. He looked up.

"Wanda?"

"Who else?"

"Ah," he said, as if remembering the taste of a favorite food. "*Wanda.*"

"Wanda knows everything."

"Yes." His professional assent sounded like Loving's. "I believe she may."

Pauline shifted her weight. "I could use a drink of water, Will. And the use of your facilities."

Opening the car door, once again unleashing the bells, she reached inside for her small soft duffel, in which were packed, she feared, not nearly enough clothes for the up-and-down weather. She turned the ignition on, sent the windows back up and took the keys, dropping them in her purse. The bells stopped.

Will excused himself for being rude and invited her in, Jesse leading the way. Near the house, under the trees, the temperature dropped. Will held out his arm, ushering her in.

Pauline's confidence flagged. She thought she had tucked

Russell Loving safely away, but at the moment he felt as distant as that small airplane disappearing into a sugar-spun cloud to the east.

A new dream: psychiatrist disguised as an airplane.

In Houston, although Pauline had not understood until the last minute about the wraparound bank note, the closing on the condominium had gone well enough. The wraparound meant that the condominium was not totally out of her life. If the new owners walked, she'd get the thing back, mortgage payments and all.

"It's the only way we can sell anything in Houston these days," her real estate agent explained. "I mean, we are talking T-R-O-U-B-L-E. We take what we can get."

The couple buying the condo looked honest enough. But then, there was no telling, really.

Before the closing, Pauline and Wanda went to the Ragin' Cajun for lunch, gumbo and po-boys. That night, they ate at Tony's, Houston's poshest restaurant, to celebrate. Wanda loved Pauline's rented Lincoln. "First time," she said, patting the velour upholstery, "I haven't felt like Poor Aunt Sadie when I turned my car over to valet parking."

For a joke, she said "valette."

The valet whisked away their car like a fairytale footman and Pauline and Wanda swept into Tony's, where they ate a lavish meal, pâté and smoked salmon, veal, Dover sole, fresh asparagus and, for dessert, a six-inch-high concoction, a meringue and whipped-cream shell filled with raspberries, covered with chocolate. They agreed, the dessert was too delicious.

Their conversation ranged widely, from Wanda's coming trip to Sri Lanka to Pauline's psychiatrist and her impending move to a new apartment. Once they'd covered all that generalizing territory, they began to tiptoe through more personal ground. Lingering over cognac and coffee, they stayed long enough at Tony's to justify the steep check and, finally, to speak of Will. And sex. Husbands. Of men in general.

Of Will, Wanda said, "I loved him and that was that. But I wasn't necessary to his life. In college they have these professors called adjunct? Well, that was what I was to Will Hand, adjunct. I could take a lot of other things but not that. Especially since what I was adjunct to was the entire, everloving natural world, rain, shine, birds and dooky, disasters and caves and you name it. I'll tell you, Pauline . . . do you smoke?"

Pauline said no.

Wanda motioned their waiter over and ordered a package of Mores. "I like a brown one now and then," she said from behind a conspiratorial hand.

The cigarette was hardly between her lips when the waiter produced a lighter and held the flame beneath the tip. Wanda thanked him.

"I'll tell you what," she went on. "Give me travel over men any day. Any day, any man. I go when I like and where I like." She waved smoke away from Pauline. "Of course now, I'm no spring chicken. You shouldn't necessarily do what I do. I'm just saying."

She tapped her ashes into a china ashtray. Instantly, the waiter materialized again to scoop up the ashtray, empty it, and replace it with a clean one.

"Of course," Wanda went on, "I'm a three-time loser. You have to take that into consideration." She glanced back over her shoulder at the waiter and then leaned toward Pauline. "Don't you hate it when a waiter just *hovers*?"

Everytime Wanda spoke of Will, she got that same sharp spark in her eyes. Pauline longed to tell her of her own experience with Will, even about the baby, but whenever she felt the urge, she stopped drinking for a while, thought of Loving and kept quiet.

When they got up to leave, Pauline reminded Wanda of her cigarettes. She'd only smoked two.

"Lord, girl," Wanda exclaimed, "if I take home a pack, I smoke a pack. No, child. These two will do me for a week."

Pauline loved Wanda more than she had ever loved anyone in her life. Driving home, thinking of the hospital duty they had done together and how much emptiness had come of it, the two women were quiet. When Pauline let Wanda off at her apartment building, she waited until she couldn't see Wanda inside the glass doors before she drove away.

The two-story house looked unfinished. There was a table saw on the front porch, two sawhorses; across the sawhorses, a stack of lumber. A packed leather tool belt lay on the saw. Beneath the saw, piles of curled shavings and sawdust. When Pauline got past the oaks, she could see that the shiny building between the farmhouse and the two-story house—set behind the others so that it was out from under the shade—was a greenhouse.

Will asked what time she had left Houston and how the drive had been, how long it had taken and how traffic was, if the bluebonnets and Indian paintbrush had been spectacular or merely beautiful.

"Spectacular," Pauline replied. "A few miles beyond Brenham I nearly ran my car off the road, looking out at those hills —a pure carpet of color, just like the tour books say. I'm sure I must have seen them before, but I guess I just looked and went on. This time, I couldn't stop being amazed. I kept saying 'Look,' out loud. 'Will you look at that,' " She laughed at herself. "That car's so fancy, I was afraid it might answer me."

Will went ahead, turning back to talk and listen as he went. When Jesse got to the porch steps, she flopped down in a cleared spot exactly her size and shape, panting as lavishly as if she'd just come back from a long run.

Will opened the screen door and, standing against it, ushered Pauline in.

When Russell Loving stood against his door, he held on to the knob and watched her go by. Taking her emotional temperature, looking for signs? He said no, that he had no tricks but played the game with all of his cards on the table. Pauline had a hard time believing that. Surely he knew more than he was saying.

"Isabel's away," Will said. "My wife."

Pauline passed him. "Yes," she said. "I knew who you meant."

"Her work. She travels."

On the hammock, there were several magazines. "Where does she go? What does she do?" At the front door she waited for Will. He closed the screen door and came across the small porch toward her.

"Import-export. She goes on buying trips and to visit her stores. She has shops in Houston, Santa Fe, Scottsdale. She goes to Mexico." He coughed and waved Pauline into the living room. The cough clearly indicated his wish to end that particular line of conversation.

The living room was dark, cooler by several degrees than outside. Windows were open. Gauzy white curtains blew. A window shade rapped against the woodwork. The room was low-ceilinged and cozy. It smelled dry and papery, of old furniture and leftover ashes.

The same worn couch with the wagon wheel arms was against the far wall and across the room from the couch sat his chair and ottoman, angled away from a window. More stuffing poked from holes in the chair. The upholstery was more threadbare. An end table next to the chair was covered with a stack of mail. The chair was lit from behind by that same brass floorlamp with the yellow shade. Will's pen, uncapped, lay angled across a writing tablet, its point resting at the end of a line of writing. On the top page of the writing pad, there was a date, a salutation.

Noticing the direction of her attention, Will spoke up.

"I have so much to do out here, I write little," he said. "But I get mail."

"You answer it all?"

He looked perplexed. "Of course. Some of it is flattering, some awkward. Strangers who long to be published write, expecting help. They feel disadvantaged. Because they're frustrated they get pushy. And there are the ladies."

"What ladies?"

"From town. They send poems."

"And?"

He shrugged. "I know nothing of poetry."

"But you read it."

He shook his finger at her. "Not officially."

She held up her right hand. "I'll never tell."

Play sweetened the conversation. The room felt smaller, darker, as if the walls and ceiling were pressing in on them.

At Pauline's feet lay a small but beautiful rug, handwoven in earth colors, brown and beige and pale sand. In the center, in profile, an unexpectedly bright blue Mayan god held a pot of fire.

"Pretty," Pauline commented, running her toe across the rug. "Isn't he the corn god?"

"He is. Also life, fertility, regeneration. Thus the fire. It's one of Isabel's contributions. She imports Mexican artifacts and furniture. Not border junk; good stuff."

Opposite the chair and ottoman, to Pauline's right, was an adobe fireplace, white and rounded like an Indian hearth. The fireplace was obviously handmade and added on. Pale ashes of chalky mesquite were piled high in the grate—doubtless left over from winter. It was hard to imagine they would have any need for fires tonight. On the mantel, a wooden clock ticked loudly.

The other two walls were all books. On the shelves by the front door were farm manuals: *How to Raise Guinea Hens, Goat Husbandry, The Book of Goats, Building a Greenhouse, The Complete Book of Succulents, The Organic Gardening Encyclopedia, Growing Grapes.* The wall next to his chair held literature; next to literature, history, then philosophy, then rows and rows of Westerns, all paperbacks, double-shelved.

Will showed her to her room, down a narrow hall past the bathroom and through what he called his wine room—a narrow area with a window on each wall, barely more than a hall. Two huge green jugs of fermenting grape juice sat on the floor. The windows on either side of the jugs were wide open.

Her bedroom was small and dark. In it, a bed with an iron bedstead, a chest of drawers and a small mirror, a glass-fronted gun case filled with various kinds of rifles, by the bed a small oak nightstand. Arranged against a wall, stacks of magazines. The bed was covered with a white comforter.

Pauline set her duffel down.

"The bathroom," Will said. "We just passed it." And quickly, as if afraid to stay, he left her.

The windows in her bedroom were closed. There were scatter rugs, ruffles; a musty smell, as if the room were not much used. In the mirror she checked her hair. Her cheeks were flushed. From her bag she took out a jar of bee pollen moisturizer and smoothed some into her skin as protection against the dry wind.

In the bathroom, while the commode flushed, she opened the medicine cabinet. Nothing exotic. Pepto-Bismol, razor blades, hair-setting gel, dental floss. Two brown plastic bottles of prescription pills with Will's name on the label. She closed the cabinet and washed her hands. Returning to the living room, she found Will standing in the middle of the room, staring out a window.

"Well," she said.

He came to, as if just noticing her. "Would you like iced tea?" he asked. "Then we can take a walk. I'll show you my rocky paradise. If you like."

"I do."

On his way into the kitchen, Will turned around so abruptly Pauline almost ran into him.

He took her by the shoulders. "I'm sorry, Missy," he said, "but I almost forgot. You had a phone call."

Pauline pointed at herself. "Me?" she said. "Here?" He nodded. "Who would call me here?"

"Your agent, Arlene something? She said you knew the number."

"How did she know I was here? I didn't tell her."

"I'm listed. She knew. She wants you to call."

"When was it?"

"Maybe an hour ago."

"In a little while. After we drink our tea."

What could Arlene want to tell her that was so urgent she had to call here? And how did she know where Pauline was?

"The phone's in here in the kitchen." Will shook his head. "I'm just glad I remembered. I'm getting so damned old."

The kitchen was small and ordinary: enamel sink with a window over it, old blackened stove jammed between counter tops, leaning refrigerator, a kitchen table with ladderback chairs. Open cabinets with no doors contained dishes, canned goods and staples. Just inside the kitchen door to the right was another door, the top half of which was all glass. Pauline peeked through.

"Was this here when you moved here?"

"Lord, no," Will said. "When we bought the place, all there was was this rock house and the barn, a couple of outbuildings. I added the greenhouse and the two-story house next to it, which isn't finished. I'll never be done. You know me."

Up close Pauline could see he wasn't the same after all. Shadows revealed differences. The crease running across his forehead had deepened and become more pronounced. His shoulders had a slump to them, caved over his chest as if in protection of it. The peacocky walk had been a pose. Vanity— his holdout against age and time—was deserting him. Had he been sick? He looked a little frail.

He opened the refrigerator door and took out a squat ceramic pitcher, dipped tea bags from the pitcher, squeezed the bags and dropped them in an oatmeal-colored bowl, then placed a green imitation Fiesta plate on top of the bowl. He turned away to get glasses.

Pauline returned her attention to the glass-paneled door.

The floor of the greenhouse was concrete, with planked walkways in the aisles. A box fan in the center of the room turned slowly. Crude shelves had been nailed together variously, going this way and that, not all in the same kind of wood. At the opposite end of the walkway, another glass-paneled door led to the two-story house.

Strangely shaped plants in various stages of growth had been placed on the shelves, some in flats, some in small starter pots. Others hung from the ceiling, or sat on the floor, some so large they took over an entire section of the room. The plants grew in unkempt directions, wild and unwieldy, like creatures in an outer-space movie.

One—possibly an aloe vera—was as large as a floor lamp. Others seemed to be forms of cactus, some with blooms, most not; one was twisted in a tortured knot as if about to turn in on itself, another proceeded from an ordinary stem into a Japanese fan of tissuelike ruffles. Many resembled body parts: a minute brain, an oversized thumb, fingers everywhere, and one like babies' toes in a pile. What flowers there were were waxy and exotic, in the brightest colors imaginable: a delicate magenta with a corn-yellow center, a pomegranate orange, a waxy translucent white, a rosy impossible pink.

"What are they?" Pauline asked. "I've never seen anything like them."

Will abandoned his iced-tea preparations to come to the greenhouse door.

"Isabel," he said. "She's big on exotics. She got me interested. Now I'm hooked and . . ."

Reaching past Pauline's chest, Will opened the door and they stepped inside.

And what? He had stopped himself. Was Isabel really on a buying trip, or had she, like Lotto, up and left? Pauline drew strength from the new mystery.

The room smelled damp and slightly fetid. Many of the plants grew in pots filled with rocks and sand. Some airier types clung loosely to hanging bits of wood. When Will closed the door, the plants seemed to shrivel into themselves, as if to withdraw from the intrusion. It was like walking into a room full of talking people only to find, once you step in, everyone grown quiet, looking up to see who you are.

Plant arms—it was hard to think of them as stems or branches—reached out into the aisle.

"Succulents, mostly," Will explained. "Some bromeliads. Some you've likely seen." He pointed. "Aloe vera's a common bird. Euphorbia's at every Safeway. Some are rare. Over there" —he indicated an empty corner—"I'm going to start orchids. Isabel is bringing pups her next trip to Mexico."

"Remember the snake?"

"Which snake?"

She hadn't meant to be the one to mention it first. "I was thinking of the one we watched in Snake Creek that time. The cottonmouth."

"Yes." He waited.

"Seeing these plants made me remember how self-satisfied and indifferent that snake looked." She held her hand up perpendicular to the floor and, fingers closed, moved it through the air in a wavy pattern. "Whipping down the water with his head up like chairman of the board."

"Indifferent is correct," Will said. "Nature doesn't give a damn what we think."

"I don't see how you stand being at its mercy so much of the time."

"But I'm not. Look." He presented the greenhouse like a magic act. "This is no act of nature but a simulation."

"Still."

"Surely on the merciless-and-indifferent scale cities are no better."

"Poisons to choose."

"Exactly."

The box fans wheezed.

"I finally read your books."

His eyebrows went up. He could not disguise his pleasure. "You're one up on me. I've still not seen you in a play."

"I felt like you were in the room with me. Reading *The*

Legend of Snake Creek, I kept hearing you tell the story that day. All those deaths. It was you on the page, exactly."

"I take that as a compliment."

"You should." She smoothed her hair.

"You've let your hair grow."

She dropped her hand and tossed her head. "I just stopped paying attention."

He ducked his chin. "Oh?"

She refused to give him a girlish response. "Yes. It's just there. And you?"

"What?"

She reached over and lifted a silvery curl. "Don't say you haven't noticed." She let the curl drop. "I know better."

He reddened slightly.

She moved down the aisle, ducking to avoid colliding with a particularly voracious-looking creature spilling down out of a hanging basket. "Like a man-eater in a jungle movie," she said, giving the creature wide berth.

Will picked up a tiny watering can with a long thin spout and carefully poured a thin stream of water into the very center of another plant with long red arms ending in sharp points. When the plant's cup was full, he withdrew the can.

"Bromeliads," Will explained, "feed from their centers." He was lecturing again. "That's why in South America you find them clinging to tree trunks." He replaced the watering can on a shelf. "If I ever get ahead, which is unlikely, I'm going to Africa. That's where succulents come from. But I doubt I'll do it." He ran his hand down the center of his shirt, across the pearl snaps that locked it shut. "I seriously doubt it."

Pauline took a step forward, to cup in her hand a bloom so bright and flashy it looked like a plastic dime-store trinket. Holding the flower gingerly, she bent her head toward it.

"Most don't have smells," Will said. "Just looks."

Pauline let the flower go.

"Your books," she said, "it seems to me, like your lectures, are to a great extent about the loss of water, the drying up of old sources." Will crossed his arms over his chest. Not interest but etiquette stilled his tongue.

"That's one thing they are about, yes. But what does that have to do with bromeliads?"

"Being here in the greenhouse is in a way like being underwater, in a new world where nothing is familiar. The plants use water differently. Since water is contained within the plants, the source is different." She was a fool, trying to analyze his work. She wasn't even sure she was making sense. "Do you think you'll write about . . ." Pauline thrust her long arm out in a wide circle, in the process nearly knocking down a piece of driftwood on which a bromeliad was delicately perched. She straightened it. "This?"

Will put his hands in his blue jeans pockets, leaving the thumbs hooked outside.

"I haven't learned enough about them yet," he said brusquely but without annoyance. He wasn't angry. He simply did not know the answer to her question. "When I do, *if* I do, I might. I can't say." His thumbs tapped a nervous beat.

"It's the strangeness. Like being in a new world."

"Plants, Missy. Just plants."

She looked up. He leaned against a shelf. She reached behind her and pushed her hands down into her back pockets.

"As I said," Will repeated, "I haven't figured it yet."

He clapped his hands as if giving Jesse an order. "Come," he said, herding her back into the kitchen. "Let's have some tea and then if you like, we'll go for a walk. Unless you're hungry." He checked his watch. "If you are, we can fix lunch. I don't mean to starve you."

Pauline followed Will out of the greenhouse.

"No," she said. "Let's walk first, eat later."

21

While Will filled their glasses with ice, Pauline looked out the window over the sink. Behind the house he had planted several rows of grapevines. The vines wound around wires connected to T-shaped supports resembling miniature telephone poles.

"My vineyard. Tonight we'll have some of my wine. It's not vintage. But it's ours."

The grape vines were leafless. They looked dead.

Will poured tea from the crockery pitcher. When one glass was filled, Pauline reached to take it, but Will held up his hand to stop her. He picked out a lime from a bowl of fruit behind him, cut the lime in slices, and hung a green wheel over the rim of her glass.

"Isabel's big on limes," he said. He handed her the tea glass. "I've gotten to where I am too."

Nervous about the caffeine, Pauline took only tiny sips.

Will filled a glass for himself. Halfway to his mouth the glass began to shake. Ice cubes clinked. Will set the glass back down. He lowered his right hand to his lap. The tremor was slight, but uncontrollable. With no change in his expression, he picked up the glass with the other hand, downed his tea in one gulp and set his glass firmly on the counter.

"Ready to take Jesse for a walk? We'll check on my wheat and I'll take you to the ridge where they found the dinosaur tracks. We'll end up at what we call our waterfall, though it's only a small drop, from one rock to the next. You might want to take a dip. Being as how you once were a leggy mermaid if I remember correctly."

"You do." She was amazed.

He tapped his temple. "Memory," he said. "It's my business."

Pauline slid off her stool. "Mine too," she said. "But that was a long time ago."

"I'm not sure you'll need that sweatshirt. It'll be hot once we get going."

Pauline crossed her arms over her chest, and, taking care not to grab her T-shirt at the same time, held the band of the sweatshirt between the thumb and forefinger of each hand and lifted it. She laid the sweatshirt on a stool and smoothed her hair behind her ears.

"That's some shirt, Missy."

Pauline looked down.

"I always forget what I'm wearing."

Under the sweatshirt she wore the purple T-shirt Wanda had bought her. In bright yellow letters across her chest, the T-shirt said RAY HAYS' CAJUN PO-BOYS. Beneath the lettering was a flaming yellow picture of Ray Hays cooking crawfish. Pauline rubbed her arms.

"Are you sure I'll be all right? It feels cool in here."

"No," Will said. "It's always cool in here, because of the stones. By the time we get past the first gate, it'll be hot."

Will jammed a red baseball cap with BAMA FEEDS on the crown at an angle down over his good eye. On the porch, he picked up his walking stick, twirled it once and, Jesse at his heels, went toward the hills. Halfway across the front yard, Pauline stopped.

"I almost forgot," she said, "Arlene." He tapped his walking stick against the ground. Pauline turned toward the house. "I should call," she said, "before she goes to lunch. I'll only be a second."

In the house she dialed Arlene's number collect. When Pauline told the secretary who she was, the secretary said, "Oh, yes, Pauline. She's right here." In seconds, Arlene came on.

"Sweetie."

"How did you know where I was?"

"You'll never get too far for me to find, sweet pea. Besides, you told me."

"Told you what?"

"That you were planning to see your uncle in Texas. You've mentioned his name. I put two and two together and there you are."

"What a snoop."

"Now listen." Arlene was always in a hurry. "I don't mean to interrupt your trip but there's an audition you should get back for. They said Thursday but I put them off. You'll be back by Friday, right?"

"I'm supposed to, yes."

"Good. I told them Friday."

"Arlene, what?"

"Macon McAllister, remember? Ancient history?"

"Now how would I forget Macon?"

"He's doing another play, did you read about it? It was off-off-Broadway for a while, got a lot of attention, about a saxophonist in a hotel band?"

"No. A saxophonist? How awful."

"Well, it wasn't. I saw it. This guy—the playwright—played in a hotel dance band his whole life. He thought he should've gone to Juilliard, so he wrote this play. It's pretty funny. The whole thing takes place in a ballroom with one of those mirrored balls shining blue lights on everybody's face. Meantime, funky music in the background. People dance different dances to show time passing. Anyway, there's a sister. Two sisters. One is nothing. The other is rich and beautiful. She's also the heavy. Many boyfriends, several husbands. She refuses to give little brother money to become a serious saxophonist, a very funny scene. They've got money to recast the show and bring it not exactly to Broadway but close. One of those new-old theaters way over west that the Tonys have to recognize."

"And?"

"Macon wants you. It's a great part, sweetie. It'll get you off the serious Sonya hook and move you into new territory. Which is what you need."

Arlene paused, a rare telephone experience. Pauline said nothing. In the background, she could hear Arlene tapping something.

"Now don't go silent on me, Pauline. I have a gut feeling about this one. You get to do the tango, no less. With a Puerto Rican dance instructor. Great makeup. Red lips. Trust me."

"It's not that."

"Now you do have to do a reading for the producer. I have a script right here. They're wondering why you haven't done anything in so long. But Macon's made excuses and he's as good as let me know you can probably have the part if you want it. Remember, I said probably."

Pauline stared at the wall. A small brown paper grocery sack had been thumbtacked next to the telephone. On the bag, in pencil, a list of names and telephone numbers.

"Well, let me get home first, Arlene, and I'll see."

"Sweet pea, listen to Mama. Say yes."

"You said I had until Friday."

"Well, all right. But he's anxious. *I'm* anxious."

"Arlene, don't worry. I'll be back."

Arlene said nothing. The *shush* of long distance.

"And . . . well, never mind."

"What is it, sweetie. Tell me."

Her voice shook. "I'm feeling positive, Arlene. I just have to check out some things first."

"Say yes, that's all."

"I just have a few things to check out."

"All right. I'll stall. Now come get the script the minute you're home. I have to go."

"You're terrific."

"I have another call. Good-bye, love."

She hung up.

Pauline pressed her forehead against the brown paper sack

on the wall. When she felt calm, she went back outside, letting the screen door slam. Will was looking in her direction.

"Anything important?"

"Not really. New Yorkers like long distance."

Will opened the first gate. Jesse went in first, sniffing at the ground. Pauline followed. The sun felt extraordinarily direct.

"Wait," she said and she unclasped the barrette holding her hair behind her ears, stuck her hair on top of her head and reclamped the barrette. From her pocket, she got out a square cotton scarf, folded the scarf in a triangle, then twisted it like a rope. She tied the scarf around her head, knotting it at the base of her neck, then pressed it back so that her forehead was uncovered. She rolled the sleeves of her T-shirt as high as they would go.

With the tip of his walking stick, Will killed a scorpion crawling menacingly up the gate. The scorpion fell to the ground. Will ground it into the dust with his foot. "You like the sun?"

"You can't imagine what a freezing spring it's been up East. Okay. I'm ready. I hope we don't see any more of those." She nodded toward the smashed scorpion. "Do you want me to get the gate?"

"No. I'll do it." Will closed and latched the gate.

"This way," he said. He pointed his walking stick in the air and then leaned down to smack it against a low-growing bush of purple sage.

"Watch out for rattlers," he warned. "They come out this time of year." And he smacked the bush again, as if to produce one. "Later, it'll be too hot. Now's the time to be careful."

Against the rocks, Will's city shoes made a swift clicking sound one beat ahead of his stick.

"We'll go to the graveyard first and then the wheatfield," he said, talking back over his shoulder. "It should be up."

"The wheat, not the graves, I assume."

"Very funny."

Needing no tour guide, Jesse went ahead until she disappeared.

Past a flat place, Will climbed a rocky escarpment. At the top, he stood a minute, posing, and then reached back to help Pauline. He was more out of breath than he wanted to admit.

"You have to be a mountain goat," he said, "to live out here."

Pauline took his hand and let him help her.

From the top of escarpment, they could see everything, blue skies, planted fields, limestone, horizon to horizon. In a cedar brake, the goats nibbled. The white clouds looked thick and creamy, like wads of Cool Whip. The tiny airplane was gone.

"Like king of the world," Pauline said.

He took her to an old graveyard where an entire family was buried, all of them including babies having been wiped out in a yellow-fever epidemic. He showed her where the dinosaur tracks had been found. In his wheatfield, Will knelt down to inspect the tender new shoots.

"Damnation," he said. "The greenbug." And with his thumbnail he popped one off to show her. Pauline saw nothing except the damage to the leaf; yellow spots, up and down the length of it.

There was nothing to do when the greenbug got into your wheat, Will explained, but hope for better next year; this year's crop was as good as gone. And, in the fatalistic head-down step of a seasoned farmer, he walked away.

Stunned by the force of his pessimism, Pauline stayed in the middle of the softly blowing field until finally, he turned around and came back to find out what was wrong.

"Will," she said. "This is crazy. Your whole crop. There must be something. I can help. We can spray or dig, whatever it takes." The wind pulled pieces of her hair from her barrette and fanned it across her face.

Will laughed. "That's country life, Missy," he said. "If pestilence doesn't get you, the weather will. At least I don't depend on wheat for my livelihood, like some."

The walk ended with a quick dip in a narrow river running through Will's property. The river was clear and swift, no wider really than a creek. Jesse went first, sprinting to a high rock and throwing herself off, hitting the water on her belly with a loud splash.

Pauline took off her shoes, rolled up the legs of her jeans and went for a wade. The water was colder than Snake Creek and quite swift. While her back was turned, Jesse stole her socks. Will finally found the socks behind a wild redbud tree, wet with slobber and river water.

They hung her socks on the line to dry. After eating a sandwich, Will took her to see his latest project, the two-story house he called the house of bedrooms.

The first bedroom he took her through might have been plucked all at once from a Victorian dollhouse. The furniture was dark, immaculately kept and uncomfortable: curved garnet velvet chairs and sofa, ornate double-decker handpainted bubble lamps, lace cloths on the end tables and against one wall, a small spinet piano, Debussy on the piano stand, a lace coverlet on the bed. The windows were adorned with delicately tatted lace curtains. Beside the bed on the floor lay a thick Persian rug, flowery patterns in wine-red and rose-pink.

"Isabel has expensive tastes," Will commented.

"I can see that."

The second downstairs bedroom, behind the stairs, was small and starkly furnished. Single bed, the covers thrown back, beside the bed a pair of worn rough-out work boots. No rug. Western shirts thrown over a chair. More books, magazines. And on the bedside table a small picture in a gold filigree frame of a handsome, dark-eyed woman. The woman's black hair was pulled straight back from her head. With long earrings, bare-shouldered, the woman was looking straight at the camera, smiling. As Wanda had said, Isabel was exotic and flashy.

Pauline pointed toward the stairway. "What's up there?"

Will went first.

At the top of the stairs were two more bedrooms, small, neat, one painted pale blue, the other a soft pearl-gray; one lace and ruffles, the other modern, with tailored white spread and miniblinds. Both rooms had rock-and-roll posters on the walls.

"Whose are these?"

Will turned and, seeing her astonishment, apologized.

"I thought you knew," he said. "Isabel has daughters."

A flush of heat dashed across Pauline's face. "How would I have known that?"

"Wanda. How else?"

"Don't make fun of Wanda."

"You're upset. Why?"

She went into the door of the first bedroom and blocked it, to keep him from following.

"Not upset. Just surprised. How old are they?"

"Aggie is in college up East. Sarah's in boarding school. Isabel thought the local education poor. And it is." His voice faded. "Nothing if not poor."

Over the tailored bed, David Lee Roth did the splits in the air.

"They like music, I see."

"Past tense," Will said. "They've gone on to other heroes."

In the other bedroom, a poster of Sean Cassidy in concert attested to the truth of his statement.

"Which was which?"

"Sarah's the Cassidy fan. Aggie liked the other. Sarah's our princess. Aggie's more inclined toward the outdoors. I thought Aggie might love it out here. So did she. But a girl who's grown up in town is not prepared for full-time isolation, no matter how countrified she thinks she is. The weekends and the winters get very long."

Pauline couldn't think of anything to say.

Will seemed to sense her discomfort. "Well, we'd better feed," he said. "If I don't get at it soon, I'll hear."

He closed the bedroom doors behind him and they went outside.

Within an hour, the world turned yellow. Sitting on a fence rail while Will fooled with a Nubian named Butter, Pauline watched as an angry band of dark clouds boiled up from the west. The clouds, separated into dark horizontal streaks, covered the setting sun and then, as the sun dropped, rose above it.

The colors of the clouds ranged from a slash of gunmetal gray to several thin swipes of pale blue-purple. The sun, a blurry ball, rested near the horizon beneath the clouds, on its way out of the picture.

"Look," Pauline said, pointing toward the sky.

Will looked up at her and, following the direction of her finger, glanced briefly toward the sky.

She shifted positions on the fence rail. From beneath the dark gray streaks, a new group of clouds, yellow as jaundice, rolled in to cover the sun. Sunlight filtering through the clouds fell in a sheet across the pasture. Limestone boulders became lumps of soft margarine. Chickens looked like experimental creatures under glass, running harum-scarum in artificial light. The kids began to agitate among themselves.

"Dust," Will said over his shoulder. "Probably"—he scooped up a bucket of feed—"all the way from Lubbock."

He lifted the bucket and, closely followed by Butter and her two kids, carried it across the pen.

When he dumped the bucket of feed into Butter's trough —half a car tire nailed to a square of plywood—the Nubian nanny and her babies almost knocked him down getting to it.

Butter was elegant—head like a llama, her coat a velvety brown, her feet as delicate and pointy as a ballerina's. When she ran, her long full bag swung against her legs and her torso jiggled, but, like a practiced high hurdler, she kept her head level and steady.

Will tapped the bottom of the bucket to dislodge a few clinging morsels of grain.

"Actually," he said without looking up, "I've been thinking. There is somebody I can call about that greenbug, an old boy near Stephenville."

"That's great. So call."

"In the morning."

"What's wrong with now?"

"It can wait."

Butter raised her head. Unwilling to give up a morsel of grain, the Nubian had nudged her kids out of the way to take the center position at trough. When she lifted her head to chew, the babies dove in, scrambling for crumbs dropped from her mouth, fighting over access to the trough. But Butter stood firm. However they shoved at her, she refused to budge.

Chewing, she fixed her sweet soft gaze on Pauline. The kids ate fast. One nudged the other from the trough.

"You'd think they were starving."

"They're like that every night."

All around, in separate pens, animals waited to be fed. Cows, chickens, horses, Spanish goats. Will's feeding ritual was so firmly established that each animal waited its turn without complaint until the animal one ahead of it was served. Their signals were subtle: the click of a gate latch, the sound of grain against a trough, the thud of a bucket against a post. Some of the troughs were commercial washtubs made of galvanized aluminum. Most were rigged from salvaged junk. Tires. A bathtub. A rusted-out red wagon.

"Why do you keep them?"

He scratched Butter's behind. "Butter's a pet. I bought her for Aggie."

As if to hurry her master along, Jesse appeared from behind

Butter's shed. She raised her chin and stretched a back leg, then went and stood at the gate, waiting.

"But she's not coming back." Pauline meant Agatha. Off his guard, Will answered a more pressing question.

"She'll bring the orchid pups and come for visits. Not for long. It was a mistake, thinking she'd like it out here. It's too remote almost for anyone."

Butter's eyes were dark and soft. She watched Pauline closely, as if making sure Pauline understood she was not just an ordinary run-of-the-mill goat.

Will shifted his feet. "Anyway, Butter's a great producer," he said. "Some people in town have a baby who's allergic to cow's milk. They come out. And there's a rich band of hippies over on the Edwards Plateau who entertain mystical notions about the milk of Nubians. She supplies them. I sell the kids or give them away to Mexicans who come out and help me. They cook *cabrito*. Butter is more than a pet. She has purpose."

"She's certainly beautiful."

"Yes. Well, we have to keep at this or darkness will catch us. All right, Jess, we're coming."

Will opened the gate. Jesse went through. Jumping down from the fence, Pauline followed Jesse and then waited for Will to latch the gate behind her. Again she offered to do the openings and closings of gates.

"I appreciate the offer but no thanks. If I don't do it the same way every time," he said, "I'll get overconfident and forget."

They went through a narrow passageway of wooden fences, past an aluminum chute where calves were trapped to be castrated or doctored. Will opened another metal gate leading to the other goats' pen, and the barn. The entire barnyard was a series of fences defining paths, keeping one animal away from another and all of them away from the house. Some of the fences were wooden, some smooth wire, others barbed. The electric fence kept the livestock out of the garden and the yard.

Following Will, Pauline looked once again at the sky. It had darkened to a deeper yellow, like a week-old bruise. She wondered which of the clouds had dust in them, the gray ones or the yellow.

Will scattered hen scratch on the ground for the chickens. Pauline kept her distance. She didn't like birds. Jesse walked harmlessly among the chickens, sniffing the ground sharply.

"She doesn't eat them?"

"She wouldn't dare."

The dog poked at the ground with her nose, going in this direction and that, making sharp turns as if on the trail of something new.

"We'll turn on the news when we get inside," Will said. "To see if there's a storm. I don't think so." He had not looked back at the sky. "I think it's just dust."

They fed the Spanish goats from the barn, emptying feed buckets into a long wooden trough. When the grain hit the trough, the goats scattered, burbling among themselves, gathering in protective bunches. When the sound died, they quickly retrenched and came back to the trough, raising their front feet up onto the railing of the trough, poking their necks through the rails. Pauline looked for the queen nanny. But the goats all looked the same.

"Do they always spook from the sound of their own food?"

"Always. But you can't blame them. Goats are prey."

He dipped a Bermuda grass seed can into a sack of Purina Omolene for the Active Pleasure Horse and took the can into another stall.

"All right, Mama," he said. "All right."

The horse, Daughter Two, was a large roan mare, thick and hefty, with a pinkish silver mane and tail. Her mane was matted, her tail filled with burrs.

Pauline stood in the stall door watching as Will fed the mare. Daughter snorted, her dark nostrils quivering. She glanced at Pauline then looked away.

Will squatted down to look under the mare's belly. "Not yet," he said.

"When's she due?"

"Any day. She's made bag. I'm watching to see when it gets waxy. She's a sturdy mare but she has trouble giving birth. I like to be on top of it."

"She needs grooming."

"Next on my list."

He rubbed her side then lay one hand against her bulging stomach.

"The colt is still," he said. "It'll come soon."

Pauline shivered. On a farm, reproduction was everywhere. There was no way to avoid it. In the city, if you managed it right, you never even had to look inside a baby carriage.

Daughter stuck her nose in the red plastic bucket and munched without pause. Will brought a hose into the stall and filled another plastic bucket with water.

Daughter stamped her feet. Jesse nibbled at Daughter's droppings, picking out undigested seeds. Will spoke lovingly to the horse. "Easy, Mama," he said. "Now easy."

The barn was open to the pasture on one side, walled up on the other. The closed section was divided into three parts. There was a door in the section of wall nearest where Daughter was; in the middle an open space; toward the house, two more stalls. The closed door had a white porcelain knob.

Will took the hose to an aluminum tub.

The open section of the barn was filled with a wide assortment of paraphernalia: a machine for grinding wheat, a large freezer, numerous cases of empty wine bottles, a lathe, a vise, a stack of old tires, a Rototiller, a wheelbarrow with the wheel off, a beautiful peeled bark canoe, what looked like an ancient sewing machine, and hundreds of magazines—*Organic Gardening, Farm and Rancher, The Smithsonian, National Geographic*—all neatly stacked in bundles, tied together with wire.

"I go to flea markets and estate sales," Will explained. "I buy too much. I don't reread the magazines. I also can't seem to bring myself to throw them away."

Pauline asked what was behind the door with the porcelain

knob. Will said to feel free to look for herself. She had the feeling he wanted her to go in. She opened the door and went up the one step into the room.

A flat-top oak desk sat in the middle of the room, behind it a matching chair with rusty springs. On the desk, a portable typewriter, a stack of white paper, some large gray-and-red ledgers with stiff covers. On the spine of each ledger, a label had been pasted, the title written in ink in Will's spidery hand. One said WATER; another WINE. Then SEASONS. SUCCULENTS. SOLITUDE, WIND, WEATHER. CHANGE. On the wall, Will had tacked up graphs and diagrams; a map of the world showing ocean currents and wind directions, and one of the moon; a geological cross section of the Edwards Aquifer; a startling and brilliant slick magazine photograph of a bromeliad, another of two rock-red mountains separated by a green field on which grew a blanket of wildflowers. There were cobwebs in the corners, dirt-dauber nests in the cracks, dust everywhere.

A writing spider had built a perfect web in Will's chair. In the center of the web, the spider delicately lifted its long spiky legs, picking its way from one silken thread to the next. There were no windows. Pauline lifted the tail of her T-shirt and wiped her face. Why would he want to work in such a miserably uncomfortable place? The room was in fact not a room at all but only an end section of the barn, walled off.

"Isabel says . . ."

Pauline jumped. "Will!"

Will laid his hand on her shoulder, as if to hold her to the ground.

"I'm sorry," he said in a low voice from behind her. "I didn't mean to startle you. It's only me, Missy."

She laughed and circled her head to relieve the tension in her neck. "I was looking hard. And thinking."

He pressed one hand against her cheekbone. Automatically, Pauline dropped her head into his hand and lowered her eyelids. With abstinence, Pauline had not missed sex. She had thought perhaps she had lost the need. Not so.

The writing spider lifted a delicate front foot and moved toward the center of its web. Pauline turned to Will.

"Isabel says I have created rat heaven," he said. He looked tired. "And I suspect I have." He lifted his hands, took a step backward, then turned and left. Like the goats from their food, he spooked from her touch.

He had made a path through the stacks of magazines and books wide enough for Indian style walking, one foot in front of the other. The ream of paper next to his typewriter was blank.

She opened the ledger on succulents. More charts and diagrams, records of growth, sketches of emerging blooms. From the center section of the barn Pauline could hear Will banging a bucket, whistling a nameless tune as he went about his work, finishing up. She turned to another page. A flower petal had been inserted, waxy and flat and bright pink. On the page beside the pressed bloom, Will had written: *2-1-84: bloom emerges. Morning, suddenly, like sunrise, while the world slept. Color, an unimaginably electric pink, nigh on to fuchsia. Unearthly. What a world, in which nourishment comes from within and beauty overindulges itself, risking vulgarity. How to imitate, replicate, describe???*

Will stopped whistling. Pauline closed the ledger. Dust rose. She sneezed and, rubbing her nose, left his office, quietly closing the door behind her. Will waited at the far end of the barn, his back to her, hands on his hips. Softening evening shadows fuzzed Will's outline, lending it a vulnerable sweetness. Jesse sniffed the ground next to Will's feet.

The sun had dropped behind the edge of the horizon. Its last rays lay on limestone rocks like a child's version of sunshine, in distinct and separable pie-shaped portions.

In his gentleman's gesture, Will placed the tips of his fingers against Pauline's spine.

Pauline moved in closer. " 'Will you, won't you, will you, won't you, won't you join the dance?' "

Will took his hand away.

"Hey," she said. "It was a test. Don't you remember? It's

from *Alice in Wonderland*. The mock turtle's song. People have to change lobsters and dance."

"Ah," Will said. "How could I forget." He tapped his head. "The hands go first," he said.

In the house, Will turned on the television set to check the news and weather. Pauline excused herself and went to take a quick shower and put on a fresh T-shirt for dinner. As the sun descended into the cloud of dust, the air had grown suddenly cool. She put her sweatshirt back on, her jeans and running shoes, undid her hair, brushed it, pulled it back tighter. Once again she creamed her skin with moisturizer, added a bit of mascara to her eyelashes, greased her lips with Vaseline. The dry wind was merciless. Her eyes felt tight.

She checked in her duffel to make sure she hadn't left her notebook in Houston. It was there, its bright turquoise cover shining between T-shirts.

In the kitchen, Will was wrapping small baking potatoes in aluminum foil.

His meal was excellent: lemon-basted broiled chicken, baked potatoes drenched in real butter and home-made sour cream—"I'm supposed to stick to corn-oil margarine," Will confessed, "but we're out"—a nicely tart salad. Pauline made the dressing. They ate on their laps in the living room.

When the night grew cool, Will built a small fire in the fireplace. He drank steadily, straight gin with a twist of lime. Pauline drank Will's red wine—good, if young, with a woody taste, like zinfandel—almost an entire bottle by herself.

They told stories. He talked books. She told him what she had been reading. He made suggestions. Pauline listened, nodded and eventually grew drowsy. Her head dropped. At midnight she went to bed.

23

She could not tell what time it was. There was no clock and she wore no watch and in the country with no moon or street-lights the air itself seemed black and solid. The only way to tell windows from walls was by listening, as dust picked at the glass like rain.

Except for the dust there was nothing. A buffered night, as if the house had been packed in buttons of Styrofoam. From her bedroom, Pauline could not even hear the loud ticking of the mantel clock.

Stretching her legs, she searched for a new, maybe warmer place in the bed, but the sheets—stiffly starched and ironed—were ice cold wherever she touched. Ironed sheets seemed a strange affectation in a purposefully country house. Isabel's idea, no doubt. Pauline longed for Kathleen, for wrinkled sheets dryer-ironed, for the green digital numbers of the coffee clock and her afghan. Between the stiff slabs of pure cotton she felt like meat in a sandwich.

This was what drove her crazy about the country, the te-dium, the dust, the wind going on and on. Nature paid no heed to artfulness or surfeit, it just went on.

She drew her feet up under her, holding one and then the other, massaging her toes. She should have brought more clothes, a warm nightgown. The benefits of underpacking—that feeling of sophisticated nonchalance—were not worth the price.

She'd been dreaming when the dust and the night air wak-ened her. In the dream, she'd given birth to a litter, four creatures. Not babies: tiny dwarflike grown men with bow legs and beards. The babies walked and talked among themselves, smoking cigars in their old-fashioned white christening gowns, long and lacy. On their heads the men-babies wore sheer bonnets embroidered with nosegays of pink flowers. Pauline watched as they walked down a long hall away from her.

Loving would have said: "Why four?"

Crossing her arms over her chest, she fingered her breasts. Her nipples stood out long and hard from the cold. It was Butter who made her dream of having a litter. And the queen nanny, her udders so long and heavy they had scraped the rock she squatted on. Daughter. All the producing creatures.

Sitting up, she clutched the white comforter around her, and—swaddled like a baby—stood. She had to know what time it was. Padding barefoot, she went across the room, taking light, quick steps as she skipped from one scatter rug to the next. Her notebook was on the chest of drawers. She picked it up, put on her blue jeans and, dropping the comforter, made her way out the room and down the steps. The wine room was freezing.

White curtains in the two open windows blew wildly. Dust was piling up in mounds on the floor beneath the sills. On her way to bed, Pauline had tried to close the window nearest her room, but it was firmly wedged open with a chock of wood. Groggy from wine, not wanting to break the thread of sleepiness that had unwound in her head, she had not done much more than take note of the arrangement. The chocks of wood were meant to stay.

She stepped in a patch of dust, went up the steps into the hall and then the living room.

Two forty. Hours to go before morning, little more than two hours since she'd gone to bed. She switched on another lamp—Will had left on the floor lamp beside his chair—and sat on the couch, covering her feet with a cushion. The greenhouse was lit up like daytime. The box fans turned lazily. She began to write down her dream.

Tomorrow, today, was Thursday. In order to catch her

plane at noon, she had to leave at nine. Ordinarily on Thursdays she went to see Loving. She wondered if he'd made another appointment to fill her hour.

In November there had been a sudden snowstorm, a near blizzard. That early in the year, no one was prepared. Buses were stalled in the street, snowplows were late, parked cars covered. It was a Monday. Pauline had an appointment. Carrying her notebook, she left three hours ahead of time. Loving's office was across town on the East Side and up twenty blocks. When she got there, he hadn't yet arrived. Her toes were frozen. She felt triumphant. If he disappointed her—did not show—wouldn't she then have justifiable reason to quit? Twenty minutes late, he arrived. From the hall, Pauline could hear the slamming doors. When he asked her into his office, he looked out of sorts and disheveled.

His office was cold. He had turned on a radiant heater at the foot of the couch.

"I want you to know," he said abruptly, before she had a chance to say anything, "there was a good chance I might not have made it here today. I tried to call but you had already left."

"Well, I hope," Pauline said off-handedly, "you didn't come just for me." This was before she lay down. Behind the glasses, his eyes were unwavering.

"I would have come just for you," he said, with great, stultifying plainness, "but no, I had other things to do as well."

A shot of electricity which felt almost erotic stilled her ability to say anything more. She turned away and lay down.

She didn't want him to do anything just for her.

Behind her, two doors opened and slammed.

"You up too?"

In blue jeans, belt and unbuttoned shirt, Will stood in the doorway. His black-framed reading glasses were down on his nose. Head cocked, with his good eye he peered at her over the glasses. His shirt flapped open, revealing his bare chest and stomach. Beneath the suntanned V at his neck, his flesh was pale. His chest was newly divided. A scar ran down the length of it, a dark red puckered line extending from the well of his neck to just beneath his rib cage.

"I was cold," Pauline said, raising her head. "And I had a dream. I came to see what time it was." She slid her notebook beneath a pillow.

"I thought I saw you from the window. I don't sleep much."

"Me either."

In sock feet, he walked across the living room to the front door. "Damned dust," he said.

"It's like rain. Will it go on all night?"

"I told you," he said, "it's not serious. It's slacking up now. Just a bit of seasonal blowing off." He frowned. "You're cold."

"The windows are open in that room with the green jugs. I couldn't close them."

"That's my fermenting room. It has to stay cool for the wine. I told you. I told you to be sure to close the bedroom door."

Too late, she remembered. "That's right, you did. I forgot."

"I didn't mean for you to freeze. I specifically told you."

"Will. I said I forgot."

He frowned again.

"I'll get you something."

He walked past her and down the hall. Pauline gathered up her hair and twisted it into a loose braid over one shoulder. Will closed her door and came back with a red plaid flannel robe big enough to wrap around her and cover her feet.

He squinted. "How about a nightcap?" he said. Without waiting for her response, he went into the kitchen.

Pauline made socklets of the robe, enclosing each foot. Will brought her a fresh glass of white wine, himself another drink. He sat down in his chair and stirred the drink with his finger.

Pauline sipped the wine. The white was too sweet for her taste. She ran a finger up the inside of her glass to remove a bit of cork.

"Your wine is good. I particularly like the red."

"The white is sweet, I know. I'm hoping for better next year."

Without buttoning it, Will had arranged his shirt so that she could no longer see the scar. He took off his glasses and put them inside his shirt pocket.

"So," Pauline said, and she ran her finger down the center of her chest and nodded the top of her head in his direction. "What happened?"

Will reopened his shirt a bit and turned his head to study the still-angry scar with his good eye. When he touched the scar lightly, Pauline felt a chill run through her.

"They cut me open, Missy," he said. "Stem to stern. Lifted my heart out, traded my beat-up arteries for new ones. I am," and he raised his glass of gin as if in a toast, "a walking tribute to modern technology and the benefits of petroleum by-products." When he smiled, his face changed and her heart swelled. "Ain't life grand. After all these years of knocking plastic, to become dependent on it for my pulse."

"That's why you don't smoke?"

"I made the mistake of telling the damned surgeon I'd smoked since I was ten. He said if I didn't care for dying I had to quit. Then he gave the orders about salt, grease, and hootch. It's demoralizing. Also boring. So I slide. I slide particularly on the hootch."

He sipped his drink and grinned like a small boy caught at minor mischief. "Not to mention," he went on, "the others."

He held the glass in his steadier hand.

"When?"

"When what? The surgery?"

"Yes."

"A little less than a year ago."

"Was Isabel still here?"

"Some of the time, yes. As I said, it was a mistake."

"Which?"

"What?"

"Was a mistake?"

"The surgery, who can say. I wouldn't have thought I would have had to it at all, but there you go." He groaned. "But the other? I expect if it wasn't a mistake, then it was at least unfair. I knew better. I wanted to fool myself into believing what I needed to. Isabel is a lovely lady. I enjoyed her company." He corrected himself. "Still do. And the girls. It was a surprise how much I like having young people around." He sipped his drink.

Drink, and the long night, were getting to him. Loneliness was closing in. When he frowned, the crease across his forehead folded in on itself.

"So Isabel was around for the operation?"

"She would have been."

"But?"

"She didn't know."

"You didn't tell her?"

"There was no reason to. She'd been out of the country. There was nothing for her to do."

"Are you serious?"

He looked up, said nothing.

"That's awful."

"She thought so. When she came back here and found me gone, with Shorty Mahood in charge . . . Shorty of course told her . . . once she knew I was all right, you should have heard the commotion. Lord, the carryings on. Never rile up a Hispanic woman unless you're ready for fireworks."

He chuckled, as if it were all a joke, then reached to the end table and picked up the package of Camels.

"And you like that."

He pulled out a cigarette.

"I hate filters," he said, and with a pocketknife he sliced the brown tip from the cigarette and lit it.

"That's terrible, Will," Pauline said.

He drew deeply on the cigarette, then held it out toward her. "What? Smoking?"

"Not telling her. What if you'd died?"

"I'd have died, that's all." He blew a torrent of smoke out

his nose. "Don't lecture me, Missy. I'm not the man I was. I don't write much that's worthwhile any more, you must have seen that out in the relic I call my office. I write. Pieces. Nothing accumulates. I keep those ledgers you saw. I putter. And that's all. The flowers, the animals. The wheat. But I've lost something. Somewhere along in there, between the time I saw you at Snake Creek and now, I have simply lost the need and the faith. And yet . . ."

"What?"

Impatient with himself, he waved his hand. "I feel foolish going on this way, knowing I will never in point of fact actually *quit*."

"You're a late starter. You write slow."

He tapped his cigarette.

"And you like to give yourself a hard time. Writing is what you do." She sounded like Coco.

"Not everything, Missy. I'm a devoted amateur."

"Bull."

He drank his gin.

"Also . . ."

At a slant, he looked up at her. "Yes?"

"A masterpiece."

"A what?"

"You feel the need to write a masterpiece."

A wave of dust blew against the windows. Will sulked.

"If not a masterpiece then why bother. If not that then nothing, right? It's a trap. I thought you said it was slacking up."

His head swiveled sharply. He wasn't sure what she meant. He looked out the window.

"Trust me, Missy. That's just wind."

He finished his drink and smoked the last of the cigarette. Going into the kitchen to refill his glass, he staggered a little and bumped into the wall. Pauline set her wine glass on the table.

She had asked for specific advice during her last session. "Remember who you are," Loving had said. "You are not Will Hand's daughter or student or his nurse. Be his friend in whatever way you see fit. That will be up to you. You know what to do."

His optimism seemed a ploy, designed to boost her self-confidence. She hated it when he set her life in her hands like a beach ball.

Will came back. "I was sorry to hear about your mother," he said. "I liked her. She was an innocent. Innocent people don't expect trouble and so they always get hurt."

"It was hard, her death. Harder than I would have expected. I'm just beginning to understand what she meant to me."

Will sat back down. Pauline looked out the window at nothing. The panes were black. Neither spoke. They were waiting, expecting something—what?—to happen.

It wasn't going to. Will had what he needed, company for short visits only. More than likely Isabel understood that this was as married as Will would ever be and that he couldn't bear to recognize the finished thing. He *had* to believe nothing was working out. Had to hold on to his eccentricities without defining or abandoning them. Had to deprive himself. Needed the antagonism. The goats, the greenbug, the loneliness. His sidekicks.

He broke the silence. "I assume you've seen Wanda?"

"Yes. Just last night in Houston. When have you?"

"Not in years. How is she?"

"Fabulous," Pauline said. "Just amazing. She's rented an apartment in Houston in a high-rise called Parc IV. It's on Montrose Street, in a part of Houston that's close to the museums and wild with nightlife. She looks great, goes to dance class three times a week . . . when she's not traveling, which isn't often. Next week she's off again, on her way to Sri Lanka. She takes pictures, goes on treks. No high mountains, she claims. Just little ones."

Will chuckled. "She's what, sixty-seven?"

"She's younger than most thirty-year-olds. I hope I do as well."

"You probably will." He sliced off another filter from a cigarette.

Pauline shrugged. "You never can tell."

Will lit his cigarette. "That's what I told you about the poison ivy when you said you weren't allergic. That you never can tell." He blew smoke toward the door, away from her. "And I was right."

"No, you didn't. You said, 'You never know.' I remember it distinctly."

He frowned. "I don't think so."

"Oh, but yes."

"You're sure?"

"More than sure. Mama used to say the exact same thing. 'You never know, honey,' she always said, 'you just never never know.' "

Pauline laughed. Will's good eye lit up.

"I'm supposed to be the one on whom nothing is lost."

"I'm the one who memorizes lines."

"Calf rope. I like your hair grown out."

She twisted her loose braid. "My agent says I have to dye the gray."

"Why?"

"I'm not old enough to play gray-haired ladies."

"Then I expect you'll dye it."

"I haven't been doing any acting. I'm thinking of giving it up."

Unwilling to acknowledge any pessimism but his own, he shook his head agitatedly. "Don't be silly, Missy. You have to."

"I expect so. And you'll continue to write. And say you aren't."

Will sipped his gin more slowly. Between sips, he smoked. When he had finished, the cigarette was so small the ashes nearly burned his fingers.

"Have you played any more brown-haired Chekhov heroines?"

"Matter of fact, that was what Arlene wanted. Not Chekhov but a part. A saxophonist's sister."

"I don't recall saxophones in Chekhov."

"No."

"Are you interested?"

"I think so. I guess I'd better be. It's a new kind of part. Which I need."

"Why?"

She shrugged. "Beats me. Life goes on."

"When does the play open?"

"The audition is Friday. Tomorrow."

Will concentrated on his feet. His glass eye stayed on her.

"What about the house on Snake Creek? Does anybody live there?"

He looked up.

"Somebody did, until a couple of years ago, when it mysteriously burned. No one knows what happened. Or no one is saying. Everything went. Nobody's rebuilt."

"Who lived there?"

"A wild boy. He'd been in Vietnam. I think something snapped over there. I heard he and his cohorts built fires on the creekbanks and did dances. Someone said devil worshipers, I don't know. It may be how the fire started."

"Maybe they were dancing to exorcise the ghosts, the snake woman and the children."

"I thought of that."

"It breaks my heart to think of it gone. I started to drive through San Marcos but didn't have the time."

"Nothing lasts forever." He turned up his glass. When Pauline sat forward on the couch, her notebook slipped out from under the pillow. She took it out and set it on the coffee table.

"Will, did you ever consider calling me? I was stupid enough to think things had a way of always coming back around again, but you knew better. Why did you let it go?"

He snapped a pearl button closed. "I used to think about it, Missy, all the time. Standing in a line at the bank, paying for groceries, hoeing weeds, I'd suddenly see you, hear your voice. Those moments, I wanted you with me more than I've wanted anything in my life. But I could not bring myself to do anything about it. I waited for you to make the first move, to write. And then, finally, I did what I had to, hardened my mind against thinking about what I could not change. I started planning to move from Snake Creek soon afterward. I cared—care—for Isabel but not in the same way. She's my wife. You were a kind of dream. I let you go, as you did me. I think we both knew that what happened was a product of the place and the time. I'm a man, Missy, who needs not only solitude but conventions. A set of expectations to go by. I believe I have said as much to you before."

"Quoting some dead man."

He turned his seeing eye directly on her. "Yes," he said—and he smiled his cockeyed smile once again and her heart danced—"you do have a good memory."

Loving had been right. She knew what to do. She stood.

"One last question and I'm off to bed. What about—and I'm asking because I want to know; it's a real question—love?"

"What about it?"

"Where does it fit in, what do you think it is?"

He rubbed his eyes and groaned.

"What a question. I don't think I've done well by love, or possibly it by me. But I believe love to be, oh, lord, Missy, attention?, devotion?, concentration? Single-minded focus? The sense of paying notice to another human being with persistence and selflessness. That lasts. The other dissipates."

"I take it you believe in fidelity."

"Not that I've always practiced it, but yes."

"And the writing? Art?"

"The fulfillment of the rest of it, naming names, making connections. Speaking to . . ." He lifted his hand toward the ceiling. "Whoever is up there. The clichés have it right."

"An actress friend of mine used to say 'God's breath.' "

"Same thing."

"And you think you let it go?"

He started to explain. She interrupted him.

"I don't know exactly what love is either but I have felt it. I love you, Will. With attention and fidelity. I'm very much alone now. I can use some family. An uncle, and not just any: you. I won't let you slip away the way I have some others, without ever knowing exactly who they were or how much they meant. Maybe I'll even meet your wife someday and then, maybe your daughters but . . ." She turned away. "Not right away. So." Having become the lecturer, she shook her finger at him. "Be forewarned. I'll be back."

She had said all she was up to. Resorting to playacting, she swirled the tail of the flannel robe. " 'Good night, ladies; good night. Sweet ladies, good night, good night.' My exit line. Who?"

"Ophelia of course."

"Exit line only."

"No watery grave for you."

"No. See me as a saxophonist's sister."

She was in the doorway when he came to her. She held up her hands and stopped him.

Against all inclination, she went quickly back down the hall through the wine room and into her bedroom. Her room was now only cold instead of icy. She pulled the white comforter to her chin, drew the flannel robe more tightly around her and hugged her knees to her chest. Her breath felt scattered, like small insects trapped in a jar. From beyond the wine room, the greenhouse door slammed.

She focused on earth breaths. Through the nose, out the mouth. The next thing to do was leave, go home, to Coco, Kathleen, Loving, and work.

After a time, she released her knees and, facing the black windows, pushed her head down deep in her pillow and prayed for no more dreams. No baby men in dresses, no babies midair, no menacing man, nothing. Eyes tightly shut, she tried to imagine she was not in Eulogy, Texas, at the mercy of tedious nature, but at home listening to traffic.

Uptown, all night long.

She felt proud of herself. Really proud.

24

The dust had stopped. Stillness rang in her ears like bells. With the confidence of a sleepwalker, Pauline rose from her bed and went swiftly through the living room.

There was no wind anymore, not even a breeze. The night was thunderously quiet, the front porch iced with a layer of dust. Wrapping the flannel robe around her, she went down the steps and into the yard. On the front porch of the house of bedrooms Jesse stirred but did not get up.

No wonder she had wakened. Floating in her bedroom window, a shimmering white globe cast a silver light into her room. In the black starless sky, the moon had risen, bright as an unfiltered Kleig light. Except for a mashed-in place on the right-hand side, the moon was round. She'd been center stage and not known it, lit up for show as she slept.

The pasture looked like daytime. Around her, against the moonlit dust the oak trees cast dark shadows as sharply defined as if it were noon.

Something whistled in a nearby tree and then flew away.

She'd had one of her visions before dinner. They'd gone out into the night to get some wine from Will's cellar, and she'd seen a glimpse of what might be his future.

What Will called a wine cellar was no cellar at all but only a crawl space beneath the house of bedrooms. He lay down in the dirt and went in on his belly. Once he was in, she lost him. With no moon or stars in the sky, the night simply swallowed him up. Only his voice let her know he was there, as he talked on, telling her about winemaking and the growing of grapes and how touchy a venture it was. At some point, his voice grew louder and his white head appeared in the opening and he handed out a bottle of wine, white, with a plain label that said in a careful hand she did not recognize, *Hand, 84.* And then he disappeared again.

In the pasture, the animals were quiet; sated. A violet restfulness enveloped the landscape. A soft breeze rustled the leaves of the oaks and mesquite. When his voice grew louder again, Pauline looked down and there he was, halfway out of the crawl space and halfway in, up to his waist in darkness. And then . . . did he pause or did time and life itself stop? The picture was so clear, surely Jesse saw it too, surely the world itself stopped to take time to look—surely what she saw was, if not the future set down, then an extension of the present, possible enough to believe:

Will in his wine cellar some other night, alone, no wife or daughters, going for wine, Jesse on her belly waiting for him to come out. A bottle of wine clamped in his armpit, Will emerges, is halfway out when something happens, an artery exploding, the heart making an unnatural jump, the unmistakable click, and he looks up. The expression on Will's face is not one of unhappiness, exactly, only annoyance, as he thinks back over the projects he has not quite gotten around to, some half-finished, some not even begun. All the books he did not write.

In seconds, the vision was over. Real time reasserted itself, Will crawled out, handed her the wine, stood, and brushed himself off.

"I think the dust has left us," Pauline said.

"No, Missy," he said, "it's out there. There are no miracles. It'll blow in soon."

In her last speech, Sonya says, "We shall see the heavens all sparkling like jewels." A newer translation had it, "see the sky all diamonds." Pauline liked the new translation. "All diamonds" was a bit sentimental, but it pleased her ear to say the words. Dropping her head back, she closed her eyes and let the black country night wrap around her.

A fitting death. Alone with his dog. In the middle of too many projects to get to the end of in one lifetime. A man who knew exactly what he wanted.

Russell Loving had placed a jug-shaped lamp at the corner of his desk, just beyond the foot of the couch. The lamp was made of pink ceramic. Inside the ceramic, sculpted into it, a pig struggled to get free. On one side of the lamp the pig's head and feet stuck out, on the other his corkscrew tail. The pig's eyes were closed with effort, his tiny feet winningly bent. His ears were like petals. Straining, the nostrils of his fat, flat snout bellowed.

Loving had set various other meaningful and provocative objects around the office as well: mysterious stone artifacts, glass bibelots, pictures, plants; a collection of masks and funerary urns in a glass case.

The pig, however, seemed a questionable choice. The message was not hopeful; the pig would never get free.

But then Pauline didn't look at the lamp much, or at the giant mother-in-law tongue plant in the carved teak planter, or at the pictures of Freud or the abstract paintings, those wild splashes of yellow and red. She stared at the ceiling. Watched the blades of the ceiling fan, counted squiggles in the sound-proofing tile, followed the metal bands that held the tiles in place, across and then up and down in a basketweave pattern. Slid her hands up under her hips and said what was on her mind.

The baby was hers. Her secret, alive inside her, its absence real, that vacancy in the middle of her life her truest companion, resting small and safe within her like a knot of blood. She would not share.

She opened her eyes.

Nothing like "the sky, all diamonds" seemed likely tonight. The moon's brightness canceled lesser lights. She wondered if the bear was up there, deep in darkness, Ursa Major looking on. No way to know. She could never remember how to identify the stars or recognize the shapes books said were up there. She could look them up one night; by the next she would have forgotten.

Anyway the bear was not real. Constellations were a myth, a child's primitive game, like fill-in-the-dots. If you drew a line from star to star and supplied the gaps with an imaginary shape, you might come up with a bear and you might not. You might see only stars.

She hugged herself and went back in. Jesse's tail banged the porch floor. Four thirty. At noon she'd be in the sky herself, flying home.

In bed, she turned on the reading light and dated a new page in her notebook.

April 11, 4:30 a.m., Eulogy. The moon was there all the time. Behind the dust.

When Will's noisy kitchen cleaning woke her up for the last time, the sun was up and Pauline was still sitting up against the iron bedstead with the light on, her notebook open on her lap.